MELODY OF MANA

✦ BOOK 4 ✦

MELODY OF MANA

✦ BOOK 4 ✦

WANDERING AGENT

Podium

Cover design by Podium Publishing

ISBN: 978-1-0394-4383-9

Published in 2023 by Podium Publishing, ULC
www.podiumaudio.com

CHAPTER 1

SILVERSTONE PORT

It had been a long and rather peaceful trip to get here. Composed primarily of recent graduates from magical and knightly academies, our crew included some of the best and brightest of our generation. After a three-year-long training process we were finally off on our first big mission.

Off across the sea and to the Elven continent we would go, seeking out information about teleporters our government sorely wanted to be able to recreate. Each member of our team had practiced skills in their chosen fields, but few could stand up to my personal mastery of the magical language because, unlike most of the people in this world, I had a head start and knew a few cheats. This was my second go at the game of life, and while my first might have ended badly, this one was . . . well, not easy or peaceful, but going well. The knowledge that I'd retained of my first world—and the fact that many of the ancient mages of power seemed to be like me in this regard—would do me all kinds of favors.

We rolled up to the gates, letting them check our papers. Despite being fairly generic, the documents were necessary because we were obviously bringing a sizable number of casters into town. The guards gave us a once-over and, after deciding that they didn't want a fight, just waved us through. Normally this would have been impossible after sunset, but if you've got all the right things in order almost anything is doable.

We weren't the first to arrive, but the second of the three caravans to roll into town full of mages and gear. Something they couldn't outright ignore.

A man in slightly fancier armor than the other guards greeted us as we made our way through, stopping the little caravan. I had my window open and was looking around a bit, so I got a good view of what had happened. He went over to Olnir's carriage.

"How can I help you," the little wizard asked as he leaned out toward the guard.

"Just a few questions, sir, if you don't mind too much. What is your business and where are you headed?"

"Ah, I understand your position, but those details are need to know, and quite frankly, you don't need to know."

I winced. Olnir was right in that he didn't have to answer the guard's questions, and their town mayor would be able to confirm that we were official, even if rather low key.

"You're bringing in a large group, after dark, and from what our man on duty tells me, with lots of magic. I may not need everything, but I have my duty to perform," the guard responded, sounding rather peeved.

"Then ask your superiors." Olnir was really doing us no favors as he still refused to answer.

An hour later, the runner who was sent to get info from the mayor returned, seeming in no hurry. I suspected that the head guard here had told the boy specifically to take his time and make us wait. It was a petty move on his part, but my boss was also being a little jerk. The page handed an envelope to the guardsmen and a few moments later we were let out of the entryway.

It was only after the third inn told us that they were full, I began to see the heart of the guard's plan. This late in the evening most places to rest were either closed or full, particularly in a busy port town such as Silverstone. Well aware of this, the guard's decision to delay us at the gate meant that the only place we could find to rest was a stable.

I'd slept rough before, and the carriage that I shared with the other ladies was by no means the worst sleeping arrangement. As a matter of point we'd slept in here several times during this trip already, since we often couldn't spend the night in a sizable town. Sleeping rough wasn't the issue that kept me up grinding my teeth; it was the fact that Olnir—my boss on this trip—couldn't muster the slightest hint of diplomacy.

As the sun rose the next day and I began to work out the inevitable kink in my neck, I looked around. I was not the first to rise, nor was I the last. The guys were all up and wandering about looking sour while the rest of my own carriage slept soundly.

After I'd slipped out and conjured up a bite for breakfast, I looked at them. "So, what's the plan for today?"

Robert stretched as he rattled off the day's events, "Olnir went off to see if the other groups had arrived. I'm supposed to head to the ship here in a moment to see if they're ready, want to come?"

He was a nice sort, and I didn't have anything else pressing. "Sure. Do you know the way?"

"Not at all! I do, however, know the ship name, so I'm thinking I can just head down to the port and check in on them," he said excitedly. Seems the idea of adventure, even small, appealed to him.

"Lead on, then." I waved toward the door. "If nothing else we'll at least get an idea of the layout."

We moved into the bright mid-morning sun and joined the small crowd of people walking to-and-fro on their various businesses. Being a port town, Silverstone was bustling, but we seemed to have missed the morning rush. I didn't mind that, as a bit of a more peaceful stroll felt more my speed for this trip.

While the city was on the upper end of what one normally saw in this kingdom it didn't compare at all to the city of Lithere, where I'd made my home for the past few years. It was also hilariously easy to find the direction we needed to go, since one whole side of the city was taken up by the various docks. Of course, that didn't mean we had any clue where our ship should be, or even how the port was organized, but that was a problem for when we arrived.

"So, I hear that you're our resident item expert?" Robert offered as an opener.

"Yeah, sort of. I mean, I'm better at those than a lot of people, but I view myself more as a general caster."

"Hey, don't sell yourself short. Dras told us that you were one of the best he knew."

"Well, maybe, but there's still a ton to learn. What about you? My understanding is that you're a really good healer." I leaned over to look at him as I spoke and he blushed, seeming a bit nervous.

"Yeah," he said, scratching his head as he spoke. "The village Leah and I grew up in didn't have any priests or anything, so I ended up patching a lot of people up. When we finally got to school, I guess I just signed up for all the healing classes and it kinda went from there. I'm no priest mind you, but I can still treat most stuff."

My guess was that Robert and his sister were a year or two older than me, but I wasn't sure. I'd never run into them at the academy, but I pretty much kept to my small friend group, so that wasn't odd.

"That I understand," I said, nodding at his story. "My village went through a rough patch too. Except with us it was the famine that was worse than any injuries." I looked off a bit as I remembered the place, which from my understanding was now nothing but ruins.

"Damn nobles didn't care about anyone but themselves." He spat. "Let the rest of us rot while they stayed in their little manors sipping wine and eating cake. Emperor Durin kicking those lazy bastards to the curb might have been the best thing to ever happen to the country."

"I'm inclined to agree. I still know a few people who were nobles, and not all of them were that bad though. One or two were decent enough people, but a lot seemed either too proud or . . . apathetic to what happened to the common folk. Personally, I think that can be worse than just hatred, because it's not that they want to do harm, it's that they just don't care if it happens."

At a quizzical look from him I gave a brief telling of how my home had been doomed by the local lord forcing us all to be locked in our city palisade, robbing us of our ability to stockpile our food, and wrecked parts of our infrastructure.

"That's insane! How did you all survive if you had to waste that much of your stock?"

"Well, I made a small mountain of bread for people, but in the end we didn't. The town isn't there anymore."

He placed a hand on my shoulder and gave me a reassuring squeeze. "I'm sorry."

"It . . . wasn't good, and not a great time for me either. On another note, I think we're about there." I pointed and waited for his eyes to follow.

We'd made it almost all the way to the port, and the ships were now clearly visible, their rigging standing over some of the smaller nearby buildings. I hadn't noticed it before now, but I could hear the gulls making their racket over the soft sound of the waves splashing against the wood and stone that lined the harbor.

There was no beach, only a small stone path that led to the various docks where all the vessels were anchored. The salty smell was strong and fresh, and it was with a smile that I noticed something I'd seen only in my old world. The cement that made up the walkway and its various small walls here had shells mixed in with it, giving it a rather unique look and feel.

We made our way down the dock looking for our boats. Most of these could be ruled out with little more than a glance, though I had to explain to Robert why.

"It's none of those, look at them," I said.

"They're all too small, and the nets. Those are fishing boats, not merchant ships. You'd never be able to cross as far as we're going with them."

"Oh . . . have you ever been on one before?"

"No, but that doesn't mean I'm wrong. What about you?"

He shook his head. "First time at the coast too. The ocean is just so . . . big."

"More than I think either of us know. Come on, those look promising." I pointed at a grouping of many-sailed behemoths bobbing in the harbor to one side. Their dock, sitting out farther than the others, looked much more private.

CHAPTER 2

✦

INTO THE HORIZON

Our boats were all moored at the same pier.

The ship that I would be traveling on was known as *The Crystal*. Boasting three massive masts, she was the largest of the nearby vessels . . . With square-rigged sails, she resembled a carrack, but with specific differences to what I knew of Age of Exploration ships from back home. For example, *The Crystal* didn't have gunports in the hull.

The captain was an old man named Tom who looked almost carved from the same wood as his vessel. He barked harsh, rather expletive-filled orders to his crew as he trudged down the gangplank toward us, apparently now informed of our arrival.

He seemed embarrassed when he realized that a young woman awaited him. "Ah, sorry miss," he said. "The language is a bit crass and I'd've liked to have a talk with you lot first. You'll have to abide it though; the men are too dense to listen to any else."

"I can't speak for anyone else, Captain," I said, "but honestly, so long as all of us make it safely to our destination I don't give a fuck what kind of language you use."

Both men in this conversation blinked at me for a moment before the old sailor burst into laughter. "Well, ain't that somethin'? A fair breeze after a blistering day you are compared to the delicate flowers we normally see when moving noblewomen."

"There are no nobles anymore, Captain," Robert said.

Since the regime change, many saw it as a major *faux pas* to compare people to the nobility of the past.

"Aye, forgive me, lad, old habits are especially hard to break when one doesn't spend much time ashore. I know things have changed and—so far as I can tell—for the better."

Curious, I asked, "Have things changed much in your business then, Captain?"

"Day to day? Not too much change. Still folks in charge, and still folks that got shipments to run. I will say, though, that the import dues are a sight better for us, and ports seem to be runnin' a bit smoother. The coasts are being scoured . . . well some places not as well, but overall, more regularly." He scratched his chin and seemed to shake himself out of a thought. "Enough of that though. I understand some of you lot are wizards?"

"We're all magic users, though of different types."

"Oh, that's good then. Is there a priest or a weather wizard among you?"

"No priests," Robert announced. He looked to me, his eyes asking a subtle question. When I gave him a light nod, he added, "But, when it comes to weather control, I believe my companion here can be of aid."

"Limited," I offered, making sure to undersell my abilities. Better to be underestimated, I decided. "I have some control but only for a bit."

"Excellent! Best thing to have on board is a weather wizard. Shame on the priest, though, seeing as none of the Elven lads have that talent."

Robert seemed a bit flustered. "Captain, most bards can heal."

"That so? Can't say I know too much about magic."

His statement wasn't odd considering that many common folk didn't understand casters. Sure, everyone knew that priests and wizards were a thing, and most probably knew that some people could punch a hole in cement. However, the distinctions between types of caster and the particulars of magical practice were outside of what commoners needed to know. While many of Captain Tom's crew had some level of magical ability, it just wasn't at a level that could have the broader effects he was hoping for. While the elves probably possessed more skill, the captain either didn't know or didn't care.

"Regardless, Captain, we're not planning on leaving until all our groups arrive. So, at the least you'll have today," Robert said.

"Ah, the men'll be glad for that, lad. It'll give them some time ashore to . . . rest."

"And give the local brothels business, surely," I interjected. "If we get word on our time to head out we'll send it forward to you."

"Thank you then, Miss, I'll see you then." He left to inform his crew. The sailors, having received a similar message from the group that had arrived before us, were enjoying some time off at the port. As far as I could tell, the ship was crewed entirely by men. While amongst the mages there was a far more equitable feeling in the common folk gender norms much more like the past of my previous world still abounded. Almost every sailor was a man, and while in port, they were doing what sailors did. A fair percentage of the crew also appeared to be of Elven extraction, a clear benefit when sailing back and forth between our continents. This led to some interesting interactions, because while I'd been getting ogled by most of the sailors, this lot seemed rather respectful, and soon their companions noticed. Here and there, I could see the flickers of suppressed auras, and understood that these elves could see that I was a caster. From what I was seeing I was guessing that most of these were minor talents, though perhaps there was a possibility that some of them could use magic properly.

I'd been told in my classes that every elf had magic on some level. For most, this manifested as what humans would call a "minor talent," allowing them access to a simple and small ability. My first maid had been such, able to create water from nothing, so were many of the other maids. It could even be a small physical enhancements. Though not the sort of blatantly superhuman stuff my dad or brother could do, the elves certainly knew enough to push just to the edge of what would be believable on Earth. We saw ourselves off. Not that we had a ton to do today other than find a proper inn, something I hoped the rest of our party had taken to doing without us. The stroll back was slightly more difficult because of the angle of the road, but it was still pleasant and we took all the time we needed.

Olnir had returned and, as it turned out, the first group had secured rooms for us at their inn. It made things significantly easier during the three days we spent stuck waiting for the last group to arrive and make their arrangements. On the last morning I woke up extra early to enjoy a bath, probably the last proper wash I'd get for the next couple months.

The other girls agreed, and we took turns, chatting as we utilized facilities I personally would sorely miss.

"So, what's it going to be like on the boat?" Leah queried. "Do we have a room or something?"

"No idea," I said with a shrug. "I imagine we'll have something private from the guys, but I'm unsure on what all that will be. I've never been on a boat like this, so it could be a room smaller than one of those carriages."

"Surely it'll be larger than that. We'll at least have beds Alana, and a desk or something." Selene seemed to be very confused about the size of our vessel.

"I doubt that we'll have anything like a proper bed. Space on a ship is a premium thing, and ours isn't quite that large."

"Well, we'll have to have something," Leah said, looking irritated at the very idea of not having proper quarters.

"I suppose we'll see. No use worrying at this point." With Selene's final comment we finished what little packing we had to do and trooped out.

The trip from our inn to the docks was rather uneventful. The dew was still on the grass and the sun struggling up from its place behind the horizon as we boarded the ship one by one, welcomed by the captain. The crew was, for the most part, busy readying the ship to make sail, but a few of them gave a quick nod to our little group.

"Boy," the old seaman shouted off to the far end of the ship. "C'mere and show the ladies to their quarters."

An Elven lad—who looked to be no older than a human eight-year-old—came bounding out of a doorway which, I assumed, led to the lower decks. Upon seeing us, he blanched slightly and gave the captain a sharp, "Yes, sir!"

"Um . . . your quarters are this way, as for your luggage . . ."

Selene gave a light wave and our three personal trunks floated up a few inches. She'd managed this trick the whole way from the inn, and it didn't seem to bother her at all.

"Oh," the boy smiled. "That'll do perfectly. This way please."

From what I could see, the ship had several levels. There were two above the main deck at the stern, one at the bow, and, based on the heights, I would guess three more below, with a final area for the bilge. The lack of cannons probably allowed for more cargo space, and I knew for a fact that we were taking some along with us for this trip. I didn't know, or care what that was though since it had little to do with me.

The cabin boy led us to a door toward the stern that opened not onto stairs leading down but into a dark tight area. Our quarters were hardly bigger than a closet. On either wall, two stacked wooden boards served as bunk beds. The only other furnishings were a lamp hanging from the ceiling and a tiny writing desk at the back of the room. With us all inside it was quite cramped.

Selene looked stunned at the size. "This can't possibly be right."

"Begging your pardon, miss, but this is the biggest private room, save for the captain's. The mate normally has this room, and the bosun gave up his quarters for the gentlemen with your group."

She looked at the boy with a quirked brow. "Well, where are they sleeping?"

"Down below with the rest of the crew."

"It'll be fine," I interjected. This would have to do. "Is there anywhere else we can be where we won't be in the way?"

"There's room on the deck, miss, but the captain may be cross if you disturb the men while they are working."

"We'll head there once our things are secured, then."

He left us to tie down our trunks, and we soon joined the rest of those on deck. I personally wanted to see everything as we made our way out. In that desire, I found a quiet spot well away from anyone messing with rigging or any of the other many jobs that went into running a ship, and settled in. Leaving port wasn't a fast operation. Once we got going though, we pulled out into the harbor, making our way toward the bright ocean. Along the docks, a few women waved to the sailors as we left. Some passing men yelled as well, wishing us luck on our journey with a smile and a raised hat.

So, into the great blue sea we moved. Moment by moment, the land shrunk behind us as we made our way out toward the horizon.

CHAPTER 3

✦

FIRST DAYS AT SEA

It took us a few hours for the shore to fade to little more than a line. This boat wasn't particularly fast, and even with a favorable wind there was little in the way of propulsion. I could have helped with the wind some, but only for a couple hours at most. But on a calm day like this, it wasn't really needed. I'd been on several boats before, though only a few at sea. This, however, was slightly different, in that it was nowhere near as stable or comfortable as those. I suspected the fact that we had to sail with the wind didn't help matters.

By noon, all three ships of our expedition were well away, the horizon now looking flat and blue in all directions. I could see the captain and a few others taking occasional measurements using a watch and the position of the sun.

"Captain," I asked as he settled into a spot where he could watch over the crew. As it was, we were now cruising along happily, and they needed little of his immediate input.

"Did ya need something, lass?"

"Just a question. I saw you checking the heading, is there a reason you don't use a compass instead?" I knew such things were available if a bit uncommon on land.

"A couple. While I do have a few it's good to check by the sun. There're a few creatures out in the deeps that can throw off your heading if you go by that alone."

"What kind of monster can do that?"

"Oh, don't worry, don't worry," he soothed. "While there are some truly massive beasties out there, none see a ship our size as a meal. The ones messing with the compass often aren't even that big; little schools of fishes and the like."

"Oh, that's good. We had spine wolves back home. Hate to have to deal with that kind of thing on the water."

"There are monsters, but our boats are big, and wooden. We don't look like food to them unless we go for a dip. There are a few spots where you can find something that could and would take a ship like ours, but those leviathans don't leave their home areas often, and we'll be steering well and clear of all of those."

"Probably need the mana concentration there." That comment got me a curious look, so I went on. "Most of the really big things on land only live where there's lots of mana. Under Lithere, there's a whole system of tunnels, and the deeper you go the worse it gets."

"Huh, I'd never heard that one. Makes sense though, I guess. Even at sea things tend to cluster around particular spots. Some deep in the ocean, some near reefs. There's even tell of islands that no ship can get near to without problems."

I wanted to know more about those, but from what I was hearing he didn't know much about it. That was sort of unfortunate, but I could just ask around, either when we got back or found land.

For the moment though, I had a good seat to watch how things were done on a ship. For example, the drinking water was created on board. I watched as the cabin boy and another elf moved to a barrel and added the fluid several times throughout the morning. My guess was that they were using as much mana as they safely could before returning to their duties, and it was enough water to supplement what the crew would need. My guess was that there was still some stored fresh water, but probably much less than what ships from Earth would have needed for this voyage.

Beyond that, it was also interesting to see a man at the top of the mast exchanging messages with our sister ships. We looked to only be talking to the center ship in our formation, which was a simple wedge triangle with us to the far-right side. Occasionally, a pair of red and black flags were taken out, and the crewman waved them in various patterns. I wasn't sure how developed this code was, but it seemed to have "check-in" and "reply" signals, at the very least.

Before long, the first of two lunch shifts was called. Our group was given priority in the serving line along with the captain and his officers. The food was surprisingly good, and it seemed that Olnir agreed with my assessment.

"I was told that the food on board would be rather plain, Captain, but this is about as fine a quality as you'd find in any inn."

"Oh, don't mind that, sir," an officer offered while Captain Tom chortled. "We'll be on ship biscuit and beans before too long, have no worries." He said it with such a chipper smile that every sailor present got a good laugh before our host managed his own reply.

"Normal food, lad, is mostly a mixture of the biscuit—no sane man could call that bread. Ye might also get a bit of cheese, some salted pork, and beans. Every couple days, we'll also have sweetened porridge with fruit that we'll all be needing to keep off scurvy."

I wanted to groan on how that could get old fast, particularly with the heavily watered beer that we were being given, but I'd survived on mostly summoned bread for a hefty chunk of my childhood, so there was no point.

"Oh, I see," Olnir replied sullenly. Most of my companions looked a bit put out as well.

I, on the other hand, was less bothered, something which the captain seemed to notice. "I didn't get the impression you'd sailed before, lass," he asked with a slightly raised brow.

"I haven't, sir. Not like this. I did, however, learn the lessons of sparse, bland food from my childhood, and brought my own herbs and tea." There were several very tightly stuffed jars in my luggage which I hoped held enough to make it through much of the journey.

"Ha! Takes most men at least one trip across the blue to think of that. Not worried about any of the men trying to rob you, though?"

"Any man who tries to rob me will sorely regret that poor decision," I answered. My chipper response got the old seaman laughing again.

After lunch, there really wasn't much for me to do. I returned to my cabin, resolved to either work on my core or to do some reviewing of the Guide. This, at least, didn't have me sitting in the sun all day. I sat and sunk into my own mind, letting myself drift a bit. Since hitting the second level of the core, I had noticed that I was becoming somewhat more aware of things going on around me. It was nice to be able to sense when someone wanted to come over to talk.

I spent several hours thus: making my connections, and building toward the third and final level of the core. This segment was absolutely massive, and I had little hope of finishing it anytime soon. The fact that almost nobody did probably had to do with how daunting the task looked. There would be a ton of time investment for any payoff at all, I just hoped that it would be worth it down the line.

After a few hours, I returned to the world at large only to notice that I was feeling a bit below the weather. I stood up, took a step from the bunk, and promptly doubled over, spewing what was left of lunch all over the floor. My hands grabbed for the bunk so that I wouldn't fall in my own sick.

Ah, the smell of vomit, and the wonderful things it does when you encounter it. I got a second to briefly look at the mess before another wave of horrid nausea crashed into me, nearly sending me sprawling again. Around the same time, I heard small racing feet approaching followed by quick knocking on the door.

"Miss, you sick?" It was the voice of the cabin boy.

"Yeah."

"Hold on, I'll grab you a bucket."

"Thank you," I said thickly. After retching again, I called, "Just come in when you have it."

It was only a moment or two later that he returned with the pail and a damp cloth. Upon opening the door, he groaned a bit before holding them out to me.

"Please try to hit the bucket, miss. I don't fancy cleaning up even more."

I quickly understood that he was the one in charge of cleaning our room if needed. After giving the bucket a nice warm-up, I sang a few notes.

Singing while trying to not puke was fun and all, but getting out enough to remove the mess and smell was priority if I ever wanted this to stop, which I absolutely did. I felt as I always did when sick: consumed by a deep and dark longing for ginger ale. If there was any chance of learning to make it someday, I would, if only to aid the upset stomachs of the blighted world.

"Thank you for the help . . . um . . . what's your name," I asked as I tried to keep myself together.

"It's Elian, miss. That's some spell," he added, looking on in amazement as the cabin cleaned itself. "If only I could."

"Right. Thank you, Elian. Sorry for embarrassing myself like this."

"Not at all. Happen to a lot of our passengers. The lads were taking bets on you lot, and I'm happy to say I won." He straightened, beaming proudly.

"Well, at least I made you some money."

"Oh, not on you, miss. I bet that your boss would get the ocean stomach. You should've seen the bosun's face when he got it right on his shoes!

Had to go and hide, myself. If that old jerk saw me laughing, he'd tan my backside."

"Well, I'm sorry I missed that too. Olnir's kind of a jerk."

That earned a laugh.

I spent several days cooped up in the cabin with my new and dearest friend, Mr. Bucket. The other girls had somehow managed to dodge the bullet while most of the boys had some level of seasickness. It was made clear to me that though I was feeling poorly, nothing could compare to what Olnir endured below decks. He was so bad that the other boys nearly kicked him from the cabin out of frustration. Sadly, I was a bit too busy with my own issues to witness Olnir's misery, but such is life.

CHAPTER 4

✦

DARK SKY

When I finally surfaced from my seclusion, now used to the rocking of the ocean and several pounds lighter, I had a rather sad moment. While we were still guests, very well-paying ones, dining at the captain's table, the quality of food had taken a noticeable decline. Having been consumed quickly by crew or by the natural passage of time, much of the ship's stock of greens and other perishable foods was already gone. Meats and most herbs and vegetables couldn't last much more than a week. Even flour, which I thought would be fine, spoiled. A question to my favorite cabin boy got me a graphic description of how bugs and other pests would get into it, thus ruining our supply.

After two weeks afloat, Dras approached to have a discussion with me after dinner one night.

"Hey Alana." He froze under my gaze, and I narrowed my eyes. I knew well what he wanted.

"Yes."

"Could you, maybe, help out with the food? Just a bit of fresh bread would make this so much better."

The other girls had joined us at this point, and they each gave me a betrayed look. I'd never told them that I could make food on my own.

I let my lips creep upwards into a smile that didn't reach my eyes. Before I went any further, I had questions of my own. "Dras, who have you told about my ability to make foods?"

"Well, nobody. I thought it'd be better to talk to you first."

"Good, and make sure you don't. You two either," I added with a glare for Selene and Leah.

Selene blinked. "Okay, but why? It's just for our dinner, right? Is it mana-intensive or anything? Not like we're using much."

"Well, yes and no. It's not hard at all, but if the sailors get wind, which they will if I start making much, they'll all want bread. I don't want that kind of demand, nor do I want a refusal to stir up any ill will."

"I get that," Leah said with a knowing look.

"Wait," Selene looked curious now. "Can all bards just *poof* food out?"

"In theory," Leah offered. "Back when we were littler, Robert and I learned to, but we only ever made stuff for our family, and not bread. Food prices were insane and often supply was non-existent for some things." She cringed and continued. "One of our aunties learned that my brother could make a passable cream, and she pestered him non-stop for, like, three years to supply her. Eventually, he blew up in her face and swore he'd never make her another drop."

I patted Leah's shoulder in understanding. While I normally didn't mind creating food, I'd been stuck with hungry people before and had no desire to be seen as the local bakery again. "So," I said, "you and your brother can make cream? I'd be willing to do some work in trade to improve the tea a bit if you want."

"Oh no, he can do cream. I do oil for cooking and lamps and stuff." She gave a nervous look at our little conclave. "You are not to let Brother know I told you under any circumstances. Don't ask him about anything like it, either, or he'll be beyond mad."

"Understandable," I said with a nod. If it would cause problems with the group, I could abstain, at least until I found the right way to acquire what I wanted. If all else failed, adding a new spell to my list wouldn't be the worst thing; especially since I couldn't practice teleporting on a ship full of researchers investigating teleporting.

"Not understandable at all!" Selene's tone was shrill. "If getting more food in is possible, I want to go for it as hard as we can!"

Leah, Dras and I took a moment to look at Selene with raised eyebrows. While Selene tried and failed to strike a hopeful pose, Dras went back to why he'd come here in the first place. "Selene's excitement notwithstanding, I really do want some better food. Alana, you mentioned a trade?"

"I'll talk to my brother. Privately," Leah added quickly. "As for the rest of us?"

"Sure," I answered. "I'll pitch in a bit so long as it's not much."

"I'll keep quiet if I must," Selene conceded with a sigh.

"Of course," Dras added.

Leah nodded. "Okay, then I'll toss in some oil. There's not much on the ship and most of that will be for lamps anyway."

"Very well, then," I began. "Let us now call the first meeting of the 'Bards for Better Food Coalition' to order."

I was met with groans.

Dras raised a hand. "We're not calling it that. We're not calling it anything."

"Do you not want to be part of the coalition then? It was your idea."

"No, no it wasn't. I just wanted some bread."

In the end there wasn't much to it. We managed to get Robert involved, though only through his sister's urging. Our supply was enough, and hiding all of it from everyone else was a fun game too. Sure, people would be mad at us if or when they found out, but I couldn't really be bothered to care that much. We weren't hurting anyone, and it kept us busy and out of the way.

After four weeks of seeing nothing but blue in every direction, I was starting to get used to life on a ship. The rocking of the boat hardly bothered me anymore—though, before our return trip, I would be having a hammock made—and while the food had now dissolved into the most bland and terrible fare being served publicly, we had our clandestine arrangements.

I also picked up some new songs and a dice game from the sailors, one which my roommates and I were playing as a knock came on our door. I was used to the periodic visits from Elian, who joined us for a game when invited, probably because it was a good way to hide from work, but this knock was harsher than the cabin boy's.

With a shrug, Selene stood and moved to the door, opening it slowly. "Captain? Is there something wrong?"

"Ah, probably not, but I'd like a word with Miss Alana, if I may."

He didn't bother to hide the serious note in his voice, and I quickly moved to the door.

"Something amiss?" I asked.

"I'd like a bit of help on deck. We need a bit of wind, if you could."

It didn't take me long to get ready and join the crew on deck. The mood was not one of levity. Olnir stood along the rail with the captain and a few of his officers staring at the horizon. Midnight black clouds billowed just within view, reaching up into the fair blue sky. It was unnatural the way they formed such a small area of the sky. All around that smokey bank the weather looked calm and normal. Within the churning column, dark blue streaks illuminated the roiling clouds.

"That," I said, pointing, "isn't normal, is it?"

"No," Captain Tom confirmed. He didn't seem panicked, but it was clear he sensed danger. "It looks like the doing of one of the larger beasts of the deep, and I'd rather be nowhere near it, lass. Can you sing us up a wind to speed us on ahead?"

The other ships in our convoy had pulled near. Though above us the red and black flags were being waved frantically, we were all close enough to shout to the next ship as we looked back and forth. *The Crystal* took the center position. I didn't know for sure, but since weather magic was very uncommon, I might well be the best at it in our little expedition. I began singing one of my favorite shanties the crew had taught me. Within a few words, the men joined in, and soon the gestalt got to doing its work. The captain gestured the direction our wind should blow, and moments later the sails, limp and lifeless, filled and pulled taut from the gale. With so many joining me, the feat wasn't too difficult. This ship, which had been so leisurely making its way through the waves, now cut like a sword along the ocean, all the officers at attention and pushing the men to their limit.

First, we maintained our heading, but it was no use. As we moved the little black patch on the horizon grew and grew, almost as if it was coming straight for us. Looking more disquieted by the moment Captain Tom turned the ship at the same time as the others. If it was headed the same way we were then there was no reason that we couldn't get out of its way and let it pass us by.

As if it knew our position and course, the storm seemed to move with us. If this were the work of some monster, then it may well have chosen us as its prey.

This wasn't just a small patch of darkness in the sky, no, it was massive. It was only the scale that had made me think it small, but as it grew closer and closer the size multiplied. We'd started our singing just after breakfast, when the billowing black was little more than a patch on the horizon. But by early afternoon, it obscured nearly a quarter of the horizon, the churning clouds reaching up high.

When the captain addressed me, half the sky was lost in the inky smoke. "You can stop singing, lass," he said, voice was hoarse. "Need to talk to the men."

Soon, the other vessels pulled close and ropes were sent across. Olnir and Captain Tom were shortly joined at the helm by those I assumed to be the other expedition leaders and ship captains.

"Well, no point in disputing it," one of the other ships' captains announced. "Only one thing makes a storm that big, and if it's followed us this far we're not getting away."

A mage I'd seen once or twice at Mystien's workshop stepped up and asked, "What are we looking at?"

"Hurricane Whale," Captain Tom answered grimly. "Big, nasty beasts, that live in the deepest ocean. They can make one monster of a storm, but luckily they're pretty rare. I've only heard stories of them."

"I've seen one," the guest captain answered. "We've only two choices: we can run, but we'll fail to escape."

"Or?" Olnir asked.

"Or we take the fight to it."

The third captain looked dour as he answered, "They can be killed. We've harpoons aboard, and more casters than I could hope for. It'll be a rough fight, but it's that or let it chase us."

"How will we even find it," one of the other mages asked.

"Oh, that's the easy part. It wants us anyway; we won't have to look hard." Captain Tom's face had hardened to wood, afraid—probably terrified—but ready.

CHAPTER 5

✦

AGAINST THE LEVIATHAN

The crew wasted no time getting to work. Every man on board ran to and fro; readying harpoons, making sure the sails were in proper proportion, and battening hatches. As the hive of activity roared the captain approached me with a bit of rope where I stood near the wheel.

"Pardon me, miss, but you might be needing this." He wrapped the rope around a nearby piece of railing then gingerly helped me tie it around my waist. "Can't have you getting swept away. If something goes terribly wrong and you must, pull this line here. It'll undo the knot I put in. Better safe than sorry," he added, checking his work over. It was rather impressive, the way he'd done it up in mere seconds.

I watched as all our casters were similarly secured. We were guests, but in this case, there was no getting around needing to fight. Glen was the only one who refused the rope. As our physical user, he wanted to be able to move as needed. I also noticed that the stocky young man had acquired a hefty bundle of harpoons for himself. Having seen him throw things before, I felt confident he'd use them well.

The different bards were assigned crewmen to help them with their magic, and as one our ships changed course, forming a wedge with *The Crystal* at the lead. This close arrangement would make it much easier to keep the wind and shields going in a way that benefited all three ships.

Once we were all in position, we still had to make it to our enemy, who was not at all close. As minutes passed and the stress level rose, you could see the cracks starting to form in the crew's resolve. We waited for contact with this monster we had no choice to fight but wanted to be done with.

Closer and closer to the storm we sailed. As our forces prepared to clash, I couldn't help but feel like we'd made a horrible mistake. The storm bared down on us, the clouds soaring above in a wall of insurmountable darkness. I had to crane my head up to see the top as we neared its leading edge.

In the last few moments before we broke the wall of clouds, spells roared to life. A glowing shield formed a dome over each of our ships to protect us from the worst of the wind and rain. A ball of either light or fire flared at each bow, allowing our party to keep track of one another in the gloaming. Any caster who was using a combat spell got their magic working up. I was told in no uncertain terms that since we didn't know how long this would take, my job was to maintain our wind and nothing else.

The edge of the storm looked almost solid, like it was constrained by a wall within only that area. Though the wind and rain howled, it did not stray from its designated column. As we breached containment, however, the change was immediate.

The waves, which had been getting rougher and choppier, swelled to massive heights. Around us, the sky blurred from the rain pummeling our shields. Despite the terrible visibility, we persisted.

I could feel the resistance of the storm to my own magic, but it was minimal. I got the feeling that whatever had made this wasn't actively managing all of it like I was with my wind. The majority of the power seemed to be focused keeping the clouds and rain contained while building them. It was like the Hurricane Whale was heating up the inside like a kettle, a barrier, and then the rest of the energy pumped into building the tempest.

Everyone on the ship searched frantically, eyes darting about to find our enemy. As we crested each massive wave all we could see were more lined up against us. More waves poised to sink our ships to sweep us from these small vessels and into the gullet of the waiting beast.

I flinched as lightning struck near us, but held my concentration on my song. Quite suddenly, however, maintaining the wind became more difficult. By the moment, the strain increased. The glow around the ships shone as the rain came in sideways torrents, raindrops being thrown into our shields like a hail of bullets.

"Something's happening," I shouted to Captain Tom. Moments later, the twins yelled the same as their shield came under heavier assault.

The storm reached fever pitch. The Hurricane Whale breached the surface, flying higher and higher into the air. Backlit by a dozen streaks of arctic blue lightning, the shape of the beast hung above us, water raining down from it in glittering droplets. In that instant, I and the crew around me froze in fear.

This beast was massive on a scale I could hardly process, easily as long as a football field with a horn sticking out again half of that. Around its weapon the aura it let off was visible and roaring like a swirling torrent of water. When it reached the peak of its arc many things happened at once. From our ships a dozen spells rocketed into the air, projectiles of red, blue and green leaving trails of light. The physical users were not to be out-done, though, and several harpoons flashed in the dim light on their way toward the beast at ballistic velocities. I doubted they'd survive as more than sharp scrap metal when they finally stopped. These left several vis-ible, but likely not fatal wounds in the creature's thick hide.

The monster, not one to leave such a message unanswered, hurled an absolutely monumental bolt of lightning at one of our sister ships. The streaking mass of plasma found one of the masts which, upon contact, exploded violently, the wood vaporized in an instant. Thankfully, the only screams I could hear were in my mind.

Then the chase was on. I saw the glow of the shields shift in color, indi-cating they were being altered to prevent another of us being struck. We sailed after our enemy. The Hurricane Whale outclassed us in raw power and size, but like a flock of sparrows mobbing an eagle, we were not to be denied.

The injured monster made to get more distance from us. We sailed after it as fast as we could, ships cutting through the high waves as we tracked the whale. It had underestimated us, and we couldn't allow it to slip away. Our plan was simple: to harry it until it could resist no more. Importantly, we couldn't allow it to retreat, lest the storm fight us instead.

It breached again, this time between us and the ship it had already damaged, and again our combined forces loosed fury upon it. It responded much as it had before, but the lightning bolt shattered, blue energy crack-ling harmlessly across the surface of the targeted vessel.

As it fell back into the water, a massive wave arose from its point of depar-ture. The wall of water bore down on all of us despite the shields, sweeping across our decks. Everyone had to hold on tight as the wave threatened to take us from our little wooden fortress. My hands slipped, I lost my footing and began to flail. The rope tied about my waist snapped taut, jerking me harshly but keeping me in place long enough for the water to pass.

I coughed and spat seawater while I tried to steady myself.

"You good, lass," I heard the captain ask from his spot, gripping the wheel for dear life.

"Yeah," I yelled in return.

"Good. Forward then! Let's get this beast."

"Aye aye, Captain."

"Hah!"

As I rose, I saw several men from the ships had been swept overboard. It took me a moment to understand that—to my horror—they were all at the mercy of an unnatural current sweeping away from us.

"Ropes," I yelled. "Get them ropes!"

I was too late. I watched as the Hurricane Whale came up from below, the men pulled into its gullet.

I wanted to puke as I saw them swallowed by the massive creature, lost to us now. It didn't escape with that meal for free, though, as more and more attacks pelted it from the survivors.

This process repeated itself several more times as our battle continued. We'd learned its tactics, though, and when the next wave came only one or two men fell into the dark waters to be consumed. The battle was bloody, and horrid, but we all watched, hoping against hope that some of us would make it.

It took a toll on us though. The mana to keep so many spells going was exhausting, and as the battle wore on, more and more of the rain was let through the shields in favor of keeping the lightning away. I was managing, but only barely, my mana slowly ticking away from all the continuous use, gestalt or no.

While we were waterlogged and exhausted, the whale was bloody. It looked like something out of a horror movie as it breached once more, hell-bent on our destruction. After its fall-and-wave came again, it stayed down for longer than before, and I tried to hope that it had finally succumbed to its injuries.

That was not to be, though. The creature, having sensed our weakening defenses, opted for a new attack. This time as it breached the waves, the Hurricane Whale slammed into the side of the most damaged ship, its horn leading the assault. It was sickening to see the massive spire of bone pierce the other vessel, breaking wood like wet paper.

"More harpoons" Glen shrieked, launching the last of his own horde of weapons.

The cabin boy, Elian, ran toward him with another bundle. Though otherwise trying to stay out of the way, he'd been running harpoons to the men as they exhausted their supplies. I heard the cracking of wood splintering from the damaged ship as the beast thrashed and bucked, whipping its head and flinging debris from the destroyed vessel in our direction.

Our shields, focused on lightning, were less effective, and the slabs of wood were not small. Though smaller pieces of debris splintered or deflected off of our meager defenses, larger projectiles made it through, slamming into the rigging and crunching our two rear masts. I was nearest the back mast and saw it leaning like a tree in the middle of felling. With clumsy fingers, I yanked on the knot the captain had shown me and released myself.

I jumped down to the nearby lower deck not a moment too soon. What remained of the mast crashed down. Wood and thick ropes lay in a heap where I'd been mere seconds before.

It took us all a few heartbeats to regain our composure and look, but when we did we saw a most welcome sight.

The titan had destroyed one ship, but in the process had caught itself in the wreckage. Ropes bound to the hull now wrapped around its horn like a net and I nearly cheered as I saw the massive beast struggle against their bindings, held fast to the mess it had created.

We were nearly dead in the water, but while our crew pelted the writhing beast with anything they could find, the final vessel in our cohort closed in. Flanking the creature, our sister ship's forces flung spells and projectiles in equal measure. The already bloody hide of the monster ripped and shredded beneath their angry onslaught.

The creature, though, would have its say. With a painful keening, it expelled more mana than I'd seen it use yet. Its final spell pulled in inconceivable quantities of energy, and loosed one final storm of lightning against the other ship, setting it aflame. Fire reflected in the monster's eyes as the light faded from them.

I stood on the deck, stunned that the beast had finally been taken down, a massive wave hit us.

I tumbled, thrown like a doll in the water only to come up with one hand latched onto something. One of the many, many ropes from our own ship hand made its way into my hand and, on instinct, I must have held fast to it.

I could see Elian, though, had not been so lucky. In the chaos, he was floating free. He tried to swim, but the waves and wind overwhelmed him, and it was clear he had little chance. As another wave made to break upon him, I had a choice: I could try to save him, and perhaps we'd both die; or I could let him go.

There was no choice. As the wave came down, I sang a note. I'd only ever used this spell in private, and I hoped that in the churning chaos of the storm I would remain unseen. Below Elian, I made space contort and twist, forming a passage through the water and foam to my side. Just as I planned, he disappeared beneath the breaker, only to surface by me an instant later.

I nearly swooned, my mana depleted, thankful for one thing I learned. It seemed—at this range, at least—that distance didn't affect how much mana was needed in any meaningful way, something I'd not really been able to test back home.

Even as my head swam with nausea, I managed to wrap the boy with my legs, clinging to both him and the rope. Everything hurt, and my vision blurred as I felt someone pulling us gently upwards.

In a flicker of lucidity, I looked up and saw Robert.

"The boy," I asked.

"He's alive."

As the answer registered, I felt the darkness take me.

CHAPTER 6

AFTER THE BATTLE

When I came to, I felt like I'd been run over by a car. Everything hurt, from my head to my toes, after using all of my strength in the fight. It took me a moment to realize that the hard heaving back and forth was the ship and not some symptom of my current state.

A quick check confirmed that I'd been stripped of my soaked clothing and tossed in my bed, possibly by my roommates. Leah was leaning against the nearby wall, seemingly exhausted from her exertions.

"You're awake," she said as the boat pitched at a concerning angle.

"Yeah, what's the current state of things?"

"In a word, bad. The storm isn't dying down. Any thoughts?"

As the resident user of weather magic, I'd be in charge of that disaster.

"Maybe," I said. "Let me get up." I tried to rise and promptly had to sit back down. "Woah, okay, maybe take things slowly."

It took several minutes to get dressed in something dry and clean up the worst of the bumps and bruises. I'd been slammed and tossed by several waves, and there were rope burns on my hands and waist from the various bits keeping me onboard. The stinging wasn't too bad, but it was distracting, and I needed to be in good form for whatever was going on outside.

As I opened my door, I found several sailors collapsed in the hallway outside. We were near the door to the main deck, and it looked as if the injured men—unable to make it down into the hold and barely able to move from their exertions—had collapsed in here to rest. Though some of them nodded wearily and tried to shift out of the way as I passed, most didn't acknowledge me.

There was no sound of rain, even as the waves heaved violently. As I opened the door, I understood. Outside, the sky above was a brilliant pink and gold field of light. On all sides, clouds towered into the sky, bounding it above us in a circle perhaps a mile or so wide in walls of white and grey.

Glen must have seen me coming, and he appeared at my side, offering me a hand. "Here, don't want you falling again now, do we?" He tried to lighten the mood a bit, but the smile he gave me was strained.

Our ship had been thoroughly dismasted. I'd seen two of the three destroyed by the Hurricane Whale, but the third had apparently followed while I was unconscious. Several men struggled to pull what remained back into place.

"Good, you're up."

I heard the captain before I saw him. Turning I caught a look.

Captain Tom looked terrible. He'd been soaked, battered, and hung out to dry. His eyes showed that he'd probably not slept a wink all night, and if I had to guess it wouldn't be long before he passed out. He was no young man, and these conditions were taking a heavy toll on him.

"I thought we killed the beast," he said, "but the squall . . ." His voice trailed off as he gestured to the obvious.

I sang a few notes and tried to push against the local weather. There was no resistance to the magic, not that I was trying to change much.

"I'm pretty sure we did, Captain. It's just that this storm is big enough to keep going naturally for a while."

"All right, care to explain this then?" He pointed a finger up.

"We're in the eye," I explained. "The center of the storm." It seemed odd that a well-versed sea captain wouldn't know the anatomy of a hurricane, but I didn't know the weather patterns globally on this world.

"Never heard of that . . . Good, though. I've sent out some men in our rafts to get whatever wreckage or survivors they can."

I could see one of them rowing in the distance, going after some bit of floating debris.

"Keep them close to the ship," I suggested. "Soon we'll be out of this and the storm around the eye is the harshest."

"Can you stop it?"

I shook my head. "With several dozen weather mages and a massive crowd for gestalt, maybe we could lessen it. This storm is big, Captain. Too big for me to affect in any appreciable way."

"All right, I'll get the men working." He turned and started shouting orders, his harsh voice stirring the exhausted crew to their labors.

I placed a hand on his arm lightly. "Captain, after you've told everyone what they need to do, get some rest. We won't have long before you're needed again, and you look dead on your feet."

He frowned a bit, but nodded after a second. "Don't like being told what to do on my own ship, but you may be right."

"I am, and like I said, we'll need you again soon to lead this mess." That earned me a bit of a smile.

My piece said, I retreated back inside. I didn't want any risk of falling overboard again, and besides, there was work I could do.

I wasn't an expert healer by any means, but what I could do at this point was sorely needed. I found Robert in the hold working on those who'd taken injuries. Overall, the injured were few. A couple of men sported broken bones and nasty rope burns or cuts, but nothing that couldn't be handled with ease. Sadly, we'd lost seventeen of our crew in the fight, either thrown overboard by waves or crushed by rigging in the monster's final assault. Another four survivors had been rescued from our sister ships, though, found clinging to the floating detritus or thrown near enough to haul aboard with a well-tossed rope. This quartet represented a grim truth: our expedition's losses were staggering. Of the three vessels, *The Crystal* alone had survived. The casters aboard were all that remained of our cohort. Even with our presence, without sails to provide meaningful propulsion, it seemed we were dead in the water.

As I healed those I could, I moved through the ship. There I found our faithful cabin boy, Elian. He'd fallen asleep clutching a pile of netting in the hold. I smiled at the resting child as I noticed something new.

Like all elves, Elian had some quantity of magic. For the majority of elves, this amount was small. After that harrowing experience, though, he now had a proper aura. It wasn't large yet, and would still need development as he grew, but it was there. All around him, small green ribbons snaked and swayed like kelp in the ocean, buffeted by the small waves created by the boy's slow breathing.

"You saw, too." Another elf moved to my side. I recognized him as the bosun.

"I've seen it before," I confirmed. "Lots of mana, lots of stress. He'll develop into a proper magic user in time, probably a caster of some kind."

"Aye. This may be the lad's last journey with us. It'll depend on what he wants, and what we see when we get home."

"Schooling?" I asked, unsure how the elves handled young casters.

"Perhaps. Regardless, though, this development gives him options. Options many of us here don't have."

"His previous ability was summoning water, right?" The bosun nodded. "Aye. Damn useful on a ship."

"Probably a bard or wizard then," I said, thinking out loud. "We've plenty of those on ship to give him a bit of training."

"Kind of you to offer."

"We'll need the help."

He laughed a bit and we both got back to our duties.

Prior to this, I hadn't spent much time below the main deck. Rooms full of sweaty seamen didn't really appeal to me, and they needed their privacy too. Now that I got to see it firsthand, I didn't think it was something I'd need to repeat.

We left the calmness of the eye, returning to the wind and rain. The deck was heaved with the rolling waves. So, that evening we went to have a conversation between us casters and the ship's officers. The largest room we could easily clear was Captain Tom's stateroom. We mages joined him there, accompanied by his first mate.

"All right, you lot know I hate to ask," Captain Tom began, "but these are hard times."

"We know," Olnir said. We watched as he and the officers did the whole diplomacy and pleasantries thing. "And we're willing to help where we can, of course."

The captain nodded. "Our main concerns are water, food, and moving the ship. We managed to salvage some wood, and the ship's carpenter tells me that he might be able to fashion a makeshift mast out of it. It won't be much, and it will take a bit of time to rig it up right, but it should give us some sails."

"Water is easy enough to handle, I think most of us can make that?"

We nodded in response.

"Aye, we've got food for a few weeks to be sure, but without proper sails," his voice trailed off as he studied us grimly. "I hate to have to tell you this, but our rations are going to be tighter than expected."

"What about fishing?" Robert asked. "We're in the ocean after all."

"Out here there's not many fish to be caught. Most schools stay near the coast. We can put some lines out, if you've a mind to, but don't expect much from it."

"I can help some with that." I sang a few notes and a bit of bread and cheese appeared on the table before me.

"What!?" Olnir looked over my work like a jeweler examines a gem. "I didn't know you could do that."

"There's much you don't know about me."

The captain was more practical. "How much can you make?"

With a smile I said, "I can easily make a modest loaf for everyone on board once a day. I'll want mana for other things, but if the food situation gets too bad, I'll consider making more. The cheese is not as efficient, but a little to go with the bread will improve morale markedly, I think, so I'll make a small amount."

Captain Tom raised an eyebrow, seeming to have realized that I'd dodged his question and instead given him how much I would, not how much I could. It was clear I wasn't willing to feed his whole crew alone.

"Fair," he agreed finally. "We've got stores that should last for a while, anyway. Thank you for helping extend them."

Leah stepped forward. "I'll summon a pint or two of oil a day, since we're helping." Looking a bit irritated, she demonstrated her talent in a small nearby glass.

"I can do a gallon of cream, but no more." Robert demonstrated as well, but the tone of his voice indicated he was irritated about it.

After working out a few more details, the captain nodded, thanking us once more for our cooperation. Olnir, on the other hand, didn't seem to think that was the end.

"Deliver a list of what spells you know to me." Olnir said, but he was fixed with glares.

It was expected that, as students, one would share work with teachers. For this reason, I'd had no issues previously showing others my range of abilities. However, asking a graduated mage for a list of their spells was taboo. One might as well ask for a detailed manifest of the mage's vulnerabilities. Many would be willing to tell you what they could do in the most general sense, but the specifics would remain vague. Even among friends, one had to be very close to get that sort of information. I for example, didn't have an exhaustive list of what Dras could do, nor he me.

"No," Robert answered first.

"I need to know—" Olnir tried to insist, however Dras cut him off.

"Not going to happen."

"Yeah, nope."

"You know better than to even ask."

"Not happening."

We each refused, one by one. He sputtered a bit but seemed to think better of his inquiry.

"Very well then. I suppose that's fine," he said, voice dripping venom.

We left the room at that, the sailors looking surprised and confused at our unified move.

CHAPTER 7

♦

ONE TO ANOTHER

After a few days, the storm stopped drenching us and the deck became safe to walk on again. This was both a blessing and a trial. I loved the fact that I now had so much more freedom to move about, particularly in the fresh air, however there were unexpected, unwanted consequences.

"Excuse me, miss," a sailor said. He was the third seaman in the past minute to almost run me over.

I'd found a spot as out of the way as possible, but the upper decks of *The Crystal* were a hive of activity. Men scurried like ants in an upturned hill, patching holes, mending railings, and hammering on things I could not begin to guess the function of.

Robert moved up beside me, looking on as the men tried to hoist a new mast into place. "Well, best we stay out of the way, huh?"

"Quite so. I've no desire to have another mast dropped on me."

He chuckled. "How close was it, then?"

"Well, I was standing about here, and it fell . . . actually you can see where it took out the railing."

"Scary. I've been meaning to ask the captain about the current plan."

"Current plan," I answered, having gotten the scoop during breakfast, "is to get the ship moving. Captain said he isn't completely sure where we are at the moment, but he can't be until the clouds clear up all the way. That said, he is sure we were closer to the Elven continent than ours. So, we're aiming west until we find land or get a grip on where the heck we are."

"So, we have no idea where we are?" Robert frowned a bit as he spoke, looking out at the waves. "That's concerning."

"That's ocean travel, friend. It's all based on the sun and stars."

"Do you know how to do it?"

"Not at all." I pointed up at the thick cloud cover, the last remnants of the squall. "Rather difficult to use those right now."

As we chatted, I looked toward the stern of the boat. There, at the rear railing, Selene was giving our youngest mage a brief lesson in magic. After the battle with the Hurricane Whale, Elian awakened as a wizard with an affinity toward water magic, surprising no one. I doubted there'd be many elements the captain would be happy about the boy slinging around his ship, and thanked whatever power that Elian hadn't developed fire magic.

"He's coming along," Robert observed. "Not powerful by our standards, but he's got drive."

"Yeah."

I'd been studiously refusing to teach young Elian anything. Partially because my magic was of a different form, and partially because I might accidentally give him some insight that counted as a state secret. It pained me to watch, because I was fairly sure that, with a bit of prodding, he'd turn out to be a pretty good mage.

"All right, that's a look," Robert said. "What's on your mind?"

"Just pondering. That kid could go far with the right education."

"Sure, and I'm sure the elves have schools. Who knows if he'll get into one, but what can you do? I don't think our academy would take him, not unless he becomes a citizen or something."

"That's the thing holding us back, isn't it? Everyone is always secretive about all their research and all their training. Good grief, can you imagine where we'd be if everyone who had any talent with magic or even research had been properly educated?"

Sure, it was a bit hypocritical of me to go on a rant about hiding research when I was hiding so much. But I didn't want to keep secrets. I just knew that if I didn't, people would come after me.

"That's what our benefactor was on about, too, wasn't it? You going to follow in his footsteps and make a school or something?" Robert passed me a light smile.

"Don't know that I have the temperament to sit around teaching classes all day, but setting one up, getting everything together? Maybe when I'm older."

"We've already got one academy, Alana, and a pretty good one. I've still got no clue why anyone would set up another in the middle of nowhere."

That led me to thinking: *why had Ristolian tried to build his school way to the north in the middle of jack all? Well, he wasn't really constrained because of the portals I guess, but still . . . not being in a country meant no support, no help, no . . . laws . . . He'd be totally independent, and with how he was setting those portals up . . .*

That was an interesting line of thought. While I'd not really considered it before, certainly someone else had. The people of this world were a bit behind on tech compared to Earth, but they were by no means stupid.

"Who knows," I said with a shrug. "When we get all our research working, someone will have to go around setting things up. Perhaps I'll do that. Be good fun to go and see the world."

"Gonna be honest here, Alana, I think I'm going to be done with exploration and adventure after this."

We laughed and enjoyed the day for a bit longer.

It was two more days before the clouds cleared, and the crew busily worked to install the new rigging. *The Crystal's* carpenter had worked like a dog day and night to get everything in place and secured to the new mast, but he had neither the tools, nor the proper materials for this level of repairs. Even with a crew of sailors and magical aid, it was an uphill battle.

As the sun set on our first clear sky in far too long, I once again stood on deck. I could tell it was a distraction to the sailors, but I was feeding them, and so they could suck it up.

Nearby, Captain Tom contemplated the horizon with a furrowed brow before retrieving several of his navigational tools. Some ships had a navigator separately, but he now fulfilled both jobs. He marked down the time of sunset, verified by a small watch that was covered in runes. That task done, Captain Tom turned his gaze to the stars, searching in earnest, using clocks and a sextant to measure their angle from the horizon. The whole process looked rather complex.

When he decided he was finished, the old man retreated to his quarters to run numbers as he did most nights. On deck, the men lit the lanterns, and prepared the night's watch.

With a minor spell, Elian lit the lamps. There were only a few lanterns—just enough illumination for the deckhands to see by—but I was thrilled to see him using every opportunity he could for a bit of practice.

"Good evening, Miss Alana," he said as he came to join me. "How are things?"

"Quite well. Yourself?"

"Good, good. Um, I didn't get to say it before, and I haven't had a chance to talk to you, but . . . thank you. I thought I was dead back when I got thrown into the drink."

"Don't worry about it, I'm sure you'd have done the same for me." I kept up my vigil of the stars. With no lights out here other than the few on our ship they were truly magnificent.

"Like to think I would. How did you get me anyway? I thought I was too far out; did you use a grabbing spell like I did on the lanterns?"

He'd managed to find the one subject I wanted to talk to him the least about. "Similar, bard magic works a bit differently, but the wave carried you to me as well."

"Could you teach me how to do things like that? While I can only manage lamps now, I'm sure that with work I could pick up a man overboard with this spell Miss Selene taught me. But, if I could also learn other ways—"

I silenced him with a raised hand. "Elian, I told you. Bard magic works a bit different. My technique is also weird, even for a bard. Learning that isn't really in the cards for you. When you're older, perhaps it would help you, but right now I think it would only cause confusion."

"Ah, sorry for asking." He looked down, nearly slinking away.

"I'm not angry with you, Elian. I merely think you should focus on what you have now." I thought for a moment. "When I was little, my teacher taught me something important, and I think it will help you."

He looked back up with hopeful eyes. "Oh?"

"It's best to focus on one thing at a time: learn it, perfect it, master it. That's how I do things anyway, I learn one spell and work on it until I'm happy, then I move to another. Many young mages try to learn as many spells as they can right away, but it only weakens their power. Why don't you try to improve your spells to make water and move things for now, then try to learn more?"

He made just the cutest face as he thought about that, finally nodding. "Okay, thanks for the advice!" Elian was a nice kid. Actually, with how long elves lived he might well have been born long before me despite his boyish features. While I considered making it an early night, Elian stayed on deck and practiced floating one of the pins used for rigging.

"How'd you end up on the ship, anyway?" I asked, breaking the silence.

"Parents abandoned me."

"What? Why in the world!?"

"My family was pretty poor. And, well, for the longest time, I had no talent, no magic at all. That . . . that doesn't really happen for elves, you know? Pretty much all of us have something, and so when my brothers and sisters needed food, they got it, but me? Not so much."

He took my stare of stunned silence as a cue and continued. "Without magic there was no future for me. No woman would marry someone without any mana at all and the jobs I could take would be almost nothing. There was a big fight and they just sort of . . . threw me out after. My talent manifested not too long after, but there was no way I was going back there, not after all that."

"That's . . . that's really terrible Elian. I don't really know what to say." I reached out to hug him lightly.

"Eh, the captain took me in when my talent manifested 'cause there's always need for someone who can create fresh water on a ship. And look at me now! I'm a proper mage. My family hasn't had a real mage in generations. Maybe one day I'll go back and show them what they lost. You know what it's like being an orphan?"

"The Order of The Shield runs a lot of the orphanages back on the human continent, and while I never went through anything like you did, I did have to spend a bit of time in one."

"Really?"

"Mmhmm. A lot of bad things happened when I was a kid, and I got separated from my family. I wasn't sure if I'd ever see them again for a while."

"But now you're, like, really strong." This made me laugh. "I don't know about all that, but it worked out well enough in the end. After several years, I did find my family.

"While I understand that you're mad, try to forgive them, you may not like them, or want to be around them, but you can still let go of what they did to you."

"I'll think about it, he said."

While I didn't know if he would, he seemed like a good kid. I thought he'd work it all out in the end.

As Elian and I finished talking, I saw the captain leaving his quarters and going below deck. That was pretty odd, as he generally didn't go down there, and that way went toward . . . . He returned a few moments later with the ship's carpenter and Olnir in tow. All three looking highly agitated.

It was hard to make out, but I thought I heard the captain grumbling something to the effect of, ". . . south . . . fucking . . . doldrums."

CHAPTER 8

✦

FOLLOW THE BIRDS

After a few minutes, Olnir returned. His gait was stiff, indicating that while this wasn't something that would have him running, it was indeed some kind of important matter.

As he approached, I called out from my swath of shadows. "Something wrong?"

Olnir turned and looked in my direction. "Ah, just who I was looking for. There are some logistical issues that we need to speak about, if you have the time."

"Sure, not like there's much going on anyway."

With a wave, I bid Elian a pleasant night and followed Olnir to the captain's quarters.

The mood inside was heavier than I would have liked. Several charts lay spread out. Captain Tom scribbled away on a small pad.

"We're back," Olnir announced.

"Good, we've quite a lot to go over," the captain said over his scratching pencil.

"Sounds like we're having even more problems then?" I asked.

"Sadly, yes." It was the carpenter who answered this time.

"Well, lay it on me then."

The captain took a moment to finish writing his thought before he regarded me. "It would seem that our altercation with the Hurricane Whale sent us quite a bit off course. My calculations say our friend and their storm must have sent us into this current here." The captain jabbed a finger to a spot on one of the charts. I could see this was a map with lines that indicated a direction of flow. "Now, with our days of drifting alone, it seems we've moved significantly further south than we should have, and that's a problem."

"Are there more monsters or something?"

"A somewhat higher number, yes, but we're still well away from that particular trouble. The issue we have currently is, well, current. We've entered the Doldrums, an area of the sea where the wind is often unreliable. Could find ourselves beset by nasty squalls, or might find a fright calm for weeks on end."

"I'm not a sailor, Captain, could you explain?"

"No wind, lass. Without that we're not going anywhere."

"We were hoping you might be able to help," Olnir said.

"I could, but I'm also making a good bit of food, doing both at once would be very stressing."

Captain Tom, pensive, mulled over the various charts and diagrams before him. Once or twice, he made notes or scribbled a few quick calculations.

"We can't sacrifice the food," he determined. "And if we try to sail north, we'll be going against wind and water, can't say that'll work without more constant of a wind. I propose we have you making us a due west wind periodically as we go. There aren't many reports because nobody likes sailing without wind, but from what I do know we should slowly drift west anyways, least till we're closer to the coast."

"That's far from the normal route, Captain," the carpenter protested. "And our maps of that region are scant at best."

"Don't I know it, but it seems our best choice. We go west until we get close enough to see land, then we head north along the coast." Captain Tom turned to the carpenter. "Can you get sails up by noon tomorrow?"

"The job'll be fast and not too pretty" the old salt grinned. "But we can have that mast dressed before you've your lunchtime grog."

Upon waking, the bakery opened—so to speak—as I tended to the process of making the day's food. It wasn't too much of an issue for me, but I would never tell others that lest they want me to do it more.

After the hurried affair that was breakfast, I emerged onto the main deck to see a flurry of activity. The rigging was being run and positioned long banners of cloth hidden in one of the holds lain out and prepped for their upcoming duties.

The carpenter had the attention of all as he directed each man where to stand and what to attach. He clearly knew his business when it came to improvised rigging. Though he grimaced as he did so, he made sure all was acceptable.

It was nearly lunch as with a heave the sails were pulled into place. Slowly at first, then with gusto. After much pulling and securing, the large square cloth hung above the deck, sagging limply. When they were satisfied, the captain and his woodworker nodded to me.

I'd had ample opportunity to learn several sea shanties from the men on board. One such tune—"The Long Way Home," as it was called—spoke of celebration and bestowing thanks for the journey being bright and sunny. Seemed the perfect piece for this moment. With a deep breath, I launched into song.

Slowly, I funneled a gentle breeze into the eager belly of the canvas. The carpenter raised a hand warily, and I maintained my spell while he examined the rushed work, ensuring that it held under the strain. He cautiously waved to me to continue, which I did for a time before he gestured that I hold again. Thus, it continued haltingly, the sail swelling bit by bit I increased the wind.

It didn't take long for the voices of the crew to join mine. A breath became a breeze, and that breeze grew into a gale, until soon—the air abuzz with the singing of men—a strong easterly wind inflated the sail to its fullest, and cheers of celebration rang out as we set out on our own power once more.

As we moved into the later afternoon, we changed things up a bit, the crew and I. Call-and-response songs became the method of the day with myself acting as the caller and the many sailors providing the return. I even took the time to educate them on "Drunken Sailor." This seemed to be their favorite number, particularly after I let them offer their own verses. They learned a new tune, and I learned that this raunchy lot had several inventive punishments for an inebriated seaman.

The next few days passed in much the same way. After breakfast, I'd spend several hours maintaining the winds that ferried us to our destination. The routine was good and most everyone seemed happy.

The moment came, though, when a cry alerted us from atop the mast. There was no proper crow's nest yet, but a few sturdy boards served as a perch from which a sailor could sit and keep a lookout for anything that might be amiss on the horizon.

From on high, he shouted, "Bird!"

All action stopped.

"Where at lad!?" The captain looked ecstatic at the news.

"Just off the port bow, Captain."

The old man took the wheel and spun it gently to the right. With a slight nod, he indicated that I should change the direction of our wind to match, and slowly *The Crystal* adjusted her heading. Moments later, a small brownish dot appeared overhead. It circled three times before lazily drifting down and alighting on one of the railings. The men backed off carefully, not wanting to spook the creature.

"Kill the wind lass, and a bit of bread if you can." Captain Tom requested.

A few notes later and he approached the bird slowly with the small loaf in hand. He gingerly tossed a bit nearby which the animal hopped down to check out. Piece by piece he fed the seabird until the food was all gone.

The animal in question looked a bit different from a standard seagull. The bill was too long and its body was mostly brown, with a few black-ish marks here and there. Still it had the distinctive shape of body and wing that indicated that it was a creature of the ocean. It was also less bothered by the presence of men than most birds would have been in my experience.

"Come now lad, mind showing me which way you live?" The old captain cooed to the little avian. "Just lead your ol' pal Tom to land and we'll be right grateful."

The bird petered around a bit, investigating our boat before finally taking back to the wing and flying slightly south of our former trajectory. As the bird retreated, the hushed silence that had held *The Crystal* was shattered by the heavy thunk of the captain's boots as he marched to the helm. "Where's Sharp-Eye," he barked. "I want him up that mast quick as lighting!" The aforementioned Sharp-Eye was one of the crew. An elf who, much like my friend Charles back home had an aura around his eyes, not to the same extent, but something. I was sure the elf had a proper name, but as he rushed up the mast to the improvised viewing area I decided it didn't matter much.

"That's good right?" I asked.

"Very good. Get the wind going for us again if you please." For the rest of the afternoon we sped on, the wind allowing our ship to slice through the waves. More birds appeared in the sky, some dipping down to the waves in search of food while others strutted along the railing. With each new arrival, the captain became increasingly giddy. I even saw him do a little jig with the first mate!

"Captain, clouds," Sharp-Eye called down, one out-stretched arm aiming west. "And the sunlight is reflecting off something!"

The crew cheered, and with haste we made for the way we'd been pointed. As we lumbered along, more birds filled the sky, their cries offering a strange—albeit squawking—counterpoint to my melody. I was running on fumes, though, and it looked like everyone could tell. Even as the sun fell lower toward the horizon, I pushed myself to continue.

And then . . .

"Land! Land on the horizon!"

"Anchor," the captain shouted. "Drop anchor! We can't well try to get ashore in the dark, lads, but come first light we'll bring her in as close as we dare."

"Is it the Elven continent?" Dras asked as we began to finish up for the evening.

"No, an island. We're still far from reaching our destination. We may be able to get wood, though, and replace the missing masts, and perhaps even a bit of fresh food." Captain Tom nodded to me, "Not that we don't appreciate your work, miss."

"No, I'd rather like some fruit myself," I added. "Perhaps a bit of fresh meat, too." That got me a few chuckles from those nearby.

"Not liking my cooking then, Your Ladyship," the cook called jokingly as he doled out the porridge that constituted the majority of our current diet.

"Oh, how could I ever," I asked as a goopy lump landed in my bowl. "Just hoping for something other than salted pork and burgoo," I replied as I took my serving of the aforementioned goop.

Salted pork stayed fairly soft even after all the time we'd spent since it had been packed, but it just wasn't the same. Even after all the time since it had been packed, the salted pork remained tender, but there was no escaping the fact that it was just salty as it could be, and none of the cook's culinary experiments could remedy this. Also, after weeks of eating the stuff, my mouth was, frankly, bored. I doubted we'd get beef, but perhaps there was something on that island that could help us vary our diets just a little bit.

◆

CHAPTER 9

MAKING SHORE

As the sun broke through the clouds, we began the laborious process of scouting the island. It would be foolish to just land, no matter how much we wanted to, and so the first thing we needed to do was get a rough idea of what we were dealing with. This place, which wasn't on any of Captain Tom's charts, wasn't a single island but three separate pieces of land jutting out of the shallows. Based on what we were seeing, there might be land bridges between them during particularly low tides. The smallest segment was less than a quarter mile across, and seemed to be almost completely comprised of rock cliff faces with vegetation on top. It would have been possible to land smaller boats at one little beach, but we were hesitant to risk running up on the rocks.

The second island was also fairly rocky. About twice as big as its neighbor it squatted in the water with less-imposing cliffs, but spiky boulders littered the beaches, which nobody cared to chance. We did catch a bit of movement in the greenery, but nobody could accurately identify what exactly it was.

Roughly circular and perhaps three miles in radius, the third and final island was not an insignificant little piece of land presenting cliff faces and stony shores. However, the mouth of a small stream led into a little lagoon. We couldn't pull *The Crystal* into it, but after a few checks it was found that one of the landing boats should suffice.

Captain Tom looked out at the gathered crewmen. "All right, lads. We've got a lot of work that must be done ashore first, then we'll see about everyone getting a chance to stretch their legs a bit."

There were several cheers at that since we all craved a bit of space.

The first mate took over. "We first need to replace our lost masts, so the carpenter and a few lads will go search for some suitable trees. We also need a few men to replenish food stores with anything that might be edible."

"Aye," a deckhand shouted. "I think we could all use something other than salt pork, lads!"

"Volunteers?"

Though everyone—crew and guest alike—practically itched with the need to get off the ship, we all knew that our land-loving cohort would be going ashore with later groups. For now, I struggled with a bit of fishing tackle, intent on catching any of the many tasty-looking morsels darting and swimming below. If the rod and line didn't pan out, I'd just electrocute the little buggers and float the lot out of the ocean. I, too, was tired of salt pork.

After an hour or so, the sailors off on their business, I dropped off a few fish to the cook and went to see the first mate. Despite our tight confines over these weeks, I didn't know him all that well. But, since he had taken charge of the shore assignments, it seemed a conversation was in order.

"Excuse me," I asked. "Could you kindly tell me when my chance to visit the island will be?"

"I think Olnir was handling that, miss, but likely this afternoon or tomorrow morning."

It wasn't far to go and see Olnir. It was surprising to me, though, when I got to the quarters he shared with the other men in our group and found a heated discussion in progress.

"I think that we'll need to go one at a time over the next few days," Olnir said, "Just in case." It was clear from his tone that he was trying to keep most of us nearby and failing.

"We don't know how long we'll be here," Selene countered, adamant. "And there is no way I'm missing my chance to go ashore for the first time in over a month." This statement earned her nods of emphatic agreement from a few others from our gathered casters.

"I understand," Olnir said, voice pained, "but we've already lost too many on our expedition, and I must insist."

Dras lifted his eyes and asked, "Are we still planning to continue with it?"

"That remains to be seen."

"Well, that aside," Robert said. "I am going ashore with my sister tonight."

"That is not your decision," Olnir sputtered.

"I think that you'll find that it is," Leah said, her voice hard. "Try to stop us. We'll stop making food. Not a dollop of cream nor a drop of oil. We'll also tell the sailors why. I'm sure they'll be thrilled."

Now that was a threat. We all knew that the food situation basically sucked, and if any of our bardic staff decided to tell everyone to suck it up, they'd all be sucking it up. It was also likely that anyone pissing off the crew that badly would be thrown off the bow and swimming his way to the Elven continent. A caster he may be, but Olnir couldn't stand against everyone on his own.

"Very well," he said sourly through his teeth. "We'll split into two groups then. I'll go with the two of you," he said indicating the twins. I chimed in from where I stood in the door. "Personally, I think I'll wait until morning." Dras, Selene and Glen all began to speak at once, voicing their agreement with me.

"Fine then," our manager conceded. "Let us prepare. I'll speak to the first mate about our departure." Olnir squeezed past me and scurried away.

Within the hour, Olnir and the twins joined a few sailors and took the short paddle to shore. As I watched their boat slide through the darkening ripples, I felt Selene's presence sidle up beside me near the railing.

"I noticed you didn't want to go with them tonight."

"I don't like Olnir," I admitted plainly.

"Okay." Selene seemed confused at my answer. "Any particular reason?"

"He just grates on me. Like sandpaper," I added, a small growl of frustration sneaking in. "It's not even that he's always wrong, it's just that he's . . ."

"Stubborn?" she offered. "A bit of an ass?"

"Yeah. Like when he told them that he would be making the decision. I mean, sure, he's supposed to be in charge, but at this point he should know that we need some time off this boat. Or the whole thing on asking about our spells. It's just rude."

"I suppose so. We must finish this expedition, assuming we continue with it."

"I plan on finishing. After that, though, I'm not working with him again." She laughed lightly. It was pleasant as we bobbed there off the shoreline, keeping an eye on the forest and trying to get a few more fish for dinner.

Since the scouts hadn't explored much of the area, we couldn't guarantee a safe evening's rest ashore. Under the captain's insistence, everyone returned from the island to spend another night aboard *The Crystal*. The captain didn't meet much resistance to this. Safety, of course, was a concern of ours, but the ship had one amenity the tempting island lacked: beds. We casters liked our comfort.

Our dinner was a veritable feast. Though the beach only offered coconuts, I hadn't been expecting this tropical delight and was more than happy to experience it. The cook used it to great effect in a course of fried fish, a luxury even on the mainland with how much oil it required. He'd toasted some of my bread and reduced it to crumbs that he mixed with shredded coconut. Using a bit of cream made by Robert, our culinary master coated the fillets before tossing them into a piping hot pan with oil provided by Leah. It was the best meal we'd had in a month, and there was enough that no one aboard was forced to endure another meal of salted pork.

That night, as I took up my normal spot to watch the stars for a bit, I was greeted by the unexpected. As the shroud of night fell upon the forest, a faint halo suffused the trees in an array of colors, painting a brilliant scene with the sky and sea around it. The land glowing between star and rippling wave, the crescent moon hanging high above, the view before me was nothing short of magnificent.

"Can't say I've seen one like that before," the captain said from where he stood nearby.

"It's beautiful," I announced on a breath.

"Aye, that it is."

I was up and ready the next morning to have my chance on shore, and there was nothing and nobody who would stop me. Seeing me bouncing in my seat, the sailors laughed as they lowered the little dinghy down from the side of *The Crystal*. The ride to shore was a short one though rough. When our little vessel slid up onto the coarse shore, Glen was kind enough to help me climb out with what remained of my dignity intact.

"All right, everyone. We know our jobs. If we're all good and ready, let's go." Divided by tasks, our landing parties split and began to move into different directions. The carpenter took his deckhands to a host of trees they'd felled yesterday. These fairly large specimens would make for good masts once they were debarked and shaped up a bit.

The group that had my eye, though, was headed not towards the trees, but the forest.

Struggling to walk on the shifting sands, I called out, "Where are you lot off to?" I asked.

"There's a little creek bed here the lads saw yesterday," a sailor explained. "Figured we'd follow it and see if there is any sign of game on the island."

"Mind if I tag along?" I asked.

Glen nodded as he came over. "That sounds fun actually, been awhile since I was hunting."

"If you want, you're welcome. I'm sure with you we could take down anything we find with ease." The sailor smiled at us, and he wasn't wrong; between our magic and their crossbows, we could be a lethal team.

All around us was a tropical paradise. A few small birds could be seen among the hulking, bright green trees. The creek bed was dry as a bone and cut a wide, sinuous path into the jungle.

As my feet failed me and sent me sprawling for the second time in as many minutes, a few of the sailors in our party chuckled. I certainly wasn't the only one struggling to walk after a month on the ocean, but judging from our collection of awkward gaits, I fared the worst.

Glen helped me up and we continued our little trip.

A solid twenty minutes in and one of the hands at the head of our party called for us to halt.

He pointed to a small section of forest. "Something moving there."

As a group, we edged forward quietly to the outskirts of the dense jungle. The ferns and vines slowed our progress, but we all kept an eye for our scout had seen. On one of my scans of the area, I spotted a pair of huge, bright yellow bulbs peeking from deep within a shaded bush. I fixed my attention, squinting.

They blinked.

A moment later came the horrid scream.

CHAPTER 10

ISLAND INHABITANTS

The noise that emitted from the brush around us was a wild war-scream. The nearby trees came alive with the sounds and flurry of birds suddenly taking wing. The yellow-eyed creature leapt from its blind, coming straight for me.

Glen didn't specialize in speed, but he was a physical type magic user regardless, and his reaction time put my own to shame. In a flash he stood before me, the blade in his hand having swept in a glittering arc.

Dark blood sprayed. A small green body, cut from shoulder to rib, fell limply at his feet. The goblin had a tiny shell-bladed knife clutched in its hand. A blade which matched, I noted, the weapons wielded by the horde of child-sized figures who poured out of the nearby trees with shrieks of their own. Their initial attacks landed many blows on our ambushed crew, however, their crude tools could do little but make bloody shallow cuts. .

A single kick or strike from one of our number was enough to cause significant damage. Their sailors swung their cutlasses and clubs, smashing heads and splitting flesh. Our bowmen loaded their crossbows, took their aim, and loosed on the little green swarm moving on us from the rustling brush.

"Back to the riverbed!" I yelled.

We retreated to the winding path as more goblins flooded out of the jungle. Out of the dense foliage, I brought up my hands and sang into existence a stream of pure alcohol, my will igniting the booze as it sprayed along the tree line. This gave the goblins pause.

Individually none of the little beasts was a real threat. Their numbers, however, and the possibility of being swamped by the creatures provided the main threat. Using the fire, I made walls that stretched to either side of us, enough to slow our enemies with forced choke points we could manage. While the sailors gathered around me and kept the monsters at bay, Glen charged at the oncoming tide. Even without his armor, the tank of a man cut down the goblins like grass beneath a scythe.

When the shrill war cries and sounds of battle abated, fifty or so tiny corpses lie on the ground.

"What the hell are those," one of the seamen asked as we tried to catch our breath.

I looked down at the body by my feet. Around three feet tall, each green-skinned individual had and overlarge head with pointed ears. Though almost all of those here wore only a loincloth, some bodies also had covered chests and extended bellies which indicated females fought alongside their males.

"Goblins," I spat. "Breed fast, but they're weak."

"What are those?" Glen asked. "I've only ever heard stories." A brief silence was long enough to remember some of those tales, particularly those detailing what the goblins did to captives. The shiver that raced up my spine stirred me to action. "We need to get back to the boat. Quickly."

"Fall in then," Glen said, taking charge. "I'm at the lead. Alana, you're just behind me. You lot, make sure they don't come from behind."

Perhaps Glen wasn't their actual commander, but none of these men was foolish enough to question the orders of the trained knight.

As we fled down the dry creek bed, I felt wary joy that we seemed to have driven back the whole of their raiding party.

As we burst back onto the sandy beach, the hands tending to the tree trunks regarded us with surprise at our speed before a few of them noticed the weapons drawn or the hard look on the warrior's face. The carpenter, as the leader of the work team, raced to us.

Glen didn't even let him speak before laying down his orders. "Get the men and the wood, we're leaving as soon as possible. Where are Dras and Selene?"

"They went that way down the beach," the carpenter said, aiming a thumb to our left. Footprints led a few hundred feet down toward where large rocks broke up the landscape. Within seconds, the pair of mages sprinted into view. Selene led a panicked Dras who whirled around and loosed a veritable firestorm behind him. The high, keening wails growing louder left no mystery as to who pursued them.

I moved after Glen in a hurry, trying to get close enough to be of use while still near to the boat for a quick getaway. The crewmen, on the other hand, took up defensive positions while a few of the workers hastened their work with the logs sailors' hands blurred, lashing the needed lumber into a bundle of logs. Quickly they heaved and hauled the load to the shore before shoving the wood into the surf.

Before I was more than thirty paces down the beach a second group of goblins charged at us from our riverbed path, screeching and baring their teeth like madmen as they came. At this distance, my best attack was the old reliable scream. After drawing a deep breath, I released the magic on them. Thirty or so green skins dropped to the ground clutching their ears in pain. It always surprised me how much that particular spell had grown from the minor stun it was in my childhood to something that could stop a group and drop them on the spot, but I was never unhappy for it. I guessed somewhere around

While Selene had no issues, Dras tripped and fell face first into the sand. Glen, not bothering to wait for the wizard to pick himself up, hoisted my friend like a bag of flour and carried him back to our boat.

With most of us packed into the dinghy, crewmen shoved the craft into the oncoming waves before scrambling aboard themselves. As the sailors rowed us out to the awaiting ship, a few of the faster goblins howled their way to us. Three casters, though, were more than enough to deal with any lingering threats.

We were still breathless and too shaken to speak as *The Crystal's* men hauled our packed dinghy out of the brine.

"Anyone hurt," the captain yelled down to us.

"Few minor injuries," Glen responded, "but we should be able to deal with those."

As I was helped back onto deck, I could see the twins gazing at the shore.

"What are those things?" Leah asked.

Odd, I thought, *being that she and her twin were our resident experts on flora and fauna.*

"Goblins," I answered.

"Something you've seen before?" She looked genuinely curious. After I nodded, weary, she sped on. "They're humanoid, and with tools. Probably intelligent, then. Can they communicate?"

"Before today, they were stories, Leah. Even if they can communicate, they're vicious and supposedly stupid."

"That sounds like prejudice, Alana, though I suppose at this point we really can't talk to them. Not after you guys messed them up so bad."

From this distance I couldn't see too much of what the little green jerks were doing, but nobody watching missed the sight of one particularly old specimen shuffling onto the beach with a staff in one hand. Well, I guessed the creature to be old due to their faded, almost grey flesh, and the way the skin seemed to sag, visible even at this distance. The other goblins scattered to clear a path before them, allowing us to see the colorful feathers and other undiscernible items that decorated their loincloth.

"Oh, an elder," Leah said, brimming with hope. "Perhaps they do want to talk."

As if to deny her, the ancient goblin raised one hand. A fireball bloomed to life in the air above their palm. All of us were quick to react. When the boulder-sized flaming projectile shot toward us, it shattered on our shields in a blast of heat and light.

For a moment the crew—and even a few members of my team!—stood frozen in shock.

"What are you idiots gawking at!?" Captain Tom shouted. "Stow the rowboat. Haul in those logs!" This ship buzzed with activity. Though the old goblin wizard kept pelting us with projectiles, our casters maintained the shields so that the wizard only succeeded in depleting his own mana.

I provided wind for the next couple of hours. Even with the infested atoll behind us, Leah chatted on excitedly about how discovering a new species was huge, and how we'd need to mark down the location in case we could get another ship out here for a deeper investigation. She even interviewed a few of the sailors for details on the goblins, what they were using as tools, their height, strength, any noises they made. I appreciated her hard work, but it was seriously annoying until she got caught up in sketching the creatures in a little notebook.

Though my work had allowed a reprieve from my fellow bard's enthusiasm, she cornered me when I took a much needed break.

"You said you'd heard of them in stories," she began without preamble. "Are they in some book or other, or did someone tell you about them? Were there any other details?"

"I don't remember all of the details, but in some of the stories they reproduced really fast. If they caught human women, they would . . ."

My voice trailed off as I considered how to continue. However, my silence or expression must have said enough.

She grimaced. "Oh." We shared an all too brief beat of silence, then she asked, "Any thoughts on why they attacked? Did you guys stumble on their settlement or something?"

"No idea. Maybe we got too deep into their jungle, or came too close to their home. Or perhaps they decided that since we weren't spending nights on shore, they would strike when able. Frankly, I just never want to go back there again."

"I'll make notes. There was nothing in any of my bestiaries, and I'm sure I'd have remembered something like those from lecture. Maybe there's some information on the Elven continent about them."

As I watched the carpenter carefully work on the task of changing a log into a mast, I leaned back, thinking that our journey could not end fast enough for my liking.

CHAPTER 11

✦

ARRIVAL

The customs boat bobbed next to us. Since our run-in with the goblin island, the trip had been fairly uninteresting. The wood we needed we could now repair and get back on course. I of course spent several weeks making wind while my fellows trained the cabin boy in magic as best they could, but by and by nothing major had happened.

We sat off the shore waiting for all the paperwork to be done before we could land. This had started with a few shouted conversations and moved into the nearby boat now giving us the once over. They had cargo to check for contraband, and of course they wanted to have a brief word with all the casters on board. Much of the bureaucratic hassle was expedited because we had several people on board who could cast healing magic, and therefore the chances of any sicknesses having been brought over with us were as near zero as it could be.

The first person aboard our ship had still been a priest who'd given us all a brief check over with some kind of sensing spell before we could continue. Once the youngish Elven man finished up, the rest of the inspectors came aboard looking for narcotics, slaves, anything flagrantly illegal really.

Our cargo, which I hadn't given much thought until this point, was mostly bulk fiber, wools, and linens and the like. While the Elven continent had a number of unique textiles, things like flax didn't grow so well, nor did some of the more sensitive types of woolly creatures thrive. It seemed popular to make a run here to sell these goods, which would fetch a nice price, then pick up some of the more exotic—or slightly magical—alcohols before returning. Such deals were the only way to justify the expense of the journey.

I heard one of the officials asking Olnir, "And what is your business in Atal?"

"We're here to examine a number of plants and animals. Many of our records on the flora and fauna of the region are sadly lacking, and we're quite interested in what may be in the forests. We hope to find some things which might be of interest to our new emperor."

They nodded, going into the specifics while I looked over the wonders that laid before me. The first was the customs ship; it had no sails, nor did many of the smaller ships moving around the port. I suspected that the elves, with their high number of mages and minor talents, could easily arrange for shorter ranged ships or military vessels to move by magic alone. This would be massively helpful in times of war, and it was probably one of the reasons that nobody tried to invade the Elven homeland. The other deterrent was the series of towers built into the water that looked like the perfect place for magical artillery.

Those of course paled in comparison to the capital city, so close, but yet, so far away. From here I could tell that it was built like some kind of idealized version of NYC, hundreds of shining white towers reaching probably twenty floors or more into the skyline, many connected by arches and tunnels. It made the human cities look like quaint villages in comparison.

"Excuse me, miss?" One of the officials had moved over to speak with me in a slightly broken version of the human tongue. "Are you caster? Or talent?"

"I'm a caster," I responded in Atali.

"Apologies for asking," he said in his language, "your aura doesn't look strong."

I flashed my aura out a bit briefly; not fully, but enough. "I was told that it was considered a bit rude to not repress it at all. Is that not so?"

"It is polite to tamp it down a bit, yes. Most visitors don't know that though, or our language."

"Oh, I see. The academy I attended started giving classes on the language, though, so I think most of us speak at least a little."

"How wonderful! Is it a popular class?" He seemed genuinely interested.

"It's considered useful if one really wants to get into making magical items. As I'm sure you know, many of the runic sequences are influenced by Atali quite a bit. My advisor suggested the class for me for that reason."

"Well, I'm quite glad that our culture is being shared with those less fortunate."

It hurt a bit to hear that we were considered kind of third world to the elves but wasn't surprising when looking at their city.

After a few more questions, I was handed a small form that looked not unlike a passport. I saw that while the Elven crew didn't seem to need one of these, all the humans did. I also couldn't help but notice that we magic users were given golden, rather than white versions.

"What do the different colors mean?" I asked, I had a fairly good idea, but wanted confirmation.

"It differentiates you as magic users," He answered without looking up from his paperwork. "We don't often let those humans without the gift of magic into our lands, and so the crew is given a visa that will only allow them access to the docks and related areas whereas you are far more welcome to stay."

That seemed backwards from what I would have expected. "You're less concerned about foreign magic users?"

"Well, of course. You won't be permitted in more sensitive areas, but if you wished to emigrate that would be quite welcome, particularly if you happened to marry one of our people. If you are looking, I have a brother . . ." He must have noticed my blinking in surprise and stopped. "Family is considered of utmost importance to our people, and humans are well known to be more . . . productive in that department, so having a few in your family is considered, by many, to be a blessing."

"I see, so should I expect many offers."

"From pretty much everyone except the council families, though possibly from some of their younger scions." He looked at the handful of gentlemen in our group with something approaching jealousy. "The men in your group are likely to have slightly different propositions, I think."

"Fun. Anything else I should know?"

"Other than the admonition to stay out of trouble? Not really. I suppose the old palace is a wonderful place to visit. It's mostly a museum now, but it is lovely."

"That actually sounds wonderful, thank you."

Shortly thereafter, the customs boat led us to our dock. As we landed, the differences were still striking. I couldn't get over how much fancier the elves did everything. There were fewer ships by a large margin, but those that we saw were of much higher quality. Some of the Elven designs included fully-enclosed tops with large glass windows. Seeing such spacious yachts was weird.

We disembarked. Our group had an address to the home for the emissary to our homeland and directions to a place where we could rent the equivalent of a cab. As we did, I couldn't help but notice we were joined by a certain cabin boy. As the crew had unloaded, he had split off to follow us, a small bag on his back.

"Suppose you're leaving the ship then," I asked as he walked down the pier with us.

"Yeah. Normally I wouldn't get my pay until we were unloaded, but Captain Tom told me that it'd be fine."

"He's a good guy," I mused, looking back at the old man yelling at the crewmen.

"That he is. I've probably got enough in savings to pay my way though one of the lower cost magic schools, especially if I sell some mana here and there. Who knows, maybe I'll even get into one of the state ones."

"Well, good luck. Hopefully we'll meet again." I offered out my hand and he shook it before going to speak with Selene and Dras.

I headed over to the spot where a cab pulled close to the street. We had luggage and people to move, and new places to go. I didn't know much about the emissary's place, other than that it was close by and had people who could help us out. I didn't even know if that would entail us returning home, or if we'd continue our mission as the much smaller group we now were.

As we passed through the unnaturally clean streets, it struck me how many of the elves seemed to be absolute perfectionists. The corridors were well ordered, the buildings clearly placed for aesthetic purposes as much as use, and even in the walled off dock region the architecture was intricately designed.

It was also clear that fewer people lived here as I might have suspected. Only a few other carriages and riders shared the road, and pedestrians, while present were few. It felt like a tenth of the people that could and should live in this city did, and this was kinda creepy.

As our cart exited the docks for the city proper, our documents were checked. As all of us obviously had magic of some form it was quick and easy. While that was going on, I leaned up to the cab driver.

"Are the docks normally this quiet?"

He did a double take in my direction. "Whatever do you mean?"

"There aren't many people around. Is that normal?"

He seemed a bit confused at my questioning. "Hmm? Looks about average to me."

"Erm, perhaps a better question is, around how many people live here in the capital?"

That got me an eyebrow raise, but he answered all the same. "Around a hundred thousand."

I leaned back to process. When I'd compared the skyline to that of a major US city, I meant it. This city could—and in a human country probably would—house a million or so souls. It made my own home of Lithere look like a quaint little village, however, it's population was not much bigger than ours.

With the driver continuing to give me a look, I decided to just tell him. "By human standards this city is massive for the number of people living here."

"Is it really? How many do you think would be here if we were in a human settlement?" That seemed like an innocent enough question, so I decided to answer.

"One-and-a-half million, perhaps two."

The driver seemed stunned as I spoke.

 "So, do you just all pack in like fish then? That's rather odd, isn't it," he asked.

"Honestly, I don't know."

From that point forward our ride was fairly peaceful. The architecture was lovely, and we didn't have too long to go before we reached our destination. I was expecting a house, or perhaps a manor of sorts, but it was neither. We rode toward one of the large towers I'd been admiring. There was a small garden out front lined with well-manicured flowers and bushes and fruit trees native to human lands.

As we pulled in, a servant opened a pair of behemoth doors to reveal a pleased looking woman stepping out. "Welcome! We've been waiting. Your things can be unloaded around back, as can the other carriages when they arrive." Our whole group winced.

She looked at us with a quirked brow. "What?"

"We're it," Olnir explained. "The others didn't make it."

"Oh."

CHAPTER 12

◆

EMISSARY

We spent several hours with the emissary to the elves, a rather peppy woman by the name of Joan. Much of that pep faltered as she got the retelling of our story, how we'd encountered one of the more rare oceanic magical beasts and lost two thirds of our cohort.

"My! I would expect a few lost to an intercontinental mission, but those numbers . . ."

"Quite severe, yes." Olnir responded, all business. "The question we have is this; should we continue or not?"

"I haven't been read in on the details of your project. What are you able to tell me?" The emissary looked a bit irked that she had to ask, but it was what it was.

"I'm afraid we can't tell you much, but it is considered to be extremely high priority to Emperor Durin. That is the reason so many were sent and why we've been training for this for years."

Joan sighed in frustration. "There's nothing for that then. Could I assign one or two others to work with you? I have a few contacts from the city who've traveled the lands a bit and could provide a little muscle. They could also be instructed to keep out of the details, or to silence."

"Perhaps. We were hoping to hire a guide to the area anyway. If you have someone who you think is loyal, then we can discuss it."

Olnir, I observed, was being surprisingly reasonable about this, but we really did have no choice. We needed more numbers.

"On to other things. What can you tell me about these goblins?" Joan looked at me, as I'd been the one to give the name in the first place. "I'm afraid I've not seen their like before."

"I don't know much. They are known to be violent and reproduce at an insane rate."

The emissary was obviously considering the implications of another sentient race. "Can they speak? Do they have language?"

"I honestly have no clue. They can scream, but I don't know if that is indicative of the power of speech. They were also using crude tools, so there must be some intelligence there."

"Fine. Do we know their location, or have any means to contact them," Joan continued. "Perhaps we could send someone to open a dialogue."

"I agree," said Leah. "We know that at minimum they can use basic tools and magic, though how much of the latter they use is unclear. The issue is that, based on the estimates of the captain on our ship, they were in an area known for a lack of wind and higher magic. It isn't the worst spot, but I doubt many sailors will want to go there."

Our ecologist was still excited by the idea, but I had my doubts as to their success. Regardless, that was one mission I wanted nothing at all to do with. After a few moments of consideration, Joan tapped her chin.

"I'll make note of the location and what we know so far, but for now we'll put that matter aside, then. It's not either of our main missions and can therefore wait for a ruling from the emperor or one of his subordinates."

With the exchange of a couple of sheets that bit was done.

"Do we have rooms we can stay in," I asked, adding, "I also wouldn't mind a proper place to wash."

"Yes. I live on the top floors, but there are a number of guest quarters on the levels just below. I'll get one of the servants to show you to your accommodations. I do hope you'll join me for dinner, though."

The building itself boasted an elevator that, humorously, had a plaque saying that the safety inspection was done by one Sharibari. There was even a little engraved picture of the woman. The human maid working here was, to judge by her aura, either a minor talent or a very weak mage. I watched as she used an elaborate panel of buttons to drop each of us off at our assigned floor. We'd each been granted half a level to ourselves.

Though I knew that all of this was run by magic, it clearly had other inspiration. My floor was one large suite. From the windows I could see out onto the bay we'd entered. The suite, much to my extreme joy, offered a bathtub. For the last couple of months, I'd washed only using a bucket of water and a precious bit of soap. Now though, I had a selection of sudsy options, each bottle a wondrous little product. It seemed that the emissary here was spending an absolutely incredible quantity of money on such arrangements.

Finally washed of salt, sweat, and the general grime of months spent traveling, I found that some of my clothes had been laundered for me by one of the maids. I hadn't come here for parties, but I still had one formal outfit in case I had to meet anyone important.

Around the time I finished getting myself dressed, a knock came at my door.

"Hello?" I moved over to the portal leading to the elevator and opened it.

"Ah, apologies, miss," A rather nervous maid said, peering in at me. "I came to see if you needed anything. Though you seem to be fine."

I nodded. "Yes, I'm quite well."

"Oh, wonderful. We don't quite have the staff to assign everyone a servant, I hope you understand."

I smiled at her kindly. That was preferable to me, in fact, as I found having someone hovering around could be a pain sometimes.

"Of course. I believe Joan asked us to join her for dinner later, do you know what time that would be?"

"It won't be until sunset in some hours. Would you like me to come and let you know," the maid inquired.

I told her that I planned on napping and asked for a wake-up call a little before the meal. When she agreed and left, it was time to try out the bed. I don't know that it was quite as good as the bed back at my family home, but having slept on a board for weeks on end, I didn't really care. I sank into the covers and drifted off to sleep.

After a rather unwelcome-though-requested awakening, I quickly prepared myself and headed to dinner.

I arrived with Selene—who, I discovered, was sharing my floor—to find Olnir and Joan in deep discussion. The latter looked up when we arrived, flashing a bright smile.

"Well, it appears the time for business has ended, my friend. Let's move on to more relaxed topics." The woman declared as she motioned us to some nearby couches. "You two seem to have relaxed since last I saw you."

Both of us laughed as we sat, and I looked over at her. "This place is wonderful, but isn't it a bit . . . much? I mean, our rooms are huge."

"Alana, wasn't it?" When I nodded, Joan continued. "It must be. The council here in Atal demands that buildings be built to a certain standard.

The elves put a lot of emphasis on aesthetics. Everything must be artsy and the like." When I frowned in silence for too long, she explained, "What I mean is that every major building must be an impressively large tower. If we put our embassy in some tiny structure, then our whole nation would be looked down on terribly."

"Everything is so nice too. Running water and that little . . . elevator? Is that what it's called," Selene asked.

"None of that is outside the abilities of human mages," the emissary remarked, raising her eyes a bit. This seemed to be a point of some irritation for her. "It's just that there are too few of us to waste the amount of mana it would take to maintain our society in this way. There are almost too few elves, but that's neither here nor there."

"Yes," I mused. "Making a moving platform, even a safe one, wouldn't be too hard. With a bit of work, you could do it . . . fairly efficiently. Same with the buildings. Even if you can't get materials that will survive all the stresses, if you put support magic in the right spots . . ."

"Exactly!" Joan nodded. "And the elves that run this city have had a long, long time to get it right."

"But why all the effort," I asked.

"Because they are perfectionists."

About this time, Dras and Robert came in and were motioned to their nearby seats.

Dras had apparently heard enough of our conversation that he had thoughts on the subject. "I don't know. The Elven sailors we met didn't seem too bad. A bit grumpy at poorly-made things, perhaps, but nothing extreme."

"Ah, I see your interactions have been a bit limited," Joan commented. "With the lower order workers, the drive for perfection is not as noticeable. However, as a family or individual climbs the social scale, they want things more and more impeccable. Most of those sailors were probably from poorer families, and quite young by Elven standards. The leaders aren't like that, though, and they have very particular demands."

That made good enough sense. We hadn't been told much about the leadership, only that the country of Atal, which shared its name with the city, was a magocracy, a government run by those with powerful magic.

Robert looked at Joan with serious eyes. "These leaders, do you think they'll be any issue for us? We're not here to start trouble, but if they're that demanding . . ."

"As long as you don't cause problems, I doubt it. Partially because you're unlikely to meet any of the council members. They and their families are a reclusive sort."

"How will we know if we meet one," I asked. "Is there some indication of the very important people in the town? A badge or some uniform? Or do we just look at their mana?"

"Easy," Joan said. "Look at their ears."

"Ears," Olnir asked.

"Yes. It's not well known unless you interact with a lot—and I mean a lot—of elves, but there are several different groupings. Since they had to interbreed to keep up their numbers after the empire fell, most elves that you see nowadays have some amount of human blood. However, councilors and their families are from a sect of those that never intermingled. This means that their magic tends to be stronger, that they never really age, and that their ears are far longer."

"Wait, they don't age?" I asked, incredulous.

"Not really. Those with more human blood might only live for one, maybe two centuries. Average elves fare longer, lasting many hundreds of years. The old stock, though, normally only die after thousands of years, and due to violence or accident at that. There are one or two of the councilors who claim that they met the king before his passing, though that's viewed rather dubiously even by their fellows."

"Um . . . wasn't that like . . . four thousand or so years ago," Selene asked.

"Yes. While nobody really believes them, nobody can easily refute their claims either."

"What kind of monstrous magic can someone learn in thousands of years," Dras mused, looking out at the horizon.

"There are limits to what a mortal body can hold, but that threshold is high. There is a reason that no human army has ever occupied territory on this continent. Between the weapons their king left behind and the power some of the elders can let loose, there's no way to take it."

"Why don't they rule the world," I asked. "A lot of people would try with that kind of power."

"Because every soldier they lose takes decades to replace. This city might as well be an unassailable fortress. But in war, if they lose one soldier it's a far larger blow. Due to attrition, they can't really project their power either. Which is very good for us." Sighing, the emissary shifted her attention to the ocean view. "Enough about that though. You got here in time for a special treat."

We looked up from our conversation. The sea was aglow. With every wave that crashed, another wave of azure light joined it. All along the docks, the rippling water shone blue, and the beaches just to the edge of our view looked like a strand of stars.

"The star tide began a few days ago and will continue for a while yet. I thought it would make a perfect backdrop for our meal."

At her words a pair of butlers came to serve us, laying down plates of food nearby. With the couches and platters, it looked nothing like the meals I was used to, but that was different countries for you.

✦

CHAPTER 13

THE PALACE OF THE ELVEN KING

I took a few moments to orient myself as I woke up. The room around me was empty, and I was clearly alone. Through the nearby window I could see the vast sky. I had been up quite late last night, and apparently hadn't risen until the sun had crested above the nearby sea, its bright rays bathing the space in golden light.

We had a number of meetings and plans scheduled, most detailing the region we would be traveling to. Joan mentioned that she had contacts that could get us near the area safely, but that we'd need to travel with a small merchant caravan. Since they wouldn't be leaving for a few days yet, I was determined to use the intervening time to learn as much as I could about the region, and about the ancient Elven king whose name I had never even been told.

The elves never referred to him by his proper name for some reason, and if asked, they'd either claim or feign ignorance. He was simply known as their king; the only one who'd ever been a true king of the elves, and the only one who they seemed to think deserved that title. Which was . . . kinda weird, but how they seemed to like it.

I had a line on the best place to learn about him. His old palace was still around, and knowing the elves it was probably fastidiously maintained. Should that king find himself alive again today, I imagined, he might be able to walk in and find most of his possessions where he'd last left them. Best of all, I'd been told by several people that it was possible to tour the palace, so that would be my first stop.

The other members of my team had their jobs as well. Dras and Glen would be looking at the local markets for information on magical items and threats in the region of our travel. Leah would be brushing up on the flora and fauna, since it was likely that she could get either examples or firsthand accounts here rather than just paragraphs in books. Her brother would, of course, be looking into any diseases and the like by speaking to the local priest organizations. Olnir would remain with Joan to discuss candidates for additional muscle, since we'd need one or perhaps two aids.

I considered asking to borrow one of the carriages, but the palace wasn't far, and seeing things from ground level could be useful. Navigating the well-planned city was easy, especially since I could ask anyone about the palace and literally any elf I met on the street should be able to direct me.

Despite knowing the way, I did ask a few people to gauge reactions to the question. I asked an older fellow strolling by, and he gave me the brightest smile.

"Ah, heading there, are you," he asked, looking down at me as one does an inquisitive child. "It's a lovely sight. Just four streets up to the main thoroughfare, and then follow that to your right. You can't possibly miss it. Is this your first time in our lands? If it is, your Atal is quite excellent."

"Thank you. It is my first time," I said, playing along and looking as hopeful as I could. "I heard it was possible to see the palace and was hoping that I might take a look. Do you think that will be allowed?"

"Oh, there might be a bit of a wait but if there is, you should check out the library just down the street from it a bit. It's from the same era, and is quite wonderful as well. All are welcome so long as they don't damage the books," he added with a finger wag.

"Thank you for the advice, I'll be sure to add that to my tour."

A bit further down the path, I met a merchant running a modest stall selling barbecued meat stuffed into something like a tortilla. At first, he seemed hesitant to deal with me, but when I gave my order in at least passable Atal he quickly brightened up.

"You speak our tongue? That's wonderful. I've heard some stories about friends who had a beast of a time dealing with foreigners who didn't," he said as he held out the small snack.

"I had a teacher who taught both the language and dance. Though, if I'm honest, I think she liked the latter much more than the former."

The merchant got a good laugh out of that one and shrugged. "Nothing wrong with that. I know too many ladies who've let their skills in dance slide."

"She was quite a bit better than any other I've seen, using it to focus her magic. It was quite the show."

As he nodded along, I decided to lead our conversation where I wanted. "I'm hoping to see the palace for the first time today. Anything interesting you'd point out?"

"Hmm, there are a few murals that are weird, but seem to have been important. Nobody really knows what they're about, and it's considered kind of a legend or mystery. The guides there should be able to fill you in, though, if you really want to know."

My pre-investigation was going well, but if I wanted plenty of extra time it was still best to head to the palace itself, so I moved along down the road. Soon, I could clearly see my destination. Unlike the buildings around it, the palace was rather short.

The edifice was still massive, though. Easily five stories and as large as several city blocks, the white marble building included gold accents in the stone. I suspected that those striations had been added by the elves for aesthetic effect, but how they managed it was beyond me.

The architecture was much like the buildings around it in shape and coloration, but with some elements that were distinctly older. The columns flowed upwards in gentle spirals, looking almost alive. The roof and many of the landings were festooned with flowering plants, greenery flowing over the balconies to drape artistically around doorways.

Slowly, I made my way to an area where people milled about near the front entrance. Climbing a set of stairs, I was met by officials in green and gold uniforms.

To my surprise, the female attendant regarded me and spoke in perfect Human Tongue. "Good morning! Are you here for a tour?"

"If possible, yes. This is my first time in Atal, and I was told seeing the palace was a must." She offered a gentle smile. "Certainly, I don't suppose you reserved a spot?"

I frowned at the idea of needing to return later. "No, I did not."

"Are you alone," she asked.

When I nodded, she consulted documents at a station nearby, taking her time. A moment later she returned. "I believe we can squeeze you into the group leaving just after lunchtime." I breathed out in relief. Though, with several hours to burn until then, I decided to walk around the palace grounds, which was no small task. Sadly, I wasn't able to study the spells, but I could examine the building at least.

I also found the library. It, too, was a sizable building, with appropriately huge windows spread along the flank. With its shelves, large seating area, and bustling occupants, the interior space looked much like any book repository.

I considered going in, but decided to return if my tour raised any intriguing avenues of study. I also wanted to get a good idea of how the place worked, if there was an entry fee, or book borrowing, or any number of other questions. Most of the libraries that I knew of in this world were private affairs belonging to the academy or wealthy folks. This place dwarfed those.

Enjoying my leisure, I took in the city. I could see quite clearly that birds of all kinds avoided the palace and library. A passing flock of pigeon-like avians swerved as if to dodge around invisible barriers surrounding the library.

I also noted that all of the lighting was magical in nature. Though the elves might have done this, too, in striving for perfection, I saw the practicality of using a light spell to prevent combustion in a library or historical building.

When the time came, I made my way back to the palace where I was quickly moved over to a tour group. The worker from earlier approached with a smile.

"I didn't ask before, miss, but do you need a translator," she asked.

"No, I speak Atal well enough to understand most people, but thank you for the kind offer."

"Regardless, it is policy that you be told the tour rules in your native tongue." Her smile didn't falter, and she kept on. "Please do not stray from the carpet as to protect the floors. No food, drink, or anything that might spill is allowed, of course. And we here take a dim view of any who would damage the palace."

I nodded. "Certainly. I've no desire to break anything."

"Good. Also, all spellcasting is strictly banned within. Our wards are quite thorough, and believe me, you do not want to come into conflict with them."

"Of course. Is there anything else I should know?"

"We do ask that you maintain a respectful stance, and direct any questions to the tour guide. Now if you'll follow me."

I was led to a group of elves who were being given the same spiel in Atal by another Elven woman in a crisp uniform. Most in this group were older children or elderly, and all paid close attention to the instructions.

"Any questions," the guide asked the group. When none materialized, she continued on. "Then if you'll all please follow me."

CHAPTER 14

✦

OBVIOUS HINTS

Touring large, old castles is always much the same. You get to see all the pretty rooms nobody uses anymore, with their fancy furniture and lovely art. As we drifted from room to room, I didn't see much of interest to me until we came to the banquet hall.

"Here is where His Majesty held dinners for heads of state," the guide explained to the oohing and aahing crowd.

I stood frozen.

"These tables," she continued, "are all replicas made from painstaking study of the originals. Sadly, the wood furnishings simply could not survive the years."

My eyes grew wider. And wider.

"And of course," she said, "some of you have noticed the art. What you see before you is no recreation but the original piece made to our beloved king's exacting standards. We're not sure of what it means, but theories abound. Those of you with access to cores may or may not have realized . . ."

I had certainly realized.

"It contains symbols found in one of the less understood sections of the core. Try as we might, however, we've not been able to translate them despite all these years." The guide referred to a mural depicting the landscapes of this continent and my own. It was massive, taking up most of a wall. Around the circular painting were words, ten feet in height and glowing.

Upon Elazia, and situated to the north of my birthplace of Elayatol lies my workshop. To those who shall come after me and can read these words, seek answers there. —Justin

That must have been his name. "Justin?" I whispered.

Several of the elves nearby froze and looked at me intensely, like I'd just committed some horrid *faux pas*. I immediately shut my mouth and tried to sink back into the crowd. As our tour wound down, I was still getting the stink eye from those who'd heard my questioning words.

It was obvious that the elves didn't bandy about the name of their king, dead or not, and I suspected that I'd just stumbled upon it. Had I thought before opening my big mouth, or perhaps asked earlier, I might have avoided the misstep.

The rest of the palace was lovely, but out of what I'd seen nothing intrigued me. The fancy hanging gardens and complex architecture was nothing compared to ten-foot-high glowing letters telling me where I should 'seek answers.' As the tour ended, I ran to the library. There were terms that needed looking up, after all.

To enter, I had to endure another short lecture on the rules from the kindly librarian. The older elf sported a bald head and many deep wrinkles. When he mentioned that the library was open to all, I frowned.

"Something wrong dear?"

"Ah, back where I'm from most libraries are rather restrictive on who they allow in," I explained.

"Oh. I see, I see. That is the standard for most human countries, is it then? Well, I can understand, but you see when our king first came to power, building public libraries was one of the things he pushed. We still have records of the founding of several, and his dictates about them. It was made clear that our amassed knowledge should be shared among the people."

"How wonderful," I commented. "Um, I have a few things that I'd like to look up. Could you tell me about the organizational system?" If this librarian was anything like the ones from Earth, he might just be able to direct me to exact answers, or, if not, books more likely to have them.

I was gifted with a rather kind smile as prepared to help me. "What sort of questions?"

"Well, the first is a bit odd, but something I'm confused about. All I ever hear someone call the king is simply that. Did he have a name? Is there some reason that nobody ever says it?"

"Ah, yes, that is a bit of a touchy subject, isn't it. There were several names recorded, such as the name he used when signing official documents. But that is more of a title than a name, and when translated from the older versions of our language it simply means 'the first king.' So, it's not considered proper to refer to him by that. There are also several families who insist that he was this or that of their scions, but all of those claims are unconfirmed. Then, finally, there is the name that his friends used, which at the time was considered a privilege of only those he called friends. Hardly appropriate for the likes of us to use."

"So, using any of those is . . ."

"Exceptionally rude, yes. From the look on your face shall I surmise that you did, by accident, do such a thing?"

I nodded, thinking that here at least, honesty might be the best policy. "Yes. I saw something written down somewhere and got a lot of looks when I read it."

"Curiosity is not wrong, child. I'll write down the most common names for you so that you may know in the future not to use them."

He took a piece of paper from a desk and did just that. It even had the names divided by the organizational sections of the library.

The proper title was kind of long, but, as the librarian had said, if you squinted it looked like 'the first king' in Atali. Below that was a plethora of names from various highborn families. But then, there was the name his friends had allegedly called him: Justin.

"Thank you so much," I said as I put the list away.

"Of course, any other questions?"

"A few on geography, but I'm afraid the references I'm going off of are likely very outdated." That might be the understatement of the century, we'd have to see.

They were, in fact, very outdated. Elazia was the easiest to find as it was still in use in some circles and was simply the name of the continent I was on. There was one for the human continent as well: Hediza. But because these were in Atali or its variants, this moniker wasn't used back in the empire or anywhere else I knew of.

Elayatol was far, far harder to find. I was sent well back into the town records that held copies of documents thousands of years old. Finally, though, I found a reference in one of the books. Elayatol had been a town situated in the west in a low and rather odd valley. I, of course, recognized the geography with merely a passing glance.

While the town wasn't called Elayatol in his diaries, Ristolian's own map led to the same location. It seemed I was following his path, not unheard of if he—like myself and, decidedly, the Elven king—was also a transmigrator.

There was of note another town existing there now. It wasn't known as the birthplace of the Elven king, which I guessed was by design. Its name was Eratol, and the tax records indicated that the town was decently sized but too rural for most of the government to care.

After making some notes, thoroughly satisfied that we were on the right track, I headed back to our temporary base, buying another snack on the way from the same vendor as before.

I arrived, and on my way in ran into Olnir and our lovely host escorting an Elven man down from the upper floors. This gentleman was older and more muscular than those I'd seen before. With a light sprinkling of salt in otherwise pitch-black hair, he had some of the facial features that I'd come to expect of elves. His body shape defied the pervasive lithe-and-long norm, but rather he was broad-shouldered and had a certain denoting he was used to hard physical labor. With the smallest points that I'd seen on any elf yet, his ears barely formed the triangular shape.

"Ah! Alana, you're back," Olnir said as I approached. "I was just speaking to Mr. Ulanion here about acting as our guide."

"Pleasure to meet you," he said, offering me a calloused hand. As we shook, I took a few moments to check out his aura.

There was a light green, vine-like aura growing around him, mostly focused on his arms, which were rather muscular.

"Glad to meet you, as well. I'm one of the bards on our team," I offered.

"Well, assuming you'll have me, I'll mostly be acting as a guide. I also have some skill with a bow."

"Well, do you mind stopping by tomorrow morning," Olnir asked.

Ulanion gave a smile before turning to leave, and as he did, Selene made her way in.

I liked to joke that I was a walking bakery, which in some ways was quite true, but I had nothing on Ulanion. My eyes nearly popped from my head as he walked away and as he passed I noticed Selene follow them, soon her face too joined mine in slight shock.

"He seems nice," I managed as he made his way out the door.

"Mmhmm," Selene agreed with a profound nod.

"I concur," Olnir added, oblivious. "He does seem the best qualified. Did you find anything useful?"

"Yes, actually, I did."

"Please, do tell."

I looked at Joan. She wasn't a part of our mission. But at my apologetic smile, she gave a brief nod of understanding and left us.

Before I let my team members in on my info, I took the time to set up basic privacy wards.

"I heavily suspect," I said, "that I've found what led our . . . guide to the site: a message from the former king that something's there."

With a raised eyebrow, Olnir prodded, "Details?"

"A puzzle in the palace. Without knowing a few tricks about the core, you wouldn't be able to work it out, but it says to go where we're going anyway."

Selene looked interested. "Tricks?"

"Yeah, but unless you've got several years to learn about ciphers, don't bother."

That was true enough, learning English was famously a bit of a pain.

"Hmm, this changes nothing, but it is good to know that we're on the right track. Thank you. Anything else?"

"Not as such. There's a town near our site by the name of Eratol. Middling size. Nothing too special."

"Right then," said Olnir. "If all goes according to plan, we should be able to hire our new friend and set out in two or three days."

CHAPTER 15

✦

VARIOUS PERSPECTIVES

There was no hiding the fact that a group of humans was passing through Elven lands, so instead we needed to rely on our cover of being a group of surveyors who found it much safer to travel with a merchant caravan.

On the day of our departure, we formed up around a pair of smaller carts. I noticed something new: a two-and-a-half-foot long piece of steel.

"Hey Glen, new sword?"

"Yeah," he said, polishing the blade. "Something I picked up in the market. Don't have any like this back home."

He held it out for me to look over. I couldn't see anything different from a normal blade, but I was no smith.

"Um? Magical?"

He nodded and after a moment the blade began to glow. I didn't see any runes on it but perhaps they were hidden somewhere.

"Wasn't that expensive, but with just a bit of mana it'll cut through stone like butter."

As he spoke our newest addition joined us.

"Manablades are fairly standard around here. Do you not use them on the Human continent?" Ulanion asked.

I looked up at him. "No, I don't think we have that enchantment. Would that be something we could trade for?" Though anyone making magical items would be a bit jealous of Elven methods, we certainly weren't going to be competition for them.

"Not an enchantment," the Elven man answered. "Something about how they make the steel. I'm not clear on the details, but it's widely enough known that I can't imagine you'd have any real issues finding a smith. Use the same metal in my arrows."

He produced one of the darts and passed it over to me.

Solid steel and a bit longer than I was used to, it was clearly an arrow. There was a series of runes engraved on it, a standard enchantment that simply stored a small amount of mana to be released over a controlled period. That wasn't one that we used often since the core handled storing mana on its own, but I could imagine its efficacy.

I pushed a tiny amount of mana into it and watched as the glow spread. "Interesting."

The glow shifted, moving down and forming a second blade around the sharpened head.

"Careful with that," Ulanion said. "When active, it's rather more dangerous, even if you don't fire it." Ulanion took the arrow and demonstrated by gently pushing it into the street, where it made a perfect hole.

"Point taken," I said, which got a laugh from the two warriors.

A shout of, "We're moving out," made its way down the caravan, and we all had to get a move on.

Though they appeared more advanced than humans in many ways, the elves still used wagons for overland transport. After several hours of walking along the various paths and roads, we found ourselves clear of the city's immediate area, and the traveling column went near silent.

Since most of the elves' crops grew from trees, there were no sprawling fields but rather expanses of thick, deep forest, lending a very different air to the landscape. By our first night I was feeling that nothing I knew from before would properly apply to this place. But I supposed that was a natural part of seeing different lands.

The wagons were circled in a small meadow, and everyone started to relax. A small fire was built, and the twenty or so other members of the little caravan gathered around it to tell stories.

"No shit, there I was," the old caravan leader began, "when we heard the growl, and it stalked out of the woods. Twice as tall as me, and four times as long: a forest tiger!"

He went on about how the beast had attacked his first caravan, killing several of their pack animals in its rampage before he'd buried a spear in its chest.

Everyone, it seemed, had some story or other. I gathered that the higher amount of mana and mages on this continent meant that almost everyone who traveled had met a magical beast at some point or another. Most of these creatures were just described as huge versions of normal animals, not unlike the giant rats that sometimes gathered in the Undercity back home.

"What about you lot," a merchant asked. "Met anything of note?"

"Well, we met a Hurricane Whale," Olnir stated. "That's probably the worst I've seen."

Our fellows leaned in for details and he began to dryly recount the chase before I had to stop him.

"Mind if I tell it," I asked. With an eye roll he waved me on.

As I rose, I began to dance. If they wanted a story, there was no reason to hold back. Illusion worked as the words flowed. From the darkness, someone began a light drum rhythm. I brought images of the whale's pitch-black clouds over the little meadow of our camp. At my will, the sound of wood splintering and waves accentuated the images appearing in the field.

With each verse I wove, images of our fight appeared in the field, depicting the enormity of our battle.

When I finished, breathless, I sat next to the fire and took a sip of water. That was when I noticed the wide eyes of the caravan members. Perhaps I'd overdone it a bit.

Outside the camp
Unknown

Shadow to shadow, I'd flitted throughout the day watching these blasted people. What were they up to? No survey of plants like they claimed. That was nonsense. Moreover, what did that girl know? Master had personally seen her use His Majesty's name while looking at that old riddle. What had she seen?

I'd thought it was too much of a bother to investigate this lot until I'd followed her footsteps. The librarian had been all too happy to tell me about the nice human girl who'd gone asking about places that didn't exist anymore, and how she'd not even known about her *faux pas*. Nobody would know that name without knowing from whom it came.

When I'd brought the details of her destination to my master, and told him of her reference to the village, His drawn, pale face and tight fist told me she'd found something he recognized. I thought he would confront her himself. Instead, he'd sent me.

When the quiet camp was overtaken by black clouds and small silent flashes of lightning, I'd almost turned to flee. My training, however, revealed that it was a mere illusion. An answer which spawned only more questions.

Durin

My head of intelligence brought me another thin folder.

"No location on him, then," I asked.

"No. Wherever they've gone to ground, it must be hidden."

"Hmm. Raise the reward for his capture, and let it be known that we'll pardon anyone who brings us his location—their family, too—regardless of their crimes. We can't have him wandering about."

The matter of Prince Lief was a thorn and only became more irritating day by day. There was no way I could leave someone with a claim to the throne roaming the countryside. Especially if he'd managed to recruit as many of the skilled individuals our reports indicated. It wasn't anything I had against the lad personally, but . . . well, he needed to go.

As my spymaster left his reports and headed back to his duties, I sighed wearily, rose, and paced to the window. Below, the first lamps were being lit along the streets of the capital of my empire. These people, formerly the Ermathi, were now mine. I owed them all I could give them. A place where the good and just could live in peace, where the low and weak wouldn't be abused. I would create an empire where those with talent could rise rather than being beaten down by the circumstances of their birth, rise and lead us into a new dawn.

That had been my hope all along, but in reality it was easier said than done. Even after I'd purged the worst of the predators and abusers from the previous regime, I still had to put new people in power. Sadly, though, a few of these appointees had similar failings to their predecessors, requiring yet more adjustments.

Moments later, my lovely wife entered the room.

"You seem bothered," she observed as she made her way to sit down on a couch.

"A bit, but it will pass. How are you feeling?" I sat beside Sophia, wrapping her up in my arms and resting my hand on the small bulge of her belly.

"Still a bit ill now and then," she said, leaning into my embrace, "but nothing unexpected."

As we rested there, I couldn't help but smile, my hope for the future cutting through all my sadness and fear.

CHAPTER 16

✦

THE SNAKE BACK HOME

City of Lithere
Spymaster Emil

When I was just a boy, I'd had to walk these streets alone, without family or true friends to lead me. That had been a horridly brutal life, but I'd learned things, so many things. First was to use anything that worked. What use were honor and pride to the dead, after all? I'd also learned the paths and ways of the city. Certainly, they'd changed since those days. Old alleys had been cut off and new ones built, tunnels leading here and there were dug or filled, but I'd kept up with a great many of those changes, and the general organization of Lithere remained unaltered.

As I stopped by a stall to eat, I watched the crowd. I sighed. There was no getting by it; the people were happy. Sure, there were those who'd lost loved ones still sulking, but all in all, everyone seemed well off. The merchants enthusiastically hawked their wares, some bringing in goods from across the lands. The people were adjusting well under their new emperor.

It grated on me how joyous they seemed. King Erik, a good and noble man, had done so much for the common folk—good that they would never know!—and here they were. No rebellion. No real pushback against this new Emperor of Shadows. Downright ungrateful of them.

I had to admit, however, that while His Majesty might have been kind, the same could not be said about most of the subordinate nobles. Perhaps that was the big change; those who'd been the real abusers had been removed. Didn't these people understand though? If the king had tried to take them out, he would have fallen to the Ermathi.

Well, what was done was done, and there was no point in being sore about it.

For the time being, I had a job to do. If I was to put the rightful king back in his place, there would be things that only I could accomplish. First and foremost, there were several secret entrances, some guarded by magic, some with more mundane means. Some of these passages could get me near, but only a few would take me directly to my goal. I needed to know if these old paths were still viable, and figuring that out would take some time.

There was also that matter of Princess Sophia. She might be called Queen in public, of course, where she appeared cheerful and in good health. But there were few ways to know how she behaved behind closed doors. Prince Lief insisted we start with her determining if his sibling had betrayed us, or if she was forced into her current position by Durin. Thankfully, there was one group who might be able to answer that question for me, and I was on my way to see them now. I trudged down to the temple district, the sound of my leather shoes on the cobbles keeping an even pace like a song.

The temples had been designed to be easy to find, and the Temple of Lovers was no exception. It seemed its gates were always open, always welcoming to those who needed their embrace. The priests and priestesses were all politically neutral, which, I remarked to myself as I made my way to the entrance, would be at least some blessing to me.

The young man working the entry asked as I approached, "Can I help you, kind sir?"

"Yes, I would like to see the head priestess if possible." I passed over a small envelope. "Please give her that."

The envelope contained a completely mundane note, nothing more than a simple inquiry on having a priest of Lovers go to one of the outlying villages, but that wasn't the important part. The wax seal keeping it closed, however, would be of particular interest. It was marked by Prince Lief's own signet ring. Though not something commonly seen, the head priestess would doubtless recognize it.

I had to wait, but that wasn't unusual. The leaders of the various temples in any city of this size would certainly be busy people. After an hour or two, though, an attendant came to gather me and take me to meet the elder of this order.

There were a number of books and tools along the walls, along with a few pieces of her own personal work, but the office lacked the gold and decadent decor that a noble would have had in their meeting rooms. The seat I was offered was simple but comfortable, the tea a plain but well-made mix. The attendant left us to our discussion, the door clicking closed behind him.

The head priestess gazed at me with hard eyes over her teacup. "I must say I wasn't expecting you to come and see me. To what do I owe this visit."

I was used to a bit of cold treatment, even from the orders. I couldn't say that I didn't deserve at least some of it, so I simply gave her a slight smile. "I've business in the city, of course, but . . . is this room secure?"

She raised an eyebrow as she spoke. "Would I not take pains to make sure it was?"

"Apologies," I acknowledged with a nod. "But I must ask. Sensitive subjects."

"If you plan to oppose Emperor Durin, we will not be aiding you," she said flatly.

"That's not why I'm here, but might I inquire why not? Has he been keeping the edicts of the orders so well?"

"To the letter, even against those he himself appointed to replace your nobles. While King Erik wasn't a terrible man, we both know that he let his men get away with too damn much. Do you have any idea how many girls passed through my doors after suffering at the hands of some pissant baron who we all knew would never be properly punished?" I gritted my teeth against her frustration.

"We both know it comes down to what can be proven," I said, "one testimony—"

"He hardly even investigated! And if he did levy punishment, it was only ever a slap on their wrists with an admonishment to never do it again."

"How does Durin handle such matters," I asked.

"Lad, *Emperor* Durin," she corrected. "He enforces our rules with a harshness I've seldom seen outside of our own priests."

I sighed. It was clear that while the various orders might not actively oppose the former nobility, the Order of Lovers at least had a strong preference for Durin. That was no good, as attempting a coup to return the prince to power would only ruffle their feathers.

"Well, at least the people are being well taken care of," I said. "Though if we could speak on why I am here?" The priestess pursed her lips. "Why, then?"

I couldn't guess what she knew specifically, but her order had offici-ated the wedding. She must have some information. "I'm trying to find out the truth about Princess Sophia. If she went to Durin's side willingly or if she is a political hostage. Her brother is concerned, as you might well understand. Surely you can share her condition with me?"

The old woman stared at me, calculating. She let the silence stretch on for a few moments before sighing herself.

"Queen Sophia," she chided. Propriety was important, apparently. "Stayed with us for some months before her wedding. In that time, she seemed both happy and well-disposed to her future husband. Though we offered to protect her or to spirit her away to prevent any forced marriage, she repeatedly declined. Often while laughing."

"She joined him willingly? Before he took over or afterwards," I asked.

She shrugged. "Who knows? He might have applied some leverage on her, but I never got that impression. Goodness, it was even Emperor Durin who'd pushed so hard for us to do whatever we wished to ensure there were no accusations after their joining."

I sat back, rubbing my face tiredly. After the girl, Gwenna, had gone on her little rampage, I suspected that Sophia might have betrayed us. Several nobles certainly had as well, there near the end. But there had remained the sliver of a chance that the recently-crowned queen remained loyal to her birthplace. The high priestess' claims contradicted these hopes, though. *If she'd gone to him willingly . . .* I thought to myself, the implications unspooling. My liege would be heartbroken, but her alliance with the enemy explained many things.

"Thank you for telling me," I said, rising from my humble chair.

The high priestess stood and walked with me. "Well, letting a family member know that a marriage wasn't forced isn't beyond reason. Though, you do test the line of my neutrality. Good day, lad," she said, opening the door. "I hope you find peace however things end."

I nodded to her in thanks and left. Once I returned, I'd have to give a full accounting to the prince, but for now I processed this new information.

My course remained the same, and my next days would be spent inspecting my hidden entrances. If I could get back into the palace, I would. Even if only to pop in and check for traps. When the time was right and everything was in place, however, we would put things back in their rightful order.

✦

CHAPTER 17

WATERFALL SCENE

As the days of travel wore on, a routine had been established determining when we rose and slept. Various duties and guard shifts, even the order in which we traveled, soon settled into a steady, defined rhythm. I did as I usually did, creating food to make sure we were all fed. Thankfully, with the weather pleasantly warm and the going easy, I didn't need to do much more than that.

The road itself followed a stream, hugging the bank through its twists and turns. It might have been easier to use a pre-cut path through the forests, but our route provided an idyllic scene for our trip.

Riding in the seat of one of the carts, I felt the lurch at the same moment I heard the crack.

Olnir shouted wordlessly as we were both hurled out of our daydreams and sprawling into the grass. After taking some moments to shake off my surprise, I saw Ulanion offering me a hand.

"You okay," our Elven friend asked as he helped me up.

I brushed a few spots off my clothes, but other than a handful of aches that would become remarkable bruises, there was no real issue. "Fine. How's the cart?"

Glen picked up the vehicle's front with little care for its weight. Sometimes, I couldn't help but wonder at how strong some of the people in this world could be.

After a few moments' examination, Glen declared, "Looks like we had a bolt snap.

"Fixable?" Olnir asked.

The knight shrugged. While Glen might have been able to notice the issue, he didn't seem particularly handy.

Several of the men gathered around to discuss, along with a few of the merchants. It reminded me of a common Earth sight: a group of men trying to work on a car. I nearly laughed.

The eventual conclusion was that the broken piece—a large iron rod, bolted in place to hold everything together—had snapped from one end. It was totally buggered. Without a spare on hand.

"Shit," Robert commented as he held up the bit of metal. "Might need a blacksmith."

"I can get it hot enough to melt the pieces together," Dras offered. "Maybe we could, I don't know, try to weld it together or something? If nothing else, we could set up the tools for making magical items and remake it, but either option would take some time."

"All right," Olnir declared, "we're close enough to break for lunch anyway, so let's rest for now and get back to it in a bit."

Dras and the merchants seemed to be deep in discussion about options, so I moved over to where Leah was standing.

"Thoughts on lunch," I inquired.

"No offense, but I'm about bread and cheesed out, and all of our rations are kind of . . ."

"Dry and salty?"

"Yup," she nodded.

"Ideas? You're far more well versed on local edibles," I added. It was true. She'd already proven herself a capable cook a few times on our journey.

"Hmm, we could check the creek," she suggested. "There are berries that would be nice."

After telling some of the others where we were off to, the two of us walked to the stream, checking here and there for things to add to our baskets. It was relaxing, and according to our intelligence, it should stay so. This part of the forest wasn't known for anything dangerous. After about fifteen minutes we found a waterfall that poured into a pool.

Pointing at a cluster of clams grouped at the bottom of the pool, my partner said, "Jackpot. Those are definitely edible if we cook them. Little deep though."

"Well, I haven't had a proper wash in a few days." Donning gloves and boots to protect against the sharp edges of the mollusks, we each took up our baskets and dove in. Our meal lay about ten feet below at the bottom of the bowl-like pool. We took several trips, making sure to take the largest specimens, but leaving the small ones to repopulate.

Dropping my haul on shore, I moved over to the waterfall to shower, only to be joined a moment later by Leah.

"Little cooler than I generally like my baths," I said, "but it is refreshing, isn't it?"

"Mmhmm," she agreed, lounging with me for a few moments.

Soon enough, though, it was time for us to head back. We reluctantly rose from the flat rock we'd stretched upon. As we waded to the shore, a rustling came from just over the waterfall's crest.

"Hey girls," Ulanion said, jumping to the water's edge. "We're almost—" The poor Elven man's eyes went wide as he realized that we'd left most of our clothing off to the side. My face flushed beet red as I tried to cover myself. Leah seemed angrier than I at being caught nude, and didn't even give the intruder a chance to apologize.

Her deep intake of breath registered with both Ulanion and me at roughly the same time.

He raised his hands in alarm, crying out as she loosed the patented bard scream on him.

Ulanion fell to his knees and covered his ears.

We rushed to the piles of our clothing and quickly dressed while Ulanion righted himself, staring pointedly in the opposite direction.

"You can look now," I told him once we were decent.

"You didn't have to drop me like that!" He rubbed his ears. "It's not like I intended to do anything!"

"You should have been more obvious about coming up on us," Leah retorted.

He seemed peeved. "You shouldn't have been naked in the middle of the bleeding woods!"

"That's my fault, actually," I said with an apologetic smile. "We wanted some clams, and I wanted a swim." I could take the blame here, I decided, as it was my suggestion. Having members of our expedition mad at each other would only cause problems later.

While Leah took her basket and walked the path toward our caravan, I moved over to Ulanion and sang a few notes, bringing my hands up to his ears to heal them.

"Thanks," he said. "I was worried they might not stop ringing."

I snorted. "Well, be more careful next time." I gave him a playful wag of my finger as though scolding a favorited child.

With a shake of his head, he led the way back to our carts. Leah had arrived just moments ahead of us, and several of the others were already focused in our direction. Glen in particular seemed on edge.

"Everything all right," Robert asked as we got nearer.

"Fine. Just a misunderstanding," I answered as his sister huffed off.

Our meal that afternoon wasn't half bad. Dras had managed to weld the pieces of metal together. Though the repair was ugly, it should hold until we got to a proper smith.

After a few more days of travel, we arrived at the village of Eratol. It wasn't much bigger than the place where I'd been born. The wall that surrounded the collection of houses, judging by the weathering, was no more than a few years old. The adjacent land was overgrown.

I turned to a merchant in our column, one who said he'd been here a few times over the years. "Does something look wrong to you?"

"It's been a while since I was out here," he answered, "but yeah." However, concern marked his expression.

We took a cautious approach, the Elven merchants led. The casters among us readied defenses just in case. As we approached the wall, I could see movement atop it. The rough gate opened.

A harried looking elf exited through the gate. Standing tall, he had longer-than-average ears, a sharp widow's peak, and a nervous smile.

"Finally," he said. "Welcome to Eratol. We were worried that our call for help hadn't reached anyone, but I see they sent a whole group of mages."

He stopped suddenly, stunned. He blinked a few times, finally realizing that we were human.

CHAPTER 18

✦

THE BROKEN MAN

The village elder was called Indriel. He had a long conversation with Olnir and the caravan leader.

While our leaders were talking, I got a few minutes to look around the town. The trees were connected to one another and the earth with a series of vines. The wall was well enough made, but it was clear that it was a recent construction. Something about the platforms looked green to me. Whomever made this didn't really understand defense, it seemed. Or at least it didn't seem they'd thought of attacks from humanoid creatures. There were no crenellations at all, and the platform near the top of the wall was far too exposed to protect anyone stationed there.

The people regarded us with a mixture of hope and fear as we entered. Obviously, we were not the relief they'd been hoping for. With their worried looks and nervousness in the air, Eratol looked besieged.

Sidling up to Dras, I used Human Tongue to keep things a little more private. "What do you think is going on here?"

"Kind of reminds me of the war," he replied, "but nobody looks hungry."

"That makes sense, with their higher number of casters. Even a few making food could keep a village this size going for months easily."

He nodded as the others from our party came near. Though some of them guarded their carts from the gawking villagers, a few merchants soon joined our clutch.

"What's your estimation on this?" Ulanion asked, his own eyes scanning.

The responding merchant looked nervous as well. "Something's up. The elder said they were waiting for help, but I heard nothing of that before we left, did you?"

"Not that we heard," Selene offered.

Answers came soon enough. Indriel, Olnir, and the merchant left the elder's home and stalked in our direction, none looked at all pleased.

"What's the situation," Ulanion asked.

"Well," Indriel answered, "we thought you were the help we requested nearly a year ago, but it seems not."

Olnir spoke up, motioning for the elder to lead us as we talked. "The village was attacked by some form of monster, a large wolf-shadow type. We need to speak to one of the survivors for more detail."

As we walked, Indriel filled us in. "It first appeared a few years ago. We are uncertain as to the creature's exact nature, but in its first attack it slaughtered most of a wedding party. During the event, the groom awakened his magic, but it wasn't enough. Forty of our people fell to it."

His breath caught in his throat for a moment and we followed silently.

"Our village isn't large," he continued. "We lost too many that night. Ormien was among those who managed to escape, though barely. His bride, however, did not. It affected him, to say the least. You'll see . . ."

"And, the wall," I asked.

"We constructed it to keep our enemy out, and it's worked. The beast also seems to dislike the light, so daytime is safer to be about. However, if our messengers didn't make it, I hesitate to say anything is safe."

We arrived at the house of this Ormien. The two-story home lacked the care shown to the homes nearby. The grass was full of weeds, and the interior dark.

The door swung open slowly at Indriel's touch.

"Ormien," he yelled to the resident. "Help has arrived, we need to talk to you."

When no answer came, we slowly walked through the entryway.

With a crash, an Elven man entered from some back room, his eyes red with sorrow and impotent hate. From beneath raggedy, unwashed hair, he eyed us with confusion. In his one remaining hand he held a bottle.

Staggering into the room, he slurred, "What do you want, you old bastard? Come to poke fun at the cripple?"

"We need to know about the wolf, Ormien," the elder said calmly.

Every hair on my neck stood up. Though restrained, magic flowed around this guy, and he was unstable. In the blink, he surged at the elder, reaching his hand out. Glen and Ulanion met him mid-charge.

"I told you not to mention that thing," he screamed as they wrestled to the ground. He settled into pitiful, soft weeping. "It took them, it took them all. Oh my Ilazia, I'm so sorry."

Shortly thereafter, Ormien passed out.

"What the shit," I asked. "How is he useful?"

"He fought the beast," Indriel answered. "When he's sober—which is less and less these days—he's competent. When he drinks, he gets like this."

"So what?" Olnir seemed irked at the drunk. "We have to wait until he sleeps it off to get anything worthwhile out of him?"

"No, we're not waiting," I answered.

Alana's Own Hangover Cure and Poison Neutralization (patent pending) was a spell I'd mastered years ago. Once I was satisfied that I'd removed the booze from his system, I motioned the guys to hold him tight while I lightly slapped his face.

"Uwh," he murmured.

"Wake up sunshine," I sang. "We need to know what we're up against."

It took a few blinks for the elf to come to and look around the room. "Who the fuck are you? And why are you in my house?"

"We came to your village to look into some unique flora and fauna," Olnir said, using our cover story. "Sounds like there is one in particular specimen we'll need to be rid of before we can get to our business."

That got the drunk's attention and he slowly sat up. "You think you can," he asked.

"Best chance we've got, and it sounds like all the calls for help your village sent out amounted to nothing," Olnir answered.

"Come on then. Let's talk." Our guide shakily rose to his feet, and led us into the kitchen where he smartly poured himself a cup of water. "Didn't think those messengers would make it, anyway. Didn't I tell you, old man?"

The elder seemed irked but said nothing. If he wasn't going to, though, I certainly would push this conversation along.

"Why did you think that," I asked.

"That thing, whatever it is, is smart. Too smart. When it attacked us, it took out the guards first. It's no base beast. That thing is intelligent. It thinks. It plans. Calculates. I saw it in its eyes."

For a moment he lost his concentration. When he returned to the moment, he said, "The only reason it hasn't attacked us yet is probably because we're more like its stockpile of food. Or, it just hates us and wants us to suffer."

"Any weaknesses," Dras asked.

"So far as I saw," the elf answered, "it's immune to mundane weapons. Arrows and non-magical blades just pass through it. While you can hurt it with magic, we, sadly, didn't have anyone strong enough to finish the creature."

That was bad. A lot of monsters had resistances, but I'd never heard of anything being completely immune to anything except magic. There were a few beasts that were difficult to hurt without it, of course, but that was just because they were tough. It sounded like this thing was incorporeal.

From the corner, Robert asked, "You fought it before—could you help us against it?"

"Oh, I'd love to, but if you have left-handed," he gestured to his missing right arm, "I'm still getting used to being left-handed. A condition, I might add, imposed on me by our friend out there."

"I might be able to help if we can get enough of the village together. It'll be a hack job though, and it'll hurt," our primary healer explained.

I saw something like hope in Ormien's eyes, and it wasn't pretty. He clearly saw a chance, perhaps the only one he would get, for revenge. "I'm in," he announced.

"No more drinking," Robert urged with a hard look. "If we're going to fight, you'll need to be sober for it."

"I said I was in. Whatever conditions you set, I'll honor."

While Ormien and Robert eyed each other, I could see Olnir smile. We'd acquired another soldier, and a physical magic user to boot.

CHAPTER 19

✦

RE-ARMING

Our new Elven comrade had to be force fed as much and as nutritious food as was physically possible. A handful of villagers had to be gathered as well. Leah was on standby as her twin explained exactly what he needed from everyone while we waited just outside his house.

While he prepared, Robert asked, "Alana, have you ever taken part in regrowing limbs before?"

Back when I'd been taking classes, we'd had a basic course on healing. I was at least passingly familiar with the process of regrowing a limb. Then, though, it had been a weeks-long process of fixing and allowing the body time to recover. Even when rushed, the task still took weeks.

"Yes," I responded. "We did a bit of that in school, but it was slow going. You said you could do this quickly?"

"I said I could do a hack job, and I can. Under normal conditions you need time for the body to regain energy while you regrow limbs, but we don't have that. We're going to force it. Sort of," he added quickly. Pointing to the elf—now drinking a vile-looking slurry conjured by Leah—Robert went on. "Ormien here is going to be shoving as much food as he can down his throat while I fix him up. My dear sister will be using her magic to speed his intake of food. While she does this, I need you to work on the skin. That's the easiest part and, frankly, I've never seen you work before."

"So, you don't trust me to do anything serious at the speed you need, understood." His expression was apologetic. I took no offense; this magic was his specialty and well beyond my personal capabilities. If we'd been doing illusions or weather magic, I'd probably have relegated him to something minor too.

"Oh, that tastes terrible," Ormien said, finishing this serving of Leah's mixture.

I felt I might regret the question, but I was curious. "What's in it anyway?"

"Mostly meat, salt, water, bones, and whatever sugar you can shove in," Leah answered. "We used honey back home, but here they have real, pure sugar. Reduce all to roughly the consistency of thin mud and cook well."

"It smells like barf," I commented.

"Also tastes like barf," Ormien confirmed.

"Well, don't get squeamish now," Robert said, pointing to a bucket sitting beside his sister. It brimmed with the same substance he'd just choked down. "You'll need to finish that while we're working. If you can't drink through the pain, we'll stop. But, I caution you that pausing is less than ideal."

The Elven man nodded his resolve.

"Question," I said, looking toward our healer. "If it's so much faster, why isn't this done for everyone?"

"Because you'd have to be able to use physical magic to even survive it," Robert said, rubbing his head before turning to his patient. "I'll be pretty blunt here, too, your new arm will be weaker than if we'd done this the right way. But, I don't want to wait around for weeks. It should eventually improve to where it was before your experience, and a priest can probably speed that along. This measure is to get you fighting-ready now."

As our preparation finished, the elder returned with a crowd of merchants and villagers. We had explained earlier that since this was a difficult bit of magic we would need more people for the gestalt casting. To my surprise, they'd not disappointed. A throng stood outside looking happy to see Ormien—now sober—and ready to get fighting again.

"You'd think they'd be madder at him for getting drunk and acting a jerk," I said to Ulanion as Robert got everyone split into groups.

He laughed at the look on my face. "Yeah, I notice that about humans. Thing is, elves live a lot longer."

"So? He still spent what, a year or so locked up drinking or whatever?"

"Probably, but when you live for centuries, a year or two isn't much. Not really. If someone you knew came out of a months-long depression when you really needed them, would you be glad? Or would you be mad? What if it was only a few weeks after the loss of a loved one? That's a lot more understandable right?"

I hadn't thought of it like that, but I suppose if you lived so much longer then stuff like this did seem slightly less offensive. "I suppose that makes sense," I admitted. "Particularly if he was well-liked."

The archer smiled and moved to his place in our grouping.

Robert began the work with gusto, pounding on a borrowed drum. In his seat, our patient buckled from the pain. Other than alcohol, we had nothing to dull his pain. After that initial jerk, though, Ormien gritted his teeth and straightened into position.

Within moments the skin on his missing arm bulged and popped as the bone pushed its way through, reforming without the other tissues around it. Blood flowed, only for muscles to worm their way out and around, pulling blood vessels with them on their way.

Before I could start returning his skin Ormien reached down and guzzled as much of the foul drink as he could. I could hear Leah to the side and I sighed in relief.

Soon, as he put down the bucket, I started up my own song. Backed by a number of volunteers, I sang, returning the layers of skin to his currently flayed upper arm. It was fortunate that he'd managed to get more in his system before I started, because he was getting all those nerves restored in a hurry. By the time I was halfway through, he was screaming.

As the upper arm finished, we pressed on. It was surreal to watch as, in real time, bone pulsed forward only to be covered in successive layers of tissue. The lower arm went much as the upper, but near the end I could see Robert hesitate. We'd arrived at the worst part and we all knew it.

"How many times do I have to tell you, boy," Ormien spat. "I'm in for this, keep going."

"Drink," Robert.

The Elven man drained the last of the gross bucket before exchanging a meaningful nod with Robert. The last of the work began. All the delicate bits of the hand flowed into place, snapping together speedily. This more detailed, more concentrated work was agonizing for Ormien. I pushed the limits of my own healing, letting the skin quickly build like a wave over the new flesh.

As his hand returned, Ormien screamed like a dying man. His good hand went white-knuckled on the chair, the wood splintering under his strength. While to us the restoration probably only took around half an hour, to him the ordeal must have seemed like ages. When it was finally done and we withdrew our magic, he sighed in relief. Ormien's head lolled to the side and he peered down at his new arm.

It . . . well it wasn't pretty. The flesh was fishbelly pale, as one might expect. As the elf moved his new appendage, those first motions were coltish and lacked coordination. However, matters improved as he practiced touching his fingers together.

"How is it," Robert asked.

"Kinda itches." That got a snort from several in the crowd, myself included.

"Sincerely, though," Robert pressed, "is there any pain, how is the flexibility?"

A few more flexes and taps before the gathered mass, and he looked up. "Doesn't move quite like the last one. Then again, I haven't had one to move in a while. No pain though. A bit stiff."

"I told you it wouldn't be great. It should improve with time."

With a few more quick movements and a smile, Ormien turned and walked back into his house. When he returned moments later, he carried a sword. He gave a look toward Glen, who'd taken up a position to the side.

"Mind giving me a few quick rounds to knock the rust off?" Ormien asked.

While they moved off to an open area to spar, the rest of us gathered.

"We don't know enough about this beast yet," Olnir began, "but there's sadly only one way we're getting more information. So, I want everyone to be prepared before sundown. Indriel has indicated to me that the creature often appears near the wall after dark."

Despite her excellent instincts when it came to magic items, Selene lacked skill in the fighting department. She asked, "Prepared for what exactly? We don't even know what the thing is."

I answered, "To hunt, of course."

CHAPTER 20

THE HUNT BEGINS

By twilight, everyone had gotten a chance to rest while our newest addition adjusted to his new arm. As Ormien and Glen took up a small clearing to engage in a mock battle, the rest of us sat to the side and watched.

I was no warrior, and though I could barely follow their movements, I understood that the elf was getting his butt kicked. Every time they reset, he looked at Glen with a bit of a glare. Glen on the other hand seemed unbothered, almost like this was painfully routine for him.

After a few more passes, the human knight called a stop to things. "Hold on. Who trained you?"

"The village warriors when I was a boy, of course," Ormien responded.

"But what of using your abilities? Did they teach you this?"

"No one to teach. Far as I know, I'm the only physical magic user for the town."

"Okay, that explains it," Glen said. "Your movements are fine for common swordplay without magic. But with your mana, you're stronger and faster. Techniques that would be lethal tools for a normal swordsman simply won't work for you. Even if you don't hurt yourself, you'll be open to your opponents."

Glen pulled Ormien off to lead him through some basic slashes. I could hear him explaining; how they were different and how to stand, but I knew next to nothing about using a sword other than, "pointy end that way."

While I watched, Ulanion and Dras approached.

"Hey, we're gonna go and take a look at what we can see. Mind joining us," Dras asked.

"Sure. Any reason?"

Ulanion gave me a slight smile. "Dras here tells me you're something else when it comes to invisibility, and I'd rather like to catch a glimpse of the wolf. Some illusions might help if you're willing."

"No problem."

Soon I'd rendered us invisible, and we'd made our way to the top of the wall. As the sun set, we could easily scan the horizon and see the fields around the town. The area—devoid of the trees so common in these lands—was weird. From our perch I could see that some had been felled purposely, something I'd not paid much note to before.

Sitting there was a mix of nerve wracking and painfully boring. However, after a couple of hours, as the last of the sun's light faded, we saw it. Far along the edge of the clearing, a shadow slinked in and out of the trees, barely visible. It didn't come close, stalking, patiently waiting to see what we'd do.

"Why isn't it closing," Dras asked. "For that matter, why didn't it attack us on our way in?"

"I don't think it cares who arrives," I said, "only who leaves. This thing is too smart, Dras. It's probably happy to wait for us to feed ourselves to it."

"She's right," Ulanion agreed. "From what I can see, this wall should pose no threat if the beast truly wanted over it. If it's spectral, it might not even need physical food. We need to know what it's after."

"Mind running a test for me, Ulanion?" I inquired.

The elf probably quirked an eyebrow, but we were invisible, so I couldn't quite tell. "Not at all."

"Can you try shooting it? See if we can take it out before it has a chance to respond?"

"All right, let's test its reaction speed, then. Can you kneel down a bit? Hate to put an arrow through your face."

I heard rustling as the archer prepared.

Both Dras and I flattened. I could just see over the rampart. There was a creaking beside me as Ulanion drew his bow.

"Ready when you are," Dras and I said.

His voice was strained as said, "Gonna be a bit hard to shoot without seeing it but hold tight."

The arrow flew with a shockwave. There was a whoosh of air, and my hair was tossed as the arrow hurtled at its target, trailing light and fast as a bullet.

In the distance a tree exploded as if hit by a bolt of lightning. Shards of bark flew from the point where the arrow hit, which had been reduced to little more than a bunch of sawdust. Up and down the tree the wood split as the shockwave and magic pressed out.

"Did you get it?" Dras asked hopefully, seeing the destruction.

"Not quite."

The thing let out a howl of rage and pain, and the shadow slipped back into the woods.

"Grazed it," Ulanion continued, "but the thing's fast." When it became too dark to continue our watch, we returned to ground. I regretted that we didn't have Charles along for this. With his eyes, we would have been able to spot the thing in pitch black at any distance. It didn't help wishing for what you didn't have, though.

"Learn anything," Olnir asked as we rejoined our group.

"It is particularly quick," Ulanion offered.

Ormien quirked an eyebrow. "We hit it several times when I fought it. Seemed to damage it too. What did you fire at it?"

Conversation and speculation began in earnest. From Ormien's explanations we knew that magic could hurt it, and the magically-charged arrow had proven that. Sadly, beyond that and a general understanding of physical capabilities, there was little we could do but just go and fight it.

Since most of us were casters, we set up a series of shields and headed out the gate. The plan was to begin our search at the demolished tree.

"Suppose maybe I should have waited," Ulanion grumbled.

"I would have preferred it," Olnir grumbled.

"I think it was the right choice," Glen offered. The knight didn't often disagree with Olnir, and the soldier's opinion held weight.

"We might have learned more had he waited," the older man countered. "Who knows what we lost because of that rash decision."

"Perhaps, but we might have ended the hunt early and without bloodshed. More importantly," Glen added, pointing to the ground, "he managed to damage the beast." A spray of inky black fluid marred the ground and formed a trail that dragged on into the gloaming. Not enough blood to indicate a fatal injury, but it did give us something to follow.

Even with our casters tossing out a few magical lights, the night was still spooky, like a haunted jungle with huge trees all around us. The trail was easy to follow, so much so that Ulanion and Ormien frowned.

"It's like it knows it's leading us to it. Either it doesn't care, or it's planning something," Ulanion said. "If it's as smart as you say, at least."

"It is," Ormien responded. "I also know where it's going, not sure if that helps though."

"Where?" I asked.

"The old ruins up the side of the valley. Nothing else this way."

"Do you know if monsters often come from those," Leah inquired. "Something similar to this?"

"No, never heard of a monster coming from there before," the elf answered.

For several minutes more we walked, the trees gradually clearing until they opened all around us. Before us stood a cliff, into which was carved what looked like a series of doors and openings. The main entrance was obvious by its archway reaching several feet higher than those surrounding it. The path of blood lead up to the door before stopping. This was where our enemy had come.

"What's inside," I asked.

"No idea, never been in," Ormien answered.

"What? Never?" Selene seemed more surprised by his words than me.

Our guide seemed confused by the question. "No, why would anyone come here? It's just an old empty ruin."

"Wait, even as a teen boy," Robert pressed, also confused, adding, "or whatever the Elven equivalent is?"

"No, nobody does things like that."

At the explanation we humans all kind of looked at each other. Elves were weird.

"Back on track," Olnir snapped. "Defensive formation, guards up."

As soon as we'd formed up, we proceeded deep into the lair of the wolf.

CHAPTER 21

ATRIUM

We walked through the arch and right into a vast atrium. As we examined the various entryways and exits I couldn't help but notice the two balconies above us looking down from the shadowy upper reaches. Other than the one we'd use to enter, I could see six additional outlets but not what lay beyond.

The layout reminded me of a massive office, this place was huge. I could imagine it bustling with workers in its prime. I could almost hear the footsteps of elves long past walking to and from the various rooms of this building. I wondered if they lived in the village or if there were quarters deeper in. With the passage of time it was impossible to tell.

"Hey, why are there no animals in here," I asked. "Or plants for that matter. If this place is as old as it's supposed to be, it should be overgrown, shouldn't it?"

"It should have, indeed. But why not," Leah mused.

"Questions for later," Olnir insisted. "Now we need to find and put down that wolf."

Even if I didn't like his tone, we did need to deal with that monster.

"Lights," Glen directed. He pushed mana into his own sword, setting it aglow.

Each of us conjured light in some form or another. Dras made a small ball of cool fire. Selene wore a little trinket that shed a soft nimbus. Robert and Leah produced similar-looking orbs, and I put out one of my own. With the combined ambience, we could see properly. The inside of this place looked as though someone had simply turned off the lights and left just yesterday. There was some minor scuffing and wear to the floors and walls, but otherwise it was pristine. I wouldn't even be surprised if the lights still worked if we could find them. We could clearly make out the shiny black tiles, and a large counter running along one side of the room, near to the back.

Being the only thing of note on our level, we made our way over to the reception desk and found that it still had papers on it. Papers that were completely legible and untouched by the millennia. The whole situation was really weirding me out.

"What in the world," Dras asked, carefully picking up a leaf of paper. "How are these . . . *what* are these?"

I leaned over his shoulder and read. "The dialect is different from modern Atali, but it seems to be a note detailing the export of materials. Some kind of manifest."

"This is weird," Selene said, voice quivering. "Really weird. I don't like it at all."

"Focus," Olnir chided. "We can look into that after."

From behind us came a quiet growl.

Ormien and Glen fell into defensive positions, blades flaring. Ulanion, his bow up, fired a potent arrow before I could even properly register what was happening. The arrow slammed into a column just behind the shadow-wolf, taking a fair chunk of the beast's ethereal flesh with it. As it did so our two wizards quickly produced heavy attack spells in the air before them. Something seemed wrong to me.

This thing was supposed to be intelligent, I thought, *picking off guards and otherwise being a clever, careful hunter. Why would it change now? Why would it use such an obviously stupid place to make a stand? Why alert us to its presence?*

I understood.

"STOP, IT'S A—!" The wizards let loose, their powerful bolts of fire and force screaming toward the beast before us.

The thing leapt from where it crouched in the shadows, all too ready for the attack. While it disappeared into the upper reaches, the spells slammed into the same column Ulanion had struck, shattering the stone like glass. In horror, I watched as the column fell toward us, as web-like fractures spidered up, up across the ceiling of the cavernous room.

It had led us to hitting just that spot. Clever, indeed.

I was numb, unable to cast and rooted to the spot. As the rock plummeted toward me, I briefly registered Glen scoop Dras and Selene into his arms, and bolt left. Ormien did the same with Robert and Leah.

Processing my oncoming death, I felt an arm wrap around me and heave. We blurred to the side through one of the archways behind the desk. Ulanion. I could see him out of the corner of my eye.

I saw Olnir. In a moment of extraordinary casting, the elder expelled a potent wave of force. There was a brilliant flash. Though the force redirected the column about to crush him, it was not enough to stop the several tons of rock falling from the ceiling. A boulder the size of a horse struck him from behind, reducing him to a thick red smear across the tiles.

A scream caught in my throat, soon knocked away as Ulanion and I slammed into the ground. We tumbled and rolled, finally coming to a stop face to face, with him atop me. His bow inches above my head, his other arm still wrapped tightly around my waist, our eyes met.

Panting, he asked, "Are you okay?"

"Yeah," I responded, breathless. "Olnir . . ."

He shook his head, eyes grim. "I didn't think I could get you both."

I was stunned. Grateful, but stunned, nonetheless. "You chose me?"

He almost smiled, and I was thankful to whomever was responsible for these things that I had been born as I was. "Save the ladies first, yes?"

"Well, thank you. Um . . . one thing, could you . . ." I glanced at how I was pressed into his chest.

He followed my gaze, seemed to realize the position in which we'd landed, and promptly turned red. As he moved to stand, he pulled me up with him.

It took a few moments for me to pry my fingers off of him. After the stress of a near-death experience, they simply didn't want to let go of anything.

"Once over," Ulanion said, brushing himself off. "Check yourself for injuries, and make sure you've got all of your gear."

I did as he instructed. Other than a few minor scrapes and bruises, I was remarkably fine. As far as my gear was concerned, I had everything I should: my armor, a knife, and a small packet of jerky.

I looked up to see him frowning at his quiver.

"All good," I asked.

"I'd like to have more arrows, but this'll have to do."

I peered through the archway. Well, I tried to. Rubble and dust blocked our path back to the atrium.

Taking in our situation, the elf asked, "Do you have some way to contact your fellows?" Though I had pushed for us to all be given radios like those I'd made back in school, my mentor—Mystien himself—had shot down that idea. It would have greatly improved inter-unit contact on our mission, however, it was considered too risky lest the technology fall into enemy hands. Besides, the elves were heralded for their skill at enchanting. They might be able to backwards engineer anything we brought.

I shook my head.

"All right then," Ulanion said. "We'll just have to work our way through and find them. Let's go slow though, I don't like how that shadowy bastard split us up."

Outside
Unknown

I had no clue what those maniacs were up to. First, they went to some nowhere village to pick up some random elf, then they trudged to a bunch of ruins? The fools seemed to be tracking the enormous magical beast that had been circling the town. I'd nearly shat myself when I saw it and could only pray that the thing hadn't realized my presence. Thankfully it scampered off when that archer fired upon it. The thing moved unnaturally.

As I contemplated following them into the ruin, there came a thunderous crash followed quickly thereafter by three explosions. While I watched, half of the facade crumbled. These humans were out of their minds firing off that kind of magic indoors! Had my superiors not demanded answers in full, I'd have just left these idiots to their collective fate.

As the dust settled, I pondered if I should await them outside, or follow the cadre of suicidal lunatics.

Decisions, decisions.

✦

CHAPTER 22

EXPLORING THE RUIN

We made our way down the eerily silent corridor. The monstrous wolf handily separated our party.

"Do we have a battle plan for if that thing shows up," I asked Ulanion.

"Not really. Any ideas?"

"Honestly? I'm still unsure of its capabilities. If I knew more, I might be able to come up with something. Did you notice anything that might be helpful?" He pondered quietly, his eyes constantly scanning our surroundings. "It likes to stick to the shadows. Both here and near the town, it avoided being in the light. This could be hunting behavior, but with magical beasts, it's difficult to be sure."

Not sure how to use that, I thought to myself. Aloud I said, "What about its injuries? You hit it twice. Could you see how badly it was hurt or anything?"

"I'm fairly sure that I got it good the first time, not good enough, but it was bleeding well. But that didn't seem to bother it in the second round. Some kind of healing ability perhaps?"

"Maybe," I agreed. "Might have to see if we can get lights on it and get a better look if we run into it again."

"Let's hope that doesn't happen until after we've met back up with the others."

With that, the elf walked on and we continued our search.

The hallway remained straight, dotted along both sides with rooms I guessed to be offices of some kind.

I picked a room at random and headed in. There were several small recesses in the ceiling, all aimed away from the desk. My guess was that those were somehow connected to making light. Instead of drawers, the desk sported cubbies. Empty and clean, I'd find nothing here. Still unsettled by the way everything here remained preserved despite being thousands of years old, I tested the wooden chair. It was fairly comfortable.

Closing up as I exited, we continued on until we came upon an intersection. Another hallway splintered off from our own.

"Only change we've seen so far," Ulanion observed.

I pointed to a sign near the fork. The word was written in the older style of Atali, but even as I squinted at it, I was stymied. "I'm not quite familiar with that one."

"Gymnasium," my companion offered, an eyebrow raised. " A place to work out? Why would they have that here?"

"Maybe people lived here? And that word is a weird one." Though I understood Atali, I'd never seen a term for *gym*.

"There were a few back in the capital, but it's not something you see much anymore."

"Regardless, do we go down there," I asked.

"I say we keep on and see if we can find something going in the right way."

After another hundred feet of boring bare rooms, the passage turned. I smiled at first, but when we arrived at the corner, I quickly frowned. We'd found a stairway leading down into the depths. There were a pair of signs; one read *Maintenance*, and the other *Laboratories*.

"Perhaps the gym," I suggested.

"Even if we can't find the others, we might be able to get the lights back on if we go down there."

I sighed. "Yeah, I know."

"Something wrong?"

"I hate going underground."

The elf gaped at me for a solid five seconds. "Seriously?"

"I have history."

Ulanion appeared doubtful. "History?"

"Every time I go underground things go massively horribly wrong," I explained.

"Well, you're in luck."

"How so?"

"Things have already gone horribly wrong, so we don't need to worry about that," he joked.

"Fine. But you're going first."

We slowly worked our way down the stairs, and—like most things here—the corridor seemed far larger than was even reasonable. The steps were feet wide and though they curved to form a gentle spiral, they just kept going. Deeper and deeper without doors or branching paths.

After ten minutes of this, Ulanion muttered, "Perhaps we should have gone your way."

"Oh, we can't stop now," I grumbled. "The only way out is through."

"Look, nothing's going to happen," he said.

The fool.

From behind us came a howl.

Without preamble, we sprinted down the stairs, making it to the bottom quickly where we found another corridor. Unlike those above, the walls were covered in pipes.

After a quick glance up the stairs behind us, Ulanion drew an arrow. "GO!" he screamed as he loosed it.

I didn't need to be told twice.

As I ran, I sang, pulling energy around me. I wasn't sure how shadow would respond to lightning, but it seemed effective on everything else. Before I could start tossing off bolts, though, I ran face-first into a door. Big enough for a humanoid, it was far too small for our howling pursuer.

I grabbed the handle. Looking over my shoulder, I saw the umbral beast bearing down on Ulanion. Though each arrow he loosed seemed to hurt it, nothing stopped the creature bearing down on us. Gathering what mana I could, I let loose, the blue-white flash streaking down the corridor and into the hulking lupine form of my opponent.

As my power lashed into its side, the wolf let out a horrible, pained scream. If Ulanion's arrows cut slashes, my bolt tore a gaping wound along its body. In the last of the bolt's light, I saw the creature fall back a few feet, its head thrashing back and forth. Searching. Within a blink, a pair of hateful red eyes found me.

Perhaps it sensed I was gathering power for another shot but whatever its reason, the beast fled up the stairs.

Ulanion carefully made his way over to me, marking his features.

"That worked," he commented, sounding a bit surprised.

"Big beastie made of shadows, who'd think the big spear of light would sting?"

"Why didn't you finish off?"

"It's not a fast spell. Why didn't you?"

"One arrow left."

"Fair enough."

I gestured to the door. The adjacent plaque indicated that this was the maintenance room. "Let's see if we can find something useful." The best thing about this room was that its door was too tight a fit for our wolf friend. However, this was the last positive trait I could find in our new surroundings.

From what I could see, we had found the origin of all those pipes in what appeared to be a master control room of sorts. Control for what? That would, in all likelihood, take weeks to parse. The moment we entered, the temperature dropped to freezing, and my teeth began chattering.

Ulanion went over to one of the several ice-covered tanks, looking closely. "What is all this stuff?" Pondering both my lives, I realized the room reminded me of a boiler room.

"To manage lights and heat, maybe," I offered. "Whatever else they needed for this place?" Shining through the ice, I could make out weak light. I padded to the first and carefully created a heated area, allowing the buildup to melt away. There were a number of knobs and buttons, all marked with the same technical Atali we'd seen in other areas of this place. After painstakingly translating what I could—and conferring with my partner for the rest—we concluded that this panel was responsible for energy production.

Annoyingly, though this meant that the generators continued to create a plentiful supply of power, nothing explained what source they were drawing from. Moving to the next panel, I ruminated on the potential here. We could be on the verge of discovering something that could power enchantments for millennia.

CHAPTER 23

POWER ON

Though we'd driven off the shadow-wolf for the time being, who knew how long that would last? We still needed to find the rest of our crew. And then, there were all of the tasks to be done in this room.

With our myriad problems laid out before me, I began with what I could immediately control. The panels in this space indicated that they were responsible for a slew of systems. If I could get a few of those working, I might make headway on the other dilemmas. I hoped I'd find a defense system, though I conceded that was unlikely. The first goal was to find lights and get those on again, possibly weakening our foe. If I was really lucky, we would find intercoms or cameras that might lead us to our crew. To that end, I cleared the ice from panel after panel, scanning them for any indication as to what their function. I started with the panels giving off light.

One panel controlled the cleaning system. While I didn't have the time to work through all of the details, it seemed that I'd found the enchantments devoted to preserving the spotless, ageless quality of these ruins.

Next seemed to focus on repairs. Though well beyond my current understanding, I could read that its limits were being strained at the moment. When I considered the colossal mess we'd made of the atrium, I figured that to be the most likely cause.

I sighed, leaning my head back.

"What," asked Ulanion.

"Checked all the active ones, and there's nothing immediately useful," I said.

"Have you at least found out why this room is so damn cold?"

"Sorry, not on any of these panels. I suspect it's because one of the machines makes a lot of heat when running properly, but that's just a guess."

The elf looked about curiously. "Where then?"

"How should I know? Some box hidden in a corner and covered in inches of ice? Maybe it's just set to always be like this."

I had no experience with any of these systems, in either of my lives. The archaic, technical version of their language didn't help either.

"Fine, fine," Ulanion conceded. "What's next then?"

I pouted. "I'm hesitant to leave with that monster still out there. Especially since it's just two of us. But, the way I see it, we either get things up and running from in here, or we continue searching for the rest of the team."

He rubbed his head. "We're here. Do what you can. We can decide then."

I needed to clean this place before I could even access things. "Can you help me sing for a bit?"

Ulanion smiled. "That I can do."

We wove a tune together, and within moments the sheets of thick ice melted away. Our findings proved to be a mixed bag. Though some panels prompted us to restart them, others remained opaque.

Hours passed, spent in careful study, examining and translating each. Little by little, panel by panel, I restored power to the facility. Lighting—being the most helpful to our current situation as well as the option least likely to catastrophically fail—was my primary focus. There were dozens of different settings to apply to the many sectors of the building. Once I had it mostly sorted—tiny scraps of paper serving as labels—I flipped the switch.

Nothing.

I checked and rechecked my work before sighing and staring at the panel for the trillionth time. My gaze landed on a narrow section on the side that didn't match the rest. I experimented for minutes before I finally pried open a hatch, and was able to peer into the workings of the control station.

It was, of course, full of ice. After clearing the ice, my jaw dropped. What had been hidden under the snowy coating I now witnessed. Engraved runes flared with light and connections reformed. A quick trip to the other side of the room confirmed that the repair panel had routed power to a new destination. Though I hardly understood all of this, I had a pretty good idea where that power was going.

Along the surface of the station, runes lit up, one by one, indicating the restoration of services. About halfway through its cycle, a click sounded and the whole space filled with a gentle white glow. I felt warmth emanating from the control panel.

"Success," I cheered.

"Congratulations! We can see now," Ulanion said as he smiled at me.

"Great! One down," I said, considering the tasks yet before me. My good mood dropped and I added, "Several more to go." I set to work on powering on the more useful controls next: doors, elevators. One by one I cleaned out the ice and put the settings on. I did worry about drawing too much power from the generators, but they seemed to chug along without the slightest hint of resistance. Regardless of what systems I engaged, the readings remained the same. Unlike the generators, however, I was struggling. Casting spell after spell through the night depleted my mana reserves, not to mention my physical energy. After staring at one readout for ten minutes and not understanding a syllable I'd read, I pawed at my eyes.

"You okay," Ulanion asked.

"Bit worn out is all. Give me a second?"

"Nothing wrong with being tired," he said from the door. He'd been standing, keeping watch through the narrow window and probably still would despite the locks I'd engaged on the door. "Rest for a bit then we'll get back on it."

"Yeah, okay," I agreed. "I'll just sit down for a second."

I found an open spot on the floor and tried to curl up. I was wiped enough that I thought I'd pass out immediately, but as it stood the ground was sucking heat from me and making me shiver and chatter my teeth.

On my third or fourth attempt to rearrange myself, I felt my companion come near. When I glanced up, Ulanion gave me a soft smile and draped his cloak over me. Irritated that he felt this comfortable, but I was cold. I leaned on him and quickly decided that he made a passable pillow.

On the other side of the facility
Dras

We'd coursed the beast, trying to run it down, but that proved a losing proposition. It used our pursuit as an opportunity to set traps, falling rocks and such. These had gotten significantly less effective, though. In the last hour or two, we'd only caught a tantalizing glimpse of our enemy while navigating the massive complex. As the massive form of the monstrosity flashed out of the door in front of us, we halted.

At my side, Robert asked, "Do we follow?"

"Could be a trap," Leah observed, "but there are only two doors here."

"Yeah," Glen added. "The last time it let us see it go one direction only to drop that boulder on us when we tried to take the other path." The knight, irritated by that trick, still sounded sore about it.

We received a minor miracle when the lights came on. Without the need to create our own light, we were able to conserve mana. Also, our pursuer-quarry seemed hampered by this development. Glen had been the first to note it, but I could see, too, that the wolf-beast was slowing a significant amount.

As we were discussing matters, a section along the wall lit up and made a polite *ding*. We'd seen a few odd sections here and there, but could only guess as to their use. Previously, they resembled luminous doorways, but in the darkness we saw no obvious way to pass through. However, in the full light, I could see a pair of glowing triangles—one pointing up, the other down—to the side of the outline. Selene squinted. "Is that . . .?"

"It looks just like the ones back in the city, yeah," I responded. "I'd wager the design is based on ones like this.

"Dras," Glen said, warily studying the hallway, "this place is waking up, should we be . . . worried?"

Somehow, with Olnir gone, I'd been treated as our leader. I didn't want to think on the stain that had once been our boss. Thankfully, though, Ormien swore that he saw the other elf grab Alana and bolt. Knowing that, I had my own suspicions about our miracle and all the other ways this facility stirred from slumber.

All I said was, "I don't think so."

"Do you think the lights are because we're here," Ormien asked, looking about the room.

"Honestly," I said, "I'd sooner bet it has something to do with our missing bard." This earned a chorus of nods.

"Regardless," Robert said, still on edge and scanning our surroundings. "We've got decisions to make if we're going to find her."

"I think we go down," I offered. "I'd like to regroup before we go after the wolf again, if possible."

"Elevator then," Selene asked.

I nodded and we piled tightly in. Once the doors closed, I pressed the button labeled *Basement.*

Alana

I was unceremoniously stirred by a panicked Ulanion. As he shook me roughly, I gave meager shouts of protest before I was finally able to process that he was speaking.

"Alana! Up, something's happening," he yelled in Atali. "Get up now!" Getting to my feet, I scanned the room and some of his fear seeped into me. When I fell asleep, ice had still covered much of the area. Now, however, it was sublimating at high speed.

"Where did it start!," I asked.

The archer pointed to a now fully lit control panel, and I hastened to it. I'd labeled it 'temperature controls' and left it be, instead working around it. However, the heat radiating from the nearby panels had melted the ice inside. The repairs began of their own accord and the thing now appeared to be running at top capacity. The result? An automatic system cleaning the glacial buildup, setting off a chain reaction of all of the dormant panels whirring to life.

I froze. I'd been too nervous to start that machine, but this was not what I wanted at all. Some of the waking systems were a complete mystery while others I definitely hoped would remain in stasis until I could give them more study. The most severe of those worries, I noted with terror, was beginning to power up.

"Shoot that," I screamed, pointing at the panel in charge of security.

Ulanion didn't hesitate. In a blink, his bow was in his hand and firing. The shining enchanted arrow slammed into the panel and . . .

It did nothing.

Without so much as a scratch, the panel remained, its startup sequence engaged and fully initiated. There was nothing I could do. As I contemplated all the ways this could go wrong, a section of blank wall split, revealing a lupine figure at least eight feet tall hulking in the recess.

"POWER ON," a mechanical voice said in a barely understandable Atali.

The eyes on the figure blazed with light. "Unauthorized entities detected. Commence removal."

As the golem stepped from its alcove, blades slid free from its jaw to form teeth, the protrusions lighting with red energy in a most unfriendly way. Ulanion blurred, appearing before me brandishing his belt knife.

"Identifying mana signatures," the mechanical voice continued. "Unknown royal-type mana signature detected. Ceasing hostilities."

The lupine warrior withdrew its weapons and knelt before us.

"How may I serve, your highness?"

CHAPTER 24

✦

GOLEMS

Stunned as the beast knelt there, I stammered, "Royal . . . what!?"

"Royal-type mana signature. Specification unknown," the thing said.

I looked at my companion. Ulanion gaped, eyes bulging. He was just as stunned as I was. Maybe more.

"Hey, Ulanion, why would you take this job if you're an Elven royal?"

"I am not," he replied.

"Well, I'm not even an elf. It must be you."

"I . . . don't think I am?"

"Give our friend here some orders then, my liege, and we'll see what happens."

"Okay, okay . . . um, golem, stand up," he said hesitantly.

I held my breath, waiting for it to rise from its kneeling position. Seconds stretched on with no change other than Ulanion's expression growing more bewildered.

"St-stand up," I stuttered.

The mechanical wolf slowly rose to its full height, eyes focused ahead like a statue.

Reeling, I stood there, mouth agape, trying to process what was happening.

Ulanion blurted out, "You're a princess!?"

"No, no I'm not," I argued. "I'm not important."

Thrusting a finger toward our companion, he shouted, "This seems to disagree!"

"Well, it's obviously wrong, Ulanion! I think I would know if I was a princess!"

He blinked for a moment or two, then tilted his head and asked, "Would you though?"

"Yes!"

As I saw it, there were only two options: Either I was a descendant of an Elven king a few hundred generations removed, or the system was somehow able to detect my original world. I didn't like those options, nor was I fond of the possible combination of them.

"No, really," Ulanion pressed, "would you? Humans don't live long. While my family has been cross-breeding for the last few generations, we still live for a good while. But if a line mingled for longer? You might not have any Elven traits beyond your higher-than-average magic."

"But wouldn't someone know," I countered.

"How? I'm aware of a few artifacts that can trace descent, but those are ancient as dirt, Alana. So ancient that nobody knows how to make them anymore. What if," he said, pacing as if to keep up with his thoughts. He didn't seem inclined to stop musing any time soon. "What if one of His Majesty's children somehow ended up on the human continent and it just passed down through the ages to you? How would you know? And wouldn't they be really inclined to hide it? It's not bad now, but a few millennia ago elves were not well-liked by humans."

"Please don't make this a thing, Ulanion," I sighed.

"Alana, if this gets out . . . Well, I don't know, but it would be huge! There are only a few families that can trace their lineage back to the king, and none of them have anything like his mana. If we could prove it, if you showed that," he fell into thought, eyes racing up and down the lupine sentinel. "It's not like you'd be made queen, but it would—"

"It would cause a war," I stated firmly.

Ulanion froze, contemplative. After a time, he confirmed, "You're not wrong."

I was fairly sure that this golem was sensing my extra-planar origins rather than my family tree. Regardless, there was no way that I'd be taking any throne, not unless they knocked me out and tied me to it. "I've seen war. I've seen starving children, and neighbors killing neighbors, Ulanion. I don't want to see that again. And I will sure as hell not be the cause of it."

His eyes settled and grew sad. "You know, in his writings our king said that it was those who didn't want power that were best suited for it. It was one of the things he felt was a failing in himself, his desire to rule. If things had been different, I think you'd have made a good ruler."

Unable to take his nonsense anymore, I punched him.

He staggered but didn't even have the decency to fall. It occurred to me that what I'd done was profoundly stupid. With his skill, his skin should have been hard as concrete. Strangely it wasn't, I even felt the flesh give as my fist connected with his cheek. My hand, though slightly sore, should have been broken.

"Um," I said, regarding my knuckles.

"I'm able to retract my magic you know," the smug jerk said, snickering. "Wouldn't want your golem thinking that I was trying to hurt you. Princess," he added with a chuckle.

"I'll punch you again," I threatened. I even pouted, but neither seemed to sway him.

"I'd appreciate it if you saved it for later. Regardless of what you think or want, this golem will follow your orders," he said with a nod to the creature. "And we can use that."

"You're not wrong. Golem, do you have a map of the facility," I asked.

"Yes," the mechanical voice said.

"That's something," I said. Pondering our needs, I considered my words carefully before speaking again. "We need to find someone. Do you have the ability to do that?"

"Please clarify order," it answered.

"Are you able to track people or monsters," I asked.

"This unit has a five-hundred-meter detection radius," it answered.

"Its answers are kind of clunky," Ulanion observed.

"It's a machine. That it can understand us at all is nothing short of miraculous."

And it was. I didn't know too much about how programming had worked back on Earth, but many computers struggled to carry on basic conversations.

He didn't seem bothered at all that I knew more about these beings than him. I appreciated the trust regardless. "Can't say I know much about golems."

"They're like other magical items," I explained. "It's all based on yes or no answers. Imagine how many yes/no statements I could fit into just this explanation, then try to think about language as an idea."

"That could get out of hand fast."

"Yeah," I answered. "Back to business though. Golem, protect us."

"Do we have a plan, then" he asked.

"Let's go find our people."

CHAPTER 25

✦

ANCIENT SURPRISES

Dras

With a *ding*, the door opened and our little group spilled out into the hall. We'd lucked out. This floor seemed to start here at the elevator bank. It was just us, and a little door with a picture of stacked rectangles and a little person on it. No clue what that was for.

The building continued to change around us. As I watched, fallen tiles and fixtures floated back into place, cracks sealing as the area returned to looking preternaturally shiny and new. Bit by bit, the whole hallway reformed in front of us.

Selene gaped. "Is . . . have you ever seen anything like that?"

"Whoever designed this—and I'm guessing it was the ancient Elven king—"

"Good guess," Ormien interjected.

" . . . knew quite a lot more about magic tools and how to use them than we do," I finished.

"Another good guess," the elf said, growing restless. "Let's find that wolf and get this over with."

Ormien had a one-track mind and an axe to grind.

"We're after our people first," Glen growled. "Then we go after the bastard."

"Right."

We began our search, room by room. It was very possible that they'd not come down this low, or were dead, but even if we didn't find our missing members we might find something useful. It was clear that we'd come down into actual laboratory spaces. Sadly what they were doing here was impossible to work out, that is until Leah called out to us.

"Guys, guys you need to look at this," she said, sticking her head out of one of the previously locked rooms.

All the rooms on this hall had had only one entrance, and this was no exception, while the physicals spent time keeping an eye on the hall, those of us with a bit less punch had taken to giving the various rooms a once-over.

Robert, who'd arrived at his sister's side seconds before me, stood in the doorway, stock still. After a few coughs, Robert sidled over and allowed the rest of us to pass. When I arrived, I froze too, despite Selene shoving me from behind to get a better look.

Before us stood an all-too familiar ring structure. We'd seen these before. Not only that, we'd used them, even working on its parts to better understand it!

"A travel ring," I said to no one in particular. The design differed from those I'd seen in subtle ways. For instance, the decorative bits used by Ristolian were absent, as was the top part I was used to seeing. Other than that, however, but it resembled something that could have come out of one of our labs. Hardly something to be found in an ancient ruin.

We'd come here to find the secrets of putting more commands into the core. But finding this . . . it meant that we might be able to skip that lengthy process and go right to production.

"This . . . complicates things," Selene murmured.

She received a round of scoffs from most of us. Only Ormien didn't understand what he was seeing.

Alana

This golem was frustrating as shit. It was extremely limited in its abilities to answer most of my questions. Though understandable, I suppose, I had hosts of questions that needed answers, and trying to ascertain the golem's capabilities quickly became a headache.

"No result in memory," it said for the tenth time.

"Weren't you the one that said that it being able to communicate was amazing?" Ulanion said, seeing my frustration.

"Yes, but it should at least be able to tell us what the labs are for, even generally." I studied the thing. No matter how I'd worded my questions, all it could tell me was that the labs were on floors B1 through B9.

"Golem, if I were to come in the main entrance and turn right where would I end up?" I asked, hoping that it might at least lead us toward where our group had gone.

"The first floor is dedicated to living facilities. The area indicated houses the sleeping quarters and offices for employee types one-through-four."

"Can you take us—"

I stopped. Lights blinked, several extinguishing altogether.

Looking toward Ulanion, I asked, "What was that?"

"I don't know, but I don't like it."

The lights flickered once, then failed, leaving us in pitch blackness.

"Golem, we need light. Prepare for combat."

I saw the teeth on our new companion reappear, but no lights. A glint of light at the end of the hallway caught my attention.

"Golem, attack that monster." I even pointed, hoping that it would follow my command.

The beast approached.

"No enemy detected," the lupine golem said as slowly.

"Right in front of you," I protested. "It's getting closer."

I wanted to run. I had a feeling that Ulanion might grab me and do just that if our new pet didn't act quickly.

The monster padded slowly toward us, ethereal saliva dripping from its jaws. It made it three steps before the lights flickered back on, bathing us all in light. The shadow beast took on a different aspect, one of corporeality.

The golem lunged.

Frustrating though it was, gratitude for my new robotic companion flooded me as it attacked. The shadow-wolf leapt, seeming to bounce off the ceiling before landing on the golem's back before opening its jaws wide, intent on its foe's neck. As my defender snarled and lunged, the beast's teeth bounced off the mechanical hide. For the briefest of moments, the lupine shade appeared genuinely, deeply confused. The golem snapped its bladed jaws, and the beast responded. The fight was on.

They were both close enough in size that it turned into a melee almost immediately, the two lunging and rolling over one another. Soon, the shadow-wolf used its speed to close its jaws in a tight grip on the golem's leg. Though our companion struggled with all its might, its leg remained trapped.

Fortunately, it needn't struggle for long. While the pair rumbled, I charged up my magic. The shadow-wolf seemed to notice the change in the air the moment before I fired. It released its enemy, bounding to a nearby intersection in the hall. If I had to guess, it had chosen to face us here—a place with a ready escape route should I decide to fire off any more lightning bolts.

"What was that," I screamed at the irksome golem. "Why didn't you attack it sooner!?"

"Enemy could not be located. Mana signature indicates presence of an Umbral Wolf."

"How do we fight it," Ulanion asked.

The golem, of course, remained silent until I repeated the question.

"Enemy database details Umbral Wolf is a high-class magical beast, capable of becoming incorporeal in low-light environments. While in this state, it is significantly more powerful."

That much at least seemed simple. It also confirmed our suspicions. The shady jerk was definitely stronger in the dark.

There was something else too. As I looked about, I saw that the golem's leg hung at an odd angle. Though functional, the mechanical warrior had taken a good hit.

"Your leg is damaged," I said. "Will it repair itself?"

"Damage must be repaired at the main office," the golem answered.

"Where is that in relation to here and our previous destination?"

"Accessing the main office will require a detour of 557 feet."

"Lead us to it then," I sighed.

A vast open space comprised the main office. Cabinets lined the walls to one side, and desks dotted the area. As we entered, in the golem stalked to one of the cabinets and, to my surprise, stepped in. The recess closed around our companion, then whirred and hummed. A nearby panel lit up, words forming before my eyes.

Lupine Defense Golem. Damage Detected
Repair?
Yes/No

"Why would they ask," Ulanion wondered, scrunching his brow.

My guess was that our Elven king had been a bit of a sci-fi fan. "Because you should never allow your killing machines to fix themselves, or replicate."

I pressed the little button labeled *yes*. Another prompt appeared.

Royal Mana Signature Detected Updating Settings

I stared as it dawned on me that this update might have effects. *From here on,* I thought to myself, *maybe have the elf press all of the buttons.*

When the box finished its work, it opened, and the golem stepped out.

"Are you working properly now," I asked.

"All systems properly functioning, your Highness," it responded.

"Good, good. Ulanion, you ready?"

From across the room, he called, "Look! It's a recording where the elevators went. Looks like one went down to B5, think that's our people?" he asked, pointing at one of the readouts.

I looked over, there was even a small map with labels for the elevators. Sure enough one of them had gone down, and it was in the area I would expect our friends to be.

"Odds are good. Think we should head there instead of to the top floor?"

"Start at the elevator on this floor, I think," he suggested. "Move down from there?"

"Yeah, we don't want to miss them." With a glance to the mechanical doggo, I added, "Can you take us to elevator 15?"

"Yes, your Highness," it responded.

"Please lead us there."

"Yes, your Highness," it said again.

"Um . . . you don't need to refer to me as 'your Highness' every time. Or at all."

"Settings were updated since the last time this unit was activated, your Highness." Behind me, Ulanion at least tried to stifle his giggles.

"Can those settings be changed," I asked.

"Yes, your Highness."

"Change them to the former ones," I commanded.

"Denied. User does not have adequate permissions to change settings. Please contact the administrator, your Highness."

The snickers from the elf intensified, and I turned to find him holding a fist over his mouth, desperately trying to stop his laughter.

I narrowed my eyes at Ulanion, giving him my harshest death glare.

"No laughing."

"Yes, your Highness."

I sighed.

I really should have expected that one.

CHAPTER 26

✦

THE FALL

On our way to the elevator, the lights flickered, threatening more outages. Luckily, the facility's repair system handled those matters before we were plunged into darkness. Just in case, though, I tossed up several light balls around us. Even if the power failed again, our golem wouldn't be blind to that damn Umbral Wolf. Though I had no proof, I suspected that the beast was somehow responsible for the unreliability of the lights. If it was, it would have to know far more about this place than I was comfortable contemplating.

As we neared the elevator, we saw no sign of the others. "Well, that's a bust," I said.

"Not quite, look here."

Ulanion pointed, his gesture indicating what seemed like perfectly normal floor to me.

When I shrugged my lack of understanding, he clarified.

"Scuffs on the floor. Do you see anything like that anywhere else," he asked.

"I can barely see them, so no."

"This place has some kind of auto-cleaning, right? Someone definitely came through, and since the floor is not pristine, it can't have been too terribly long ago."

"Makes sense."

I pushed the button to call the car back to us.

After a few moments' wait, the doors opened with a friendly *ding*. We stepped in, and I studied the setup.

As we started to move, I felt the carriage lurch.

"Golem," I said, uneasily peering upward. "Is the elevator shaft lit?"

"I do not know, your Highness."

That wasn't too surprising, I suppose. The machine had been built for defense, not maintenance.

Though we slowly continued our descent, the ride grew steadily more janky, our speed uneven. I didn't hesitate. Singing, I prepared a lightning bolt. Whatever that bastard was up to, it couldn't be good for us. The shaking continued, and from above the beast let out a low, rumbling growl. There was a horrid *snap!*

The elevator began to plumet. My feet left the floor, my spell faltered, and I screamed as every nightmare story I'd ever heard about falling elevators careened through my memory. Ulanion reached out, wrapping an arm about my waist while he clung with his other hand to the handrail.

With a cacophonous screech, the car came to a halt. Though I tumbled, the floor coming at me awfully fast, Ulanion held me tight. When he slowly released his grip on me, my legs buckled and I crumpled to my knees.

"Oh, I love safety features," I stammered.

"It's still up there," Ulanion warned. "Get ready."

While I gathered another lightning bolt, Ulanion kept his eyes trained on the ceiling. As I got to my feet, I heard groaning metal and another harsh snap. Within our car, nothing changed. But, then, the process repeated itself. This time, the snap was followed by a jolt. The elevator rocked, now at an obvious tilt. Without another thought, I shoved my hands upwards, releasing the stored power. As the spell left me, I tried to expand its reach as much as possible in an attempt to kill the creature I couldn't see.

Before I could prepare another volley, the elevator plunged down the shaft. Knowing what doubtlessly awaited us, I built a shield. Down we fell, faster and faster, the bottom of this place speeding to meet us. Within the carriage, runes flared, red light pouring from each one.

As another emergency braking system engaged to slow our fall, Ulanion's arm found its familiar place around my waist. We crashed into the floor of the elevator shaft.

With the requisite *ding*, the doors jerkily opened onto a dark corridor. Due to the collision, the carriage crumpled in such a way that we would need to climb up onto the floor of the hallway. Ulanion did not see this as an obstacle. He scooped me up and leapt for the exit. Following dutifully behind, the golem pounced into the corridor and scanned for enemies.

I spun the brightest light spell I could muster and tossed it above our heads.

I felt instant regret for this decision. We'd found ourselves in an area unaffected by the cleaning and repair systems. Filled with the pungent stink of rotten gore and death, the hallway was littered with bones of various shapes and sizes. We'd emerged beside a pile of small, humanoid skulls.

Children.

"This is its den," I gasped.

Behind us there was a creaking and horrible ripping. As our enemy forced the cart lower into the shaft, lurking in the door like a shadowy demon, saliva dripped from its jowls. It licked its lips.

Then came a scream of pure rage.

Glen

I was standing in the hall, looking for any danger while the bookish folks did . . . whatever they did. I knew that it was something involving those gates, but the details had never been shared. Any idiot could realize that having one here, far, far, from our home was a massive deal, but as for the specifics, I'd leave that to them.

Of its own accord, the elevator started moving, the glowing symbols above the door indicated that the car was going back up to the ground floor. Ormien and exchanged a glance and drew blades. That beast was crafty, and this had to be something it was up to.

"Look alive," I yelled to the others. "We may have incoming!"

The spellslingers poured into the hall, already chanting and charging up magic. Ormien and I took the lead. Though the elf was green, he was driven and that was enough. I knew that as long as we were after this terror's head, he'd be with us.

Several sounds came one after another. There was a weird noise, kind of like a cord being cut and falling, followed by a screeching. The elevator was still a couple floors above us and the indicator started going crazy.

"We're opening it, cover us." I got a series of nods from behind and me and the elf moved up.

To grab the door, I had to lower my shield. Even with my strength, I struggled at the seam of the doors. Beside me, Ormien strained. Together we were able to pry the doors apart enough to get head and shoulders through for a look.

From above came a crunch, followed by scraping noises. I pulled my head back an instant before the elevator careened past. Despite its high speed, there was no mistaking the flickering image of the beast clinging to the roof as it passed.

The noise as it hit the bottom was harsh, bending steel and whatever it landed on crunching.

"Spells," I screamed, pointing at the shaft.

Less than a second later, the doors started to close. I gripped the edge of one door, but even with my strength, I faltered against the will of the building. Ormien let out a scream of rage before jumping into the shaft. Without his aid, the door slipped from my fingers and snapped shut, the force shoving me back into the hallway.

Glowing symbols illuminated the door. I could speak the Elven language, even read a bit, but this dialect I couldn't parse. I shrugged toward the assembled spellcasters.

Dras stepped up. "It says, 'Elevator out of service, please use stairs.' There are stairs," he added, incredulous.

"Screw that," I answered. Igniting my blade, I thrust it into the metal door.

My blade had been forged to slice through wood, stone, and supposedly steel. I should have been able to carve through this, however, cutting proved to be a struggle. The edge just wouldn't penetrate. After three blows, the minimal damage I'd made began to heal itself. "Well shit," I said.

✦

CHAPTER 27

VENGEANCE'S END

A spear of light and fury fell from above. Ormien landed atop the wolf, sword blazing white with the mana he poured into it. The radiance pouring from the elf's weapon provided enough light that the golem could see the Umbral Wolf. My defender wasted no time, joining the fray with a leap. Ormien and the two lupine foes rolled and twisted, a howling cloud of claws, teeth, and blades.

Though I needed to maintain my light spells, I still wanted to get some hits in where I could. With that in mind, I charged up a bolt. Holding both spells at once was a pain, a real one, this abomination needed to end. Now.

With no arrows, there was little Ulanion could contribute, but he remained alert for any opening that might present itself. He reached to the floor and retrieved a broken piece of plaster. When the Umbral Wolf's head came into view, Ulanion hurled the debris, distracting the beast for the barest instant.

Individually, we'd tried and failed to best this monster. Ormien had lost his arm. The golem, nearly a leg. Ulanion and I had thrown everything we had at the thing, but it hadn't been enough. With all of us fighting together, however, the tide began to turn. Slowly at first, a few small slashes from the sword opened along the creature. Then a well-placed bite. One by one, the injuries added up while above my light spell continued to hamper the beast's abilities. The Umbral Wolf seemed to realize this, too, and as inky blood flowed from countless wounds, it kicked a bit of debris at my head. As the hunk of stone zipped at me, a body appeared in front of mine to bear the entirety of the force. Ulanion grunted, staggering backward into me.

I lost my concentration. The light flickered once before I regained my focus. In that moment our enemy struck. It aimed for the false wolf, either deciding it was the bigger threat or simply not liking it taking that particular form. With a quick snap and sound of rending metal it broke the golem's neck, shredding the metal there with a passing of jaws.

I didn't have time to give to the moaning form at my feet. Determined to recover and kill this thing once and for all, I waded into the battle. As I looked for my opening, the monster turned on Ormien, and as it did I thought I saw it smile. It grabbed him by his new arm and pulled, tearing the appendage and flinging it away. Still clutched within his severed hand, Ormien's sword clattered to the floor.

Ormien sprawled across the debris-filled hallway. The beast padded to him and placed one paw upon the fallen elf, raking its claws across his stomach. He screamed in agony.

I needed seconds more, just a bit more, and a clear shot. With a chuff, the beast lifted its head, found me with its gaze and licked its chops. Slowly, eyes locked with mine, it took a step, hatred, rage, and hunger evident in that gaze.

From behind the creature came a blazing white light, brighter than anything I'd seen on this journey. Ormien, having regained his sword, leapt and plunged the blade deep into the beast's throat. The wolf thrashed with a strength and ferocity that flung the already broken elf into the nearby wall. He hit with a sickening crunch.

My hand outstretched, I loosed the spear of electricity at the enchanted sword, still buried in the shadowy hide As the light of Ormien's mana faded from the blade, my spell landed, crackles of electricity dancing along the metal into the monster. I shielded my eyes from the blast, the room around me quaking with rolling thunder.

When I opened my eyes, the Umbral Wolf lay on its side. Strangely, as its eyes lost the last of their life, the shadows that composed the monster faded, evaporating until only bones remained.

Ulanion groaned in pain as he tried to get to his feet. When I approached him, though, he pointed to the other elf. I rushed to the side of the broken Ormien.

He wheezed, eyes wildly searching the ceiling above yet seemingly unable to focus on it. He'd already lost much blood, and though I patched and mended, his life continued to flow out of him in great gushing waves. With entrails spilling out, the missing limb and several broken bones, he was worse off than anyone I'd tried to treat before.

"Is it dead," he asked weakly.

"Yes, hold on. Just hold on for a bit while I patch you up."

I began to sing quietly, focusing on his vital organs first, as I'd been trained to do. Through my spells, I could sense that his lungs were punctured, liver too. I pressed my hands to the innards slipping out of his abdomen, trying to hold the slippery flesh in place. Sadly, as I worked, I could feel Ormien slipping away. If we'd had a priest, or even another healer, we might have been able to save him. But my efforts proved insufficient.

"My love," he murmured, reaching out with his hand. "Oh, how I have missed you, my dear Ilazia." Then, wearing a smile of absolute peace, his final breath left him on a sigh. Not for the first time, I felt the life leave one of my patients. I gasped in horror as that sensation hit me. It was visceral, so very deep. This elf, who'd seen horror and come to fight again, who'd lost so much slipped away. The healing magic ceased, beginning to slip around his cooling corpse.

I stood shakily, fighting tears as I moved to Ulanion. He sat propped against a nearby wall, and as I approached his eyes settled on me.

"He's dead." Not a question, but a clear statement of fact. I could hear the sadness in his voice as I stumbled toward him.

"Y-yeah." I reached out and began healing my still living companion.

Ulanion had taken a blow meant for me. Had it struck true, I would surely have died. However, physical magic users were made of tough stuff. Though he was injured, without my aid he'd probably have survived. The bruising was still pretty nasty, though, and taking the time to fix it gave me something else to focus on as I tried to calm my trembling.

After a few moments, he lightly touched my shoulder. "I've heard that it's bad when they die on you, but it'll be okay. You'll be okay," he added firmly.

Since coming to this world, I'd seen a lot of death, even caused a bit of it. I'd seen beasts, men, and magical creatures die. Normally, I could just shake it off, push through with a bit of dark humor, but feeling it like that was different. It was just visceral, deep in my heart and painful when I felt him go.

Falling to the wall beside Ulanion, in that dark hall full of bones and spent lives, I wept. When I stopped, too spent to continue, I leaned back and closed my eyes, trying again to calm myself.

"How are you doing, there," the elf asked.

"Not great," I answered.

"Care to talk about it?"

"I . . . when they die it's like someone ripping out my own heart."

"I knew a priest. Every time someone died on him, he emptied his stomach. Right then, right there. Said there was nothing he could do, it was just like that. Compared to him, I think you're doing pretty well."

"Thanks," I said, frowning.

"I mean it. The same guy told me that when someone died in his hospital, whoever was treating them took the rest of the day to recenter themselves. Unless there was an emergency. It's been a bad day, Alana. A real bad one. I'm no healer, so I can't really empathize with you too much, but if you need to talk, or vent, go ahead."

With that said, Ulanion waited. I could tell he was watching me, waiting to see if I needed anything. Strangely, knowing that there was someone with me helped.

"Later, maybe," I said. Changing the subject, I asked, "How's the golem?"

"Head's half off and the eyes are out. Might be able to repair it later, but we'd need to take it back up to that box, I think."

I heard him rise and start moving.

"What are you doing" I asked, watching him approach the bones of the Umbral Wolf.

"I know that it's not right, but if there's anything else waiting for us around here, I'll need a weapon. Without one, I'm basically useless."

He drew the sword out from where it lay in the skeletal remains. Over Ormien's body, he whispered a brief apology while taking the other elf's scabbard.

I rose, looking at the den around me. "This place creeps me out. Why did it bring all these bones down here? For that matter why aren't the enchantments fixing or cleaning it all? It's weird."

"Don't know. Let's take a look around." Though most of the remains were decayed, some bodies were noticeably fresher. For whatever reason, that monster had decided to store all of its victims here. While some corpses were ripped, nothing seemed gnawed upon. Nothing had been consumed.

As I saw more and more of the dead, I noticed that though there were a number of piles, they seemed grouped by relative size. The bones of children formed one collection. Adolescents another. Still larger bones formed more piles.

"Are these . . . arranged?"

Ulanion examined our surroundings, then said, "Hey. Didn't they say that it was Ormien's wedding that got attacked first?"

"Yeah," I replied. "Killed his bride and lots of the guests."

"Well, that one is in wedding attire."

He pointed toward one skeleton sitting on its own. Adorned with coins, the body wore a ravaged version of a dance costume. For whatever perverse reason, the monster had laid her corpse apart from the others against a piece of wall.

"I'm glad that thing is dead," I commented.

There were a number of magical monsters in this world, many horrifyingly dangerous. That said, in the context of attacking people they often fell into two groups: those hunting for food, and those that lashed out when disturbed. The intelligence and malice displayed by the Umbral Wolf was rare, almost unheard of. From what I could see, this beast hadn't bothered eating anything. The elves it hunted, certainly here long before it, had not ventured anywhere near this place.

Ulanion carried Ormien's limp form and laid the would-be groom beside his beloved. Since they seldom died, elves didn't have much in the way of burial rites, and I didn't know if the villagers would ever inter these people in proper graves.

I reached down to move Ormien's legs into a better position, and noticed his blood on my hands. It shocked me, but I quickly regained myself. A cleaning spell, I felt, would be disrespectful. Instead, I summoned a bit of water and scrubbed my hands.

As we continued to investigate, we found a small junction box. It was trying to repair itself and failing miserably. From the look of it, the beast had chewed it innumerable times, finally ripping enough away that the spells maintaining the building failed. At the current rate of repair, it would be days, or perhaps a week before the work was done. It also answered how that thing had kept taking out the lights, it must have understood that those boxes were important somehow. Soon, we found the sign indicating a stairwell. At that point, both of us were more than ready to leave this place. Even if it took us more time to find the others, getting away from here would be a mercy. On our ascent, we discovered that the first set of stairs had been demolished by that monster, reduced to a heap of rubble. The intact flights of stairs loomed above us a good ways up. On the wall nearby, I noticed some writing. I admit, I'd expected to find some more English, but seeing it shocked me to stillness. That king had certainly liked his jokes.

I sighed, tired of this place. Any potential exit was something I wanted. "Open sesame?" As the floor split, Ulanion jumped in front of me. We peered into the newly formed doorway and found another set of stairs descending into the darkness.

CHAPTER 28

TRUTHS

It's fine." I pushed past Ulanion, heading for the stairs. "I don't think it's a trap."

As my foot fell on the first step, I heard it from behind me.

"Who are you?"

"What?" I regarded my companion, trying to appear innocent. "It's just a trick, something a bit hidden in the core—"

"Don't lie to me," the elf said, tone rigid. "I may be mostly human, but I'm still old enough to be your great-grandfather. My people have studied the core to the very limits of what it can do, and I know those symbols. They're connected to parts of that magic that even we cannot decode."

"I . . ."

Ulanion's gaze was hard, his hand white-knuckled on the hilt of the fallen elf's sword. "People have died Alana, good people who deserved better. Ormien died against that beast, as did Olnir, perhaps even your friends. You know something, something about this." Between his stony voice and unyielding stance, I knew he would not let this go. Then what? Best case scenario: he would turn on his heel and leave me alone. Worst: he'd kill me. In a fight, at this range, there was no way I'd win.

I'd held this secret for my whole life, not telling anyone, not family, not friends. It had held me, kept everything together, at least sort of normal. Finally, I blurted out, "I didn't ask for this. Not for any of it. That monster, this place; it wasn't my doing. And telling you everything won't change what's past."

"I make no accusation, but if we're to continue I need to know who it is I'm dealing with. If you really are a princess or whatever that's nothing to hide. Not from me. We can work through this, but I need to know who you are."

I sighed. "So far as I know, I'm in no way related to your king. I heavily suspect that we're related in other ways, though. That we come from the same place. It would make sense of things like why our mana is similar and how we both understand the same language. I'll admit there's a possibility that he wasn't, but someone near him was like me."

I could see the confusion in his face as I spoke. "The same place?"

"This is my second life, Ulanion."

"Second . . . explain."

"I died in a place far from here, a place so different it wouldn't even make sense. As I died, I was reborn an infant in a small village with all my memories intact. That's how I can read these." I pointed at the words on the wall. "And, I suspect, why my mana signature is similar to the king's."

"Even if I believe that—which I'm on the fence about, mind you—how?"

"I haven't the slightest idea. Whatever happened I don't understand it either. There was a message back in the capital though, in the palace. It basically said to come here for answers. Not sure what we'll find down there, but I suspect Justin knew more."

"The others, do they . . ." he began, only for me to shake my head.

"They don't know about this. Not even my family does."

"That seems even less probable. If you displayed that kind of knowledge at any of our schools you'd be found out in an instant."

"I'm fairly good at hiding it. Most people just thought that I was a bit too smart, a bit too mature. Moreover, no matter how much they'd like to brag, the human schools are nowhere near as advanced as the Elven ones."

That got me a quirked brow.

"I'd like the whole story."

"Fine, but let's talk as we walk. I'd rather not stay in this monster's den." With that, I turned and headed down the stairs, my light following me. After all that I'd said, I wasn't sure if he'd come, but he did and I was glad for it.

"So, what kind of being were you before? Some monster, or perhaps something made of light or magic?"

"I was a human," I answered.

"Really?" Of all the things I'd said that seemed to be the one that put him off the most.

"Yes, just a normal one, didn't even have magic. Then again, nobody had magic where I was."

"Fine. Wait if that's true—"

"It's likely that the great Elven king Justin was also a human at some point," I agreed.

"Don't! Don't say that out in public unless you plan on being beaten in the street. There's a lot of people who might even kill you for saying something like that." Ulanion looked a bit alarmed at that idea.

I noticed Ulanion insisted on walking behind me. To keep his eyes on me? Had I lost some of hist trust? "Not you though," I asked.

"Like I told you before, I'm mostly human anyway. So a lot of that 'Elven pride' nonsense doesn't really bug me."

The stairs went down and down. As we traveled, I told him about my first death. While he asked about my life before, he seemed content to let most of that rest.

"So, there was no magic there," he asked.

"Not that I ever knew of."

"How did you get anything done then?"

I shrugged. "We studied the world in depth, and used what we learned to build machines that did the work for us. There was a saying, 'Any sufficiently advanced technology is indistinguishable from magic.' That was bandied about a lot."

"Sorry, you knew what magic was, but never saw it?" He seemed a bit hung up on that, though I suppose this world wouldn't really understand if I tried to explain some of the odder parts of electronics. Not that I could.

"Mmm, there were stories, but most were disregarded as myth. Oh I suppose I did see one bit of magic, when I died. Don't know if that really counts."

"Perhaps there was magic, you just didn't know about it," he postulated.

"I've considered that, but it doesn't really matter in the end."

As we kept going down, I noticed a slight glow to the rock. At first, I thought that perhaps the rock was just like this, or that it was, perhaps, an enchantment. But as we drew near, I realized it was mana. Something was putting out mana like some kind of nuclear reactor, and we were headed toward it.

"Look alive, Ulanion. I don't know what is powering this facility, but I think we're about to find out."

The elf couldn't see mana as such, but as we got deeper and deeper, he must have sensed it somehow, as his eyes started to snap around the tunnel.

"This is weird," he said. "It's like something's just out of my vision."

"This place is putting off mana like I've never seen before, and I think I'm only seeing the excess."

Eventually we came to a set of double doors. The archway above was covered in runes, but it looked, frankly, beyond me. If the king had made this place and invited us, certainly this wouldn't be a trap.

"Want to open those?" I asked, hoping that I wouldn't need to touch them.

"Oh, I wouldn't want to intrude," he answered. "May be that you need a certain mana signature not to trigger whatever is on them."

He had me there, and while I was nervous about it, there really was only one thing to do. I grabbed the handles and pulled.

With a rush of blue light, the wave of mana crashed into me, sending me sputtering back. It was almost physical how much power was locked behind those doors and the rush of pale blue light in my aura sight was just too much. Normally when magic was working you didn't see anything, even if it was pretty potent, but this, it was just too much to be ignored.

Covering my eyes as I tried to adjust to the input, I yelled, "What the fuck!"

"I can feel that," Ulanion responded.

Once I could see again, the room became clear. Beyond the doors was a vast cavern easily the size of an amphitheater or stadium. In the center was a bowl-shaped pool with symbols looping and turning around it, branching off like fractals. Symbols I could never forget.

Shocked, voice laced with fear, I whispered, "This is where it started."

CHAPTER 29

✦

THE CRATER

This was not the cave I had first died in, at least I didn't think it was. For one, this place was far too large, the ceiling barely a blur. Large hulking masses were strewn about, in an almost-organized fashion. Though it was far away, I could see what looked like a stone desk squatting near the pool—which I now guessed to be fifty meters across—in the center of the room. It stuck out like a sore thumb; it seemed to have been placed here in the aftermath of . . . well, whatever happened here.

I walked toward the center, passing vines that wound and reached across the stone. There were no stairs as such, nor a proper path, but there was ample room to avoid tripping over the reaching tendrils. Though the sensation reminded me of that dreamlike fascination that preceded my first death, what compelled me forward now was a gnawing need to know.

"Where what started," Ulanion asked, nervously following. He might not be able to see the magic like I could, but he could feel the power of this place.

"I'm not entirely sure, but whatever caused the Elven king, and me, and that mad mage. Whatever that was all started here. Let's go find out."

"Alana, this place is dangerous. We should get the others."

I barely looked back, my feet carrying me closer and closer to the center, to whatever answers there might be. "And tell them what exactly? You might have taken the truth well, but others probably won't. And regardless of how it comes out, it's likely to start a civil war somewhere as people argue about what the truth is. Some might call me a demon, or some kind of heavenly messenger, or something else altogether. No, at least not right now."

Before I could take another step, my companion rushed in front of me and fixed me with his gaze. "Alana, this place is weird, consider if it's effecting you. Stop and think. Really think."

I did as he told me, looking around. I cast my mind back to my death, to the cave, remembering how weird and comforting it seemed. Was that the mana? Was the mana here still doing something to me? After several seconds, I found a place to sit where I could avoid the pool and its glow. The elf allowed this, giving me space while still keeping an eye on me.

As I tried to mediate on what he was saying, I had to admit that pool was doing something, at least a little.

"It's like a flame attracting moths. Perhaps something about the sheer amount of mana in the air. We shouldn't stay here too long, but I still want to know what we're dealing with, at least on a basic level. There is no chance that this mana isn't what's running that facility, so we've already been exposed a bit. I think it'll be all right as long as we're careful."

Ulanion nodded at my conclusion. "We go quickly then, if you see me doing anything weird, stop me."

"Same, if it looks like I'm about to lose it, drag me out of here."

It was a good plan, flawed and dangerous.

We worked our way down and down into the center of the crater. Unsure of what they might do, if anything, I tried not to step on any of the vines or patterns on the floor. As I looked, I could tell, these were far more complex than those I'd seen back on Earth. It wasn't so obvious at first, but as they fractured from the more concentrated areas, the symbols on the stone created increasingly complex patterns.

There was a slight rise that kept us out of the bottom, but the six-or so-foot tall ring of stone proved a quick boost for me and an easy jump for him. As soon as I got over, I could see that, from this distance, the water seemed to boil, the mana I had viewed as light bubbling like a pot on the verge of catastrophic overflow.

Carefully, I approached the pool. After a few steps, a hand landed gently on my shoulder.

"Still good," he asked. At my nod, Ulanion gave one of his own and indicated the pool "Look there, in the center."

My eyes weren't as sharp as those of an elf, nor those of those of a physical magic user, so I strained to see beyond the massive quantity of magic. All I could see were strange shapes, like mottled boulders.

"What are those," I asked.

"Either very regular rocks, or very big eggs," he answered. "We might be able to get one if you want."

"I know you can't see the magic, but if you touch that water, I imagine it'll cook you. The mana looks like it's literally boiling at this distance. Big bubbles of light. Not sure what that would do to you, but my guess is nothing healthy." I cringed at the memory of drinking similar water, even trying to crawl into it if it would cool the burning of my body.

I walked over toward the little desk. It was completely out of place yet still felt as if it'd been here for ages. The facility above was still preserved perfectly, so it wasn't a great surprise that this was as well. This, however, looked like a proper mess. There were piles of papers all about it, and a teapot off to the side.

I began slowly poring over the notes. Written in a lovely English calligraphy, most of it was out of my league. These were probably the king's own notes, so of course those would be complex after more than a thousand years to study magic.

I did gain some insight though. This pool and this place were most certainly the nexus for a spell—the intricacies of which eclipsed even the knowledge of the writer. Though he did recognize that it was playing with space and time on a startling level. The vines served as energy conduits for the spell, he noted, though how someone had made organic conduits for magic was not explained.

His notes included some kind of dimensional math equation that looked like it had come from a quantum physics dissertation.

The symbols were apparently the stand-in for the runes that I was more familiar with, though even the notes indicated that they were poorly understood.

As I moved through the various piles, I noticed a faint smell and looked over to find the teapot emitting the aroma of a lovely blend. I put my hand by it and realized it was still warm. There were runes all over it, presumably to keep it warm, but a spell that durable was impressive. The ambient magic was probably enough to charge the spell into perpetuity.

I picked up the pot to give it a closer look. It might have been the only thing on the desk I could fully parse. The runes weren't hidden or anything, though there were a few sequences that I didn't recognize at all. A practical, mundane enchantment like this didn't need the kind complexity that the maker had put into it.

A few moments of rooting through drawers, and I'd found me one of several cups. Though it wasn't the sanest thing I'd ever done, I poured myself tea. After several seconds contemplating the matter, I took a tentative sip.

"Okay wow," I said, returning my attention to the notes. "That's not bad for millennia-old tea." While I continued to delve into the papers, Ulanion had been exploring a bit on his own.

"Alana, you need to see this," he said. He stood near one of the big mounds, looking past the many vines covering it.

I put down my half-drunk cup and made my way over.

"What'd you find," I asked as I approached.

"Not sure," he responded, moving to let me look. "Whatever it is, it's dead."

I gazed past the vines at the bones. It took a few minutes to find the skull, but as soon as we did, I was alarmed. With teeth like sabers and eyes I could walk through, it dwarfed both of us. The ridges on the head, the shape, the sheer size . . . I could imagine its massive wings, its breath of fire. I'd never heard stories of such a creature in this world, but on Earth it was the end-all be-all of fantasy.

"That's . . . that's . . ." I struggled.

"The bones of a dragon," a voice said from behind us.

Terror creeped up my spine. They used the same ancient dialect of Atali the golem had used for all except one word that had been English. *Dragon.*

CHAPTER 30

✦

THE ANCIENT

Standing there, aloof, was an elf with waist-length white hair. Though his body was that of a young man, his eyes held an ancient weariness. Unlike the other elves I'd seen, this one had extraordinarily long ears, the points reaching just past the back of his head. His aura, I noted, poured off him in a delicate stream of gentle green bubbles.

"Nothing to say," he asked. "Goodness, when meeting a king most people at least say hello."

I turned to look at Ulanion, only to see his eyes growing wide. I'd seen busts of historical figures, but never paid them much attention. Ulanion, however, had spent the whole of his long life seeing those. Based on his reaction, there was certainly only one identity for the elf before us.

"Justin," I asked, still puzzled.

"Normally one introduces themselves first, but yes," he said. Casually, he brought a teacup of his own to his lips and took a sip.

"You disappeared five thousand years ago," Ulanion muttered.

"I had my reasons," the ancient king said, a sad look in his eyes.

My companion exploded, incensed. "To abandon us? To let our empire crumble as it did and waste away; a shadow of what you made it? For what? To hide in a hole in the ground? Are you even real or are you some golem or programmed spell?"

Calmly, His Majesty replied, "I'm the original. Come, let's go have a chat."

As Justin—the ancient Elven monarch—strolled, small bridges of radiance appeared before him, letting us cross any and all barriers without trouble.

Trying to remember the exact wording on that mural and failing, I asked, "So . . . you said to look here for answers?"

"Indeed. I have a few to offer, though I also have some questions. I don't get to meet many like us often, and there are details that I'd like to discuss." He stopped at the desk and began adjusting the pages that I'd disturbed, adding, "Younglings. Always making a mess. Care for a refill on your tea? I did hear you saying you liked it."

"You were watching us," I asked after nodding. It was good tea.

Ulanion added, "From where?"

"I'm millennia old, archmage boy. I'm perfectly capable of being unseen if I want to be." He passed me my cup and turned again. "Let's go somewhere more comfortable, though, shall we?" Leading us to another side of the massive crater, he asked questions. Where I'd come from, what the date had been, when I'd appeared in this world, and where. This line of inquiry was followed by general questions about the president, the place where he had lived, and many other details that could confirm we came from the same reality. As we approached the wall, he waved vaguely and a door appeared.

"I'm surprised you didn't just teleport us or something," I remarked.

"While I don't *think* anything bad would happen, I am very cautious about that sort of thing near an area effected by a colossal, inter-dimensional spell." He preceded us into a small sitting room. The décor here looked nothing like what I'd seen in the palace. In a style that could only be described as "cottagecore meets Professor's study," the aesthetic favored homey touches, like the overstuffed couches arranged near a fake fireplace.

"I've answered your questions," I said, sinking into one of the poofy couches. "Now I'd like to know why you asked them."

Justin found an armchair while Ulanion—who had been fairly quiet the whole time—just stood, scowling.

"Everyone so far that I've met from our world and time," the king began, "came from the eastern seaboard. All of us were alone when we passed into this world, isolated. One reported being on a coastal island that appeared barren except for the rock and pool. She found herself turned around, walking in circles and brought back to the same spot any time she tried to escape. I, myself, had been lost in a forest, injured and alone. Trying to move away from the pool and vines filled me with unsurmountable terror."

"Same for me," I confirmed. "In a cave." After a time, I said simply, "The fruit?"

"Nasty thing. Haven't seen one sprout from *these* vines yet. No idea why." The old elf shrugged. "I believe that they were meant to bring us here."

"Why," I asked.

"I don't know."

For years, I'd gone to sleep with questions in my mind. Questions no one could answer. Now, having come so close to that information only to hear him claim ignorance? My frustration exploded. "What *do* you know?"

"I don't think the dragons are from this world. I think they're from ours. What I don't know is the *when*, or the *why*. Nor do I know *why us*, but I can tell you this: our magic is ever so slightly different than the magic from this world."

Noting our similar auras, I asked, "The bubbles?"

"Yes, all of us have it."

"Why, then, do you think the dragons are from our world?"

He looked a bit disappointed. "Didn't you notice? The eggs; they're boiling off mana. Those are the same bubbles as we have." This was a lot to process. Thinking, I sank deeper into the sofa. "So, it transferred our souls here? Is there even math for separating out a soul? That would be . . ."

"That magic is beyond anything I've seen, Alana. I don't understand much of it, and I've studied it for thousands of years."

"As for the soul," he continued, "there was a theory that people were observers; seeing and therefore—in a sense—creating reality, making the possibilities become one. We certainly weren't the only example of such beings, but does that not indicate that there's something like a soul? An observer must always observe—at least that's what I think—and what is magic but observing reality and making the conscious choice to change it?"

I had a small existential crisis as I tried to process all the implications of that little theory. I didn't know if he was right, and I suspected he didn't either. The idea did sound plausible, and I trusted that the creator of the core was no slouch.

"Why did you abandon us," Ulanion asked, filling the silence my contemplation created.

"It was for the best."

"We needed you," my companion pressed, words dripping accusation. "Most people think you're dead."

As he looked at Ulanion, Justin seemed exhausted and morose. "It's better that way."

"You led us to a bright future, only to leave us and allowed all of that to fall! You allowed people to suffer! You owe an explanation for that."

"You weren't there, child. We advanced, became stronger. But as we conquered, we did terrible things, my boy. Horrible, terrible things. With what I'd introduced, our might surpassed that of any seen on this planet. It was so easy. We became cruel. I became cruel," he added for emphasis.

"We civilized the continent first," Ulanion began. "Then, as we spread, traveling across the oceans and . . ."

"To the Human continent," Justin said, completing the thought. "I missed it at first, separated as I was from my soldiers. Many of them raided villages. They took slaves, raped women, and smashed the skulls of infants beneath their boots. They took anything of value and burned the small hamlets. When I learned of their deeds, I tried to put a stop to it, but ultimately I was not successful." Ulanion stammered. "We wouldn't—"

"We were indomitable, boy. Power corrupts, and that much power turned good folk into monsters. Never forget that," Justin warned, staring hard at the younger elf.

"But you didn't . . ."

"Things happened," the king declared firmly, "and I now live here, in exile, so that I might never commit such atrocities again."

His ancient eyes fell.

"Choosing, instead, to allow the atrocities to occur above your head," Ulanion spat bitterly.

"What," Justin asked.

"The Umbral Wolf."

"What Umbral Wolf?"

"The one that was living here," Ulanion said, "using this facility—your facility—as a den. The one that has been harrying the nearby village."

Having been down here so long, he'd missed the carnage up above. The ancient mage, alarmed, asked, "Was? Did you get all of them?"

I shouted. "All of them!?"

"Yes," Justin confirmed. To our gaping stares he added, "They're wolves, they travel in packs."

As that was pointed out to me, I felt terribly dense.

✦

CHAPTER 31

REUNITED COMPANIONS

With a flick of his fingers, a mask and hooded cloak appeared before him and we began moving. Since he knew the place well, traveling with the king was quite a bit quicker, in that he knew his way around like the back of his hand. With a flick of his fingers a mask and hooded cloak appeared before him and we began moving. As we got back into the den of the Umbral Wolves, Justin gazed at the carnage in shock.

"Oh . . . this should have never been possible," he muttered. "The security systems should have prevented . . . I need to check. You have friends here, yes?"

"Yeah," I replied. "Last we could tell, they were up a few flights. Assuming what we saw on the charts detailing energy use was correct."

He nodded and moved over to the broken golem. "Stand close. I'll take us up to ground level."

As we teleported, I was jealous. My portals worked, sure, but the little bubble Justin conjured around us popped an instant later, the transition seamless. One second, we were standing in an abattoir. The next, a pristine corridor, and I didn't even feel the shift.

"They should be just down," I said, indicating the stairwell. "We'll go warn them that there might be more."

"Good. I'll head to the control room. If we have any hope of eradicating these beasts, we'll need reliable light, at the very least." The broken golem floating behind him, the first king of the elves glided away.

I looked to Ulanion. He nodded and followed me to the stairs which we took two at a time. Our friends might be in danger.

Dras

After Ormien dove after the plummeting beast, it had taken the rest of us ten minutes or so to find the stairs. A portion of the way down we were met with a wall of rubble, the remaining flights destroyed.

With no way forward, nor a path to aid Ormien, it seemed our best option was to retreat to the portal room and set it up as a defensible position. None of us knew this facility well, and having this—a known point to begin our search—seemed to be the best plan if we were to find our missing bard and the two elves.

This situation was bleak. Though we'd found our objective, half of our team was now either missing or dead. We couldn't continue getting split up, and there might be a real need to fall back. In the increasingly unlikely event that we returned to the capital, the emissary might be able to get us backup. The portal gave us another option, if we could fix it. It was well-known that Emperor Durin's abode had a series of portals, some with missing links. Those might lead anywhere, or nowhere at all. If this gateway connected to those? A risk in any regard.

As the ladies, Robert and I planned out our defensive spells, Glen shouted from the hallway, "Activity!"

Selene and I emerged first, conjuring our strongest shields while the twins engaged light spells. I followed Glen's gaze to the stairwell. The door flew open, and a familiar bard burst into the hall. A certain elf arrived on her heels, his signature bow replaced with a sword.

"Dras," Alana yelled. "Thank goodness we found you! The wolf. It's not the only one."

I let her past my shield when she came near.

"Explains how it seemed to be getting around so quick," Glen said. "Don't suppose you found that idiot Ormien did you?"

Both of them winced. Ulanion answered. "Dead. Managed to get revenge on the beast, though."

"What's your plan," I asked the bard.

"Well, since there are more of those things around—"

Overhead, the lights flickered and went out, leaving us with only the twins' luminous spells to see. In the shadowy corridor, something moved.

Two Umbral Wolves slinked into view, shadows dancing around their bodies. They stalked forward, streams of saliva pooling at it fell.

Glen and Ulanion took the lead as the beasts charged at us. Alana retreated down the hallway, singing a spell into being, though I had no time to know what she intended.

From behind us, Selene screamed, "Incoming!"

Her shield flashed to life, warding off a third wolf loping from the other direction.

While the twins and Selene kept our backline protected, the rest of us focused on the advancing pair. Perhaps they took offense that we'd dispatched one of their fellows, perhaps their attack was nothing more than primal instinct. Regardless of their logic, they seemed to have decided we needed to be dealt with. As one, they streaked forward where they were met with blade and mana.

Individually, neither of our physical users was a match for these opponents, however, with our shields slowing them down and a potent bit of lightning from Alana, we held our position. While the bard lent her attention to keeping Ulanion from falling, I focused on supporting Glen. Behind us, Robert dropped his light spell to reinforce Selene's shield. Neither of them was trained in war magic, but we didn't need their might. We just needed them to maintain the shield and illumination.

Alana loosed another spear of electricity at the wolves, causing Ulanion's foe to slip. The elf exploited this opening by carving a solid gash along the creature's flank. When the beast hobbled into the shadows, blood oozing from their injuries stopped flowing entirely.

Nearby, the other wolf had hold of Glen's off hand, his armor creaking under the pressure of those inky jaws. I charged a ball of fire. With a burst of sight, the overhead lights flared. The lamplight grew brighter and brighter until the hallway became a blur of white, too painful to observe. Several sounds around me jostled for supremacy. Staggering footfalls on tile. A loud clanking. Opening my eyes, I saw another wolf—this one metallic, with red claws and fangs—as it bolted down the corridor.

Internally, I groaned. *The last thing we need is another accursed wolf.* "Umbral wolves found," the addition remarked. "Commencing combat." The metallic wolf lunged at the shadow-wolf tangling with Ulanion, its crimson teeth sinking into the creature's rear leg.

Alana didn't miss a beat and loosed another bolt of lightning. It slammed into a bewildered monster, passing through the thing's skull to leave nothing more than a smoking ruin.

"The golem is on our side," Alana called breathlessly. "Attack the umbral one."

Out of the corner of my eye, I could see her stagger. She was on her last legs, and to be honest, I wasn't far behind. When the other beast in front of me tried to flee, I snatched it round the leg with a spell, lashing it in place where the two angry swordsmen cut it to gory ribbons.

Two down, our front line turned as one to face the wolf harrying our rear. Though damaged, our backline's shields held fast. The remaining foe, watching us form a unified force against it, showed us its tail and bolted away.

In its path, at the end of that hall, a bubble popped and a masked, cloaked figure appeared. The monster lunged at the newcomer only to fall to the floor. It struggled beneath the invisible weight that kept it pinned in place.

"I think that's more than enough out of you," the masked figure said coldly.

The cloak shifted as its wearer raised a hand.

In my first year of school, I'd witnessed the headmaster at the time—an ancient archmage—lose his temper. A student had spoken out of turn. When the headmaster ceased repressing his aura, I'd nearly fallen over from the force. There, in the bloody hallway with its wolf corpses, I saw in my aura-sight a flood of green bubbles. I trembled. The most potent mage I'd ever witnessed, the hoary headmaster, had been but a mewling babe before this caster.

From their extended hand, a brilliant beam of golden daylight flowed over the monster, casually turning to vapor a creature we had only barely survived. As the radiance faded, I blinked the spots from my vision. Selene had fallen over, her eyes huge. Robert and Leah wore similar expressions of confounded awe.

"T-thank you, s-sir," Leah stuttered, the first to find her voice.

"Of course," our ally said. "I received a report that Umbral Wolves had been spotted in the area, and I came to clear them out." With a kind nod, he offered his hands to Selene and brought her to her feet. "I think that was the last of them, but you children might want to wait here while I investigate. Safer that way." With another popping bubble, he was gone.

After a few seconds, I regained my focus. "Okay, everyone," I said, "Whatever we do, we cannot piss that guy off."

Alana and Ulanion chuckled, earning looks from the rest of us.

"Don't suppose you found a room with chairs or something," Alana asked.

"I think there were a few in the portal room," I said, pointing.

Alana shouted, "Portal room?! Whatever," she added with a sigh. "Let's go rest in there until he comes back, then."

The metallic wolf followed Alana. It spoke, its mechanical voice using the ancient Atali dialect. "Yes, your Highness."

Alana's weary sigh was drowned out by Ulanion's howling laughter.

CHAPTER 32

✦

RUMINATIONS OF THE MONARCH

Justin

I walked through the halls I had built so long ago. Though I rarely traveled up to these areas, I could navigate it with my eyes closed having lived in this place for so long. This had been a right mess, not even including the disaster in the basement, and all the bodies of those poor children that would have to be buried, but also the intrusion.

I had always been a bit lax on security, sure, but that had been out of anticipation of having visitors in the form of others like me. What I hadn't counted on was a group of monsters making their way into my home and setting up shop while I wasn't looking. There would have to be some changes made, additional levels of security to ensure such horror never happened again.

As I walked, I pondered, attempting to see the flaws, where it all had gone awry. Most of the physical damage was fixing itself, but there were still scars. *How long has it been since I've ventured to the surface* I wondered, *a century? Two?* Approaching the old cafeteria, I tried to picture it in its prime, my friends and companions at all the seats. I felt so very old. As I aged, time only seemed to go faster and faster, slipping through my fingers like grains of sand.

My reflection gazed at me from a nearby window, the illusion I was using not bothering my eyes a bit. Effectively ageless, we pure-blooded elves did not show the physical wear of the years. The only real change from my youth had been the shift in my hair from pitch-black to silver-white. Such expressions of maturity, uncommon though they were, became a symbol that one should be regarded with respect for their vast experience. I had been a rarity then, so long ago. Now, however, I might be truly unique. Alone.

My thoughts drifted back to the Elven lad, his anger at my leaving and his frustration that I had no plan on ever returning. That said, there was still so much he didn't understand. I would have to pull him aside and talk to him, tell him a few stories. If I could not convince him of my reasoning, I would need to persuade him to keep his silence.

In regard to the girl, well, I didn't really have too much more to say to her. She seemed nice, but average. I'd mark her arrival, of course, as I had the others. I'd found neither rhyme nor reason to the arrivals. It was likely I'd missed a number of them, but even with my limited data set I felt I should have been able to discern something.

My visitors were interested in the portal room. It was useful magic if a bit primitive. I'd never used it, but an old friend seemed quite keen on the idea. Perhaps I could bribe them. Pay them in kind? Share with them this mystery that they might keep the secret of my continued existence.

As my feet carried me to the entry hall, I sighed. Even with the automated systems running endlessly, the destruction would take years to repair. With a wave of my hand, the largest pieces of rubble gently flew back into place. My magic sealed them so the wards could do their work.

Outside was silent. I took a look. Drawing my eye, the barest bit of an aura drifted from the upper boughs of a tree some distance away. Warping space around me, I moved to the bottom of the tree.

"Come down here," I said, not bothering to look up. In swift response, a little spy fell from his perch with an alarmed cry.

I gave him a once over. Standard dark, mottled gear. A couple of knives on his belt as well as a shortsword. Nothing of particular interest.

"What are you doing here," I asked.

"What am I doing here? That's funny, friend," he said snarkily, "since you're decidedly not from that village or that little expedition. Whoever you are, though, you're far out of your depth."

Trying to intimidate me with power he did not possess, I thought, *how quaint.*

"I'm from Lady Mistan's house, by the way," he added. "Whom do you serve?"

Allowing my long ears and white hair to appear through my illusion for the barest second, I said, "You're quite mistaken, child. I am indeed from that village. You would do well to respect your elders." He froze in alarm, breath hitching for a few moments. It was good to remind people, sometimes, that they needed to not pick fights. As for his Lady Mistan, we'd met, and she knew my secret. She also knew how displeased I would be if that knowledge became public. Surely, she would understand that by returning her tool to her unharmed I had offered her a great kindness and she would repay me with her continued silence. Otherwise, as my meager display had proven, I could crush this boy like an ant beneath my heel. His mistress would fare no better.

"Apologies sir," the man said, groveling. "I didn't know that the village had such an esteemed protector."

"Nor do they, as is my wish. Go now and return from whence you came."

"My orders—"

I teleported him back to the capital, or at least where the capital was last I checked.

How troublesome, I thought. *Now, what to tell that little group of humans . . . I could say that I was sent by the capital to clean up those monsters . . .* No, I chided myself, *that's stupid. nobody would believe that.*

Alana

"So what you're saying is," Robert began, brow raised, "he was sent by the capital to clean up those—what did you call them?—Umbral Wolves?"

I nodded enthusiastically. "Yup. We met him down in the basement. Nice guy."

"Well, the village elder did say they sent messengers," Glen offered. "But why didn't he tell them he was here?"

I'd forgotten the elder had tried to call for help, but I could use that to bolster my lie. With a floppy shrug I said, "No idea. But he did, in fact, help us clean them up." Desperately hoping he contradict my tale, I chanced a glance at Ulanion. He stood apart from the others, expression grim. Whatever was going through his head, it would be best if he could stick around, I rather liked him.

As my eyes flicked back I saw Selene behind me, still losing her mind over the golem that was still following me around like a slightly murderous puppy dog.

"It's so cute!" she declared, leaning in to look even closer at it. "And the design! Most golems are super basic, only being able to process a few commands, but look at how it moves! It's not even following a route or taking voice commands! Do you know how cool that is?"

"Didn't that thing call you 'your Highness' too?" Dras asked. Quickly, to cover Ulanion's snort, I explained, "A glitch in its system. It seems to think I'm Elven royalty or something. Clearly, I'm not. Obviously. But, it's a glitch I think we can overlook since it is willing to keep protecting us."

"We should take it with us," Selene said, examining the range of motion of the golem's legs.

"Maybe. Golem, can you leave the facility," I asked.

"Affirmative. This unit may move about the grounds or, in event of an emergency, just outside of them, your Highness."

I continued, "And if you are taken beyond that?"

"If this unit is removed from its operating zone without administrator approval, fail-safe systems will destroy it, your Highness."

"Okay," Leah said from a chair near the portal, "I can see how the responses could get old fast."

Wanting to run screaming from this subject lest it quickly become a running joke to Dras, I diverted to another topic. "So, you guys found another gate. Any information on how to make them here?"

"We were a bit busy, so there's still a good bit to go through. If this portal is here though, maybe we can use it to return home," Dras said.

That seemed improbable, though still possible. I knew of many gates beneath Emperor Durin's home. Most of those he kept sealed with portcullises just in case, issues for later. That seemed disconnected from the dozens he could access. If this gate could be connected in such a way . . . well, that remained to be seen. Around this time, the masked and hooded form of the Elven king returned. He briefly scanned our group before settling his eyes on Ulanion.

"Mind if I have a word with your guide for a few moments?" he asked.

Our archer gave us all a nod before heading out into the hall with Justin. While we did our thing they were out in the hall. As time stretched on, some of the others were giving curious looks, but nobody interrupted. Soon enough Ulanion returned, but he looked . . . sad, like something was desperately wrong. The king called for me next, rattling off some lie about wanting to discuss the dead downstairs. I don't know if my team believed him, but no one spoke as I crossed the room to join him. As we entered the hall, Justin conjured a small dome to give us privacy and sighed. "Let's have a chat."

CHAPTER 33

PRIVATE CONVERSATION

I talked with your friend, there," he said angling his head toward the room. "While he's not happy about it, he's agreed to keep my presence here quiet, and I'd like to think he even understands my decision."

"Good," I said, adding, "and I'm guessing . . ."

Justin nodded. "I'd like the same from you."

"Very well. If you want to keep hiding here, I see no reason for me to oppose it."

"Out of curiosity, are you and your friends after the gates?" He seemed genuinely interested in that. Ulanion hadn't known the details, but there was no harm in telling Justin. Not now.

"Yeah," I confirmed. "And the ability to add new things to the core, such as the sequences used in the gates."

After several seconds spent in contemplation, he spoke. "The last bit? I cannot give it to you. At least, I cannot grant the ability to add anything you want. That is an extraordinarily hazardous proposition if one is unprepared, untrained. I experimented. Exhaustively," he added. "Some of the early iterations were disastrous. Because of the limitations of magic, I don't think you could do anything truly apocalyptic, but I've no desire to test my luck on such matters."

"Listen," I said, weary. "I realize that if you wanted to remove us you could do so in a myriad of ways with varying degrees of complexity and unpleasantness, but we went through a lot of shit to get to this point. People died—literal shiploads—to get to this continent in hopes that we might find the secret to making more of those gates. We cannot turn around empty-handed now."

"I know," he purred, hands up in a gesture of supplication. "I know, and I'm not heartless."

"You don't know," I shouted. "Our expedition started with three teams. We were the only ones to even reach the continent. We lost our team leader to one of those damn monsters that you allowed to squat literally just over your head."

He winced, and I realized that he wasn't responsible for everything that had gone on. While he should have dealt with the wolves, he did save us. The loss of most of our people was also not his fault. He had nothing to do with the Hurricane Whale, so he couldn't be held accountable for the floating bodies left behind. Then, I thought about the infant skulls piled high outside his front door and any remorse I felt for emotionally wounding this man evaporated like mist.

"Please," he begged, "let me finish. I don't intend to send you away with nothing, merely without the ability to cause mass destruction. Furthermore, I'll not have you upending something which has helped more people over the years than any of my other inventions." At my incredulous stare he just continued. "I don't pretend to be a good man my dear, but the core, that is one thing I think I can be proud of. It's something that's helped society more than anything else I've done. So I can and will help you make the gates. It's about time for more travel in this world anyway."

Though relieved that we would get something we'd come for, I was unsure how to feel. Angry? Frustrated? There was so much good he could do! And he wouldn't! But that had been what he said to Ulanion, right? That he'd tried. That he'd amassed and used power to make the world a better place only to be corrupted by that same power and cause unspeakable pain to so many. Deeds horrible enough to drive him into self-imposed exile in an attempt to stop them from occurring ever again.

"Thank you," I said finally.

"You're quite welcome. Now," he said, offering me a small stone. "Take this."

The grey ovoid fit comfortably in my hand and I could feel it humming slightly as I turned it over. I could feel it trying to connect to my core.

"What is it?"

"Quick and dirty explanation? Think of it as a software patch. The core was designed to have some modular capabilities, to allow for growth. It shouldn't take you long—less than a day or two—but after processing your way through, you'll be able to access the commands needed for those gateways."

He paused, seeming to question himself a moment before producing another stone. "Actually," he added quickly, "have two. Your people might try to take it from you, and I'd like you to have access. Also, the guide will update with descriptions to help you along. Bit of a warning, however: if you use one of your cores to teach others after that, they'll inherit this ability."

This brought to mind a very old, very specific gripe I had long wanted to discuss with the person before me. "Your guide is a disaster, by the way. Why didn't you add any sort of organization to it?"

"You're not the first person to lodge that complaint," he admitted, "and I'll tell you what I told them. If you don't like it, make your own."

I scoffed. "Seriously? You can update it, right? Are you telling me in five thousand years you haven't even bothered to put in a contents table, or an index?"

"I hardly need it as I understand my organizational system," he explained dismissively.

Intolerable. This guy was just fine with the absolute academic mess he'd left. "Please, do enlighten the rest of us to your system of organization."

"No, it would take too long." At my glare, he frowned. "I can take those stones back, and send you lot on your way, you know. If you don't want them, that is."

"Fine, fine." I didn't think he would, but before he could take the stones, I stashed one down my shirt. Best I could do in a pinch for a secret hiding place. Darkly, I muttered, "Maybe I will make my own."

"Is there anything else you need right now?" Justin asked, clearly ready to go and do . . . whatever he did.

With a nod toward the room, I asked, "Do you know if this gate connects to Ristolian's network?"

"I think so? I never had much use for the gates. It was but a prototype back in my day. However, I do believe Ristolian put a connector in there at some point. Nice guy," visited me periodically. One of the few over the years with a sense of humor." He had smiled sadly as he spoke.

"Like putting 'hello world' in the cores?" I asked.

"That was a wonderful joke," he concluded, defending his choice. "A joke, I might add, that led many like me—yourself included—to this very place."

"And the giant letters hanging in your palace?"

"Same answer."

"Fine." After a moment's contemplation, I warned, "You may want to lock the gate down or something after we leave. If you don't, I suspect you'll find a lot more visitors in short order." My country craved an intercontinental portal, and if they could get it, I doubted that Emperor Durin would find this place to be a suitable outpost. Especially if he happened to run into Justin.

"Noted," the king affirmed.

"What happened to Ristolian anyway," I asked, curious as to my predecessor's fate.

"Got old. Nothing to be done about that, I'm afraid. Well," he added, scratching his chin, "I suspect there are things one could do if one really wanted to. With a properly trained priest . . . I am not a priest, however, nor do I know quite enough about biology to teach the skills necessary for such work. There was one of us, though. Came as a priest. I believe they were potent enough."

I'd always thought the many priest orders were rather progressive. Maybe there was something there. "One of us was a priest? Who? When?"

"I think that particular individual would have wanted me to maintain some of their privacy. Since they might still be kicking across these continents, I think I shall do exactly that."

"Why do I feel like I'm the weakest of us?"

"My dear, you're still young. Even then, based on your aura I think you'll be more than strong enough one day to change the world if that's what you want. Personally, I'm not sure that I'd recommend that course. Not without immense care."

"I'll think on that. For now, though, I think I should return to my friends."

I took a moment to hide the update stone by tucking it in my sleeve. Later, I could tell my companions that I'd found it somewhere along our twisting journey through this facility.

"If you ever find yourself over in human lands," I said, "look me up."

He chuckled. "I highly doubt I will, but I'll keep your invitation in mind."

"All right. Now, if you'll excuse me, I have to go and figure out how to lie to my friends . . . again."

"Best of luck with that. Though you might want someone you can confide in. It helps."

With that he waved me off, and I returned to the room. I moved up next to Dras who was parsing out some notes scattered about on one of the desks.

"Don't suppose you'll tell me what that was about," he asked as he looked up.

"A bunch of things. Our friend there wants his privacy, I think, and he wants to ensure that I—that we—maintain that."

He knew me well enough to sense that I was hiding things from him again, but he didn't push. "Well, feel free to jump in wherever you want. We've still got a lot to go through in here, and a limited time, probably, before whoever sent your friend shows up." There were more than enough stacks of notes to pore over. I chose a desk, surreptitiously slipping the update stone into a drawer of its neighbor. If nobody else discovered it there, I could later. But for the time being, I busied myself gathering information. We really did have a lot to be getting on with.

✦

CHAPTER 34

DELIVERING THE NEWS

We worked on the most obvious materials for several hours before collectively deciding that sleep was required. Though I instructed the golem to stand guard, no one fully trusted it or my exhausted explanations. So, a guard rotation was established. Our night passed without incident, and after waking, we dug into a basic breakfast. Though the twins remained reluctant to create food outside of an emergency, I didn't mind conjuring a bit of bread for everyone. As we planned our next moves, I munched on a sandwich spiced up with what dried meat we had left.

"I think we should go and inform the village," Dras said. "They'll be happy to know that we got the beast. Also, if we're going to stay here much longer, we might want to pick up a few things."

He wasn't wrong, we lacked bedding options of any kind and we could use some variety in our diets. There were other amenities the town offered, as well. For example, though we had managed to find a restroom on this corridor—a blessing I'd nearly wept over—it didn't have a bathtub.

"I'll go," Ulanion volunteered, drawing my focus back to the moment. "I was there when Ormien died."

"I'll go too," I added. I wanted a conversation with the elf, and this would be a good opportunity.

I got a bit of a look from the others, but everyone nodded their agreement. With the golem providing directions, finding our way to the exit was easy.

As we entered the atrium where Olnir had died, I blinked in surprise. The room was repaired. The fallen pieces were back in place, cracks were filling in slowly. It looked like the whole room would be back to an immaculate state in short order. Except for one thing.

Someone—and I suspected I knew who—had left a small wooden box. Upon opening it, we found what was left of Olnir's remains, laid out respectfully. It wasn't much, as the enchantments had clearly seen most of the corpse as something to be cleaned, but there were some bones and his personal effects.

"I'm not sure if we should bury him nearby or what," I said. "What do you think?"

"He's from your group," Ulanion answered, a salty bite to his voice. "So it's your decision."

I sang up a small privacy bubble around myself and the elf. "All right. What's bothering you?"

He gave me a tired look. "I was never too much into the whole Elven pride thing, but that doesn't mean I don't care about my people at all. I just learned that the greatest leader we ever had, the one responsible for a majority of our society's basis not only lives, but he also refuses to re-assume a throne that would be passed over to him in a second. He won't even bother to try and remake that which brought civilization to our world."

"And you think he should?"

"After what he told me, I don't know." He collected his thoughts before continuing. "I knew that we'd been rough back then. Harsh with the humans we'd displaced when we expanded from this continent. I had no idea how terrible. We were always told that he had been a kind and merciful king, gentle to all. We read it in his writings we were given to read."

"It's often a bad idea to meet your heroes," I commented.

"The writings left out a lot. Some of which, he spoke of. The things done in his name. And worse, the things he did himself, actions that would shock all if they heard. Things that, if done today, would draw the lethal ire of the orders." His fists clenched in anger.

I reached out, resting my hand on his arm. We'd only known each other a short while, but he seemed a good guy. "I don't know how to deal with that, Ulanion. I'm here if you want to talk about it, though."

"Thanks, I guess. Just not sure how to deal with it all. I mean, there's also the weird world-hopping thing."

"That I can understand. I doubt even the elves around here know of that though," I said truthfully.

"And you're probably the only person I can talk with about any of this."

I pondered that and had to agree. Though he might not get as much vitriol as I mentioning such things in an Elven city, I imagined it would still be a losing proposition for him.

"We've got the whole walk back to the village for you to ask questions, if you want. Or the trek back here so we can get home."

I smiled and we headed off, leaving the impromptu casket with our fellows.

And questions he certainly had. As we walked, he asked what my former world had been like, how things worked there. I made an illusion of a dragon, and told him that while there were many stories surrounding such creatures, the tales often conflicted with one another, or were proved to be complete fiction. On the subject of things like computers and communication, he perked up. It was easy enough to understand the basic ideas from someone who came from a burgeoning magitech society, though some of the finer implications had to be explained.

Of all the things that we discussed, the strangest to him was our governance system. There was nothing like it here. While both of our countries were considered more progressive than most, the very idea of a democracy seemed, to him, completely absurd. In this world, people weren't equal, not at all. A fact known to all.

"So," he asked, laughing, "the rich and the powerful were treated the same as the peasants?"

"By law, they were supposed to be," I answered.

"How'd that work?"

"Honestly, a lot of the time, it didn't. If you had money or friends in the right places, you could do things and get things that others couldn't."

"And you all still held to the idea that everyone was equal?"

"How do you do it in Atal?"

"Well, the law is supposed to apply to everyone, but those with power have both rights and duties. While they're unlikely to be bothered about small issues, and if their mana is high enough they can just ignore some of the most minor of infractions. They are also expected to provide more in taxes, and if there is some conflict they have responsibilities others don't."

"That's not altogether unreasonable," I admitted. It certainly beat how things had worked before Durin's takeover, when nobles could basically do as they pleased without punishment. The village sentries spotted us well before we arrived, and I could easily see that, atop the wall, our arrival was causing quite the stir. Our calm and measured pace seemed to settle the guards, and as we approached the gate opened for us. Indriel, the village elder, rushed to greet us.

The nervous elf nearly bounced as we came into polite speaking range. "I see you've returned, but not all of you?" I nodded to Ulanion, allowing for him to explain. "Sadly, not all of us made it. Though we managed to deal with the monsters, we lost Olnir, one of ours. And Ormien as well. He died."

"My condolences," he said, visibly relaxing. "Wait. Monsters? As in plural?"

"Yes," my companion continued. "What was mistaken for one wolf was actually a pack of the creatures. On the road, we met up with someone sent to deal with them. Seems your call for aid reached someone after all."

He lied easily about the last part, and while I generally didn't love having to lie, I was glad he did. I wasn't looking to irritate Justin. Though he had been generous thus far, he remained powerful enough to mess us up. This would probably save us a lot of trouble down the line.

"We cannot express our gratitude enough," Indriel intoned. "Please come in."

The elder made way for us, and as word spread the mood in the village shifted. People hugged, shedding tears as they heard the good news. The children jumped with joy and ran through the streets making sure everyone knew that they had been saved. I awkwardly accepted their words of gratitude as several people came to thank us personally.

Indriel took us to his own home, a slightly larger affair then the rest. A woman I took to be his daughter served us drinks.

Ulanion held out the sword and scabbard he'd been carrying these past hours. "This was Ormien's. Could you have it returned to his family?"

The elder considered the blade then waved his hand, indicating that Ulanion should place it on his own belt. "I'll need to speak with one or two people, but for now you should keep it. I think he'd want it to go to those who helped him avenge his love."

"As it was our initial goal," I said, "our group wants to stay in the ruins for a bit. Would you have any objections?"

Though I legitimately wanted the consent of the village, realistically speaking, we didn't need it and would stay regardless. Thankfully, Indriel remained pliant and giving. "No objections at all. Stay as long as you like."

"There are some remains," I mentioned delicately. "I don't know your culture as well as I'd like, but would you want them returned here for some ceremony or other?"

He considered a bit, though he seemed unconcerned. "I suppose we should make a small art piece celebrating the defeat of the creatures. We could then, perhaps, bury them below it."

I smiled and broached our last bit of business. "One final thing, then, before we return. I was hoping we could purchase some supplies. Our rations are dwindling and we could use a few bedrolls and such."

"No," he said. The syllable was both abrupt and final.

My muscles tensed at his denial. "Excuse me?"

"I said no, dear. Unfortunately, your money is no good here. But if you will provide me a list of what you need, I'll see to it that—if we are able— each one is fulfilled."

I wanted to laugh at myself.

After spending a couple of days in the village, we took our supplies and returned to the ruins. Upon our arrival we learned that Selene had found the most interesting stone in one of the desks.

CHAPTER 35

✦

RECRUITMENT DRIVE

Even after the stone was found it still presented a number of issues for our group. First, nobody was sure what it did. Selene knew that it was trying to connect with her core, but not why. That in and of itself was a cause for alarm since the core was solid, and not meant to be manipulated. At least, not easily. I remembered when I'd first made my core thinking that nothing could interfere with it. I was right in some sense too, it couldn't directly.

While the twins remained cautious, Selene wanted to try it out. Dras and I stood on the sidelines, refusing to add to either side. From my own work with the matching stone, I was as sure as I could be that Selene's experiments would be safe. It was interesting, in that it didn't plug directly into the original core, but rather added something like a second core altogether. They were similar in a number of ways, but still separated by a thick barrier. Neither could directly touch the other, and all communications between the two had to be done through me, which was weird.

The debate continued among the casters. Meanwhile, our guards had their own questions, particularly Ulanion. Though Glen had a limited idea of our full mission, he knew enough to get on and trust us along the way. Ulanion on the other hand, had been told next to nothing.

After the elf went to the restroom, Dras asked me, "How should we deal with him?"

"Ulanion," I asked.

"Yeah. He's not read into this, and while we've kept fairly quiet about things, by the time we're done he'll know too much. I like the guy, but we've no way to prevent that from happening. So, what is our plan?"

Though not a leader as such, Dras had become the main voice of our group. He was the most likely to forward any discussion.

"We can't tell him anything, and may have to . . ." Robert began.

"If he can't be trusted," Leah interjected, "something must be done. Our work could be world-changing in the wrong hands."

I watched, gauging my companions and their opinions. Selene, at least, seemed willing to talk to him. She said, "We need to know if he can be trusted though, as well as our options."

"We won't take him without losses, and we can't afford many more if we want anyone to return home." Glen was practical about it, and right. We needed to get this stuff back no matter what. He was a bit further away, near the door keeping a lookout.

"I think I should talk to him," I said finally. "He seems a bit disillusioned with a lot of the Atali ways, and we might be able to convince him to join Emperor Durin. Then there should be no issue, right?"

They nodded along in agreement.

"Alana you've spent the most time alone with Ulanion. If you think we should try to recruit him, so be it. Between his abilities and all the help he's been, I think the Emperor would want him on our side anyway. If not, it'll be best to let the leadership deal with him," Dras said. That suggestion got a round of nods as well. Decision made, I steeled myself.

The next day, citing that I wanted to get some more info on the golem, I managed to convince Ulanion to accompany me to the control room. He agreed and we set off along the empty corridors.

When we were well away from the others, he asked, "So, what's this actually about?"

Ah, he'd been able to read me, I thought. I conjured a barrier around us as we walked.

I asked, "What are you planning to do after we return to the capital?"

"I'm not sure, honestly. I've learned a lot on this mission, and I've got a lot of questions."

He'd kept my confidence, so I felt that I owed him some honesty. "Well, we'd like you to join us. I'll be blunt; it's not entirely for your benefit and coming with us might not work out well for you."

"Care to go deeper into that?"

"You've realized that what we're doing is pretty secretive?"

"I wasn't going to pry, but yes," he said. "You came straight here, a rather important place, and have been all *hush-hush* about everything, including whatever you're doing with that gate thing back there. What is it anyway?"

"The actual target of our search," I said, measuring my response. "It's a rather potent tool. Our group was formed to investigate it."

"His Majesty knows that you want it?" After a moment's thought, he answered himself, "Of course he knows, he saw what room you gravitated toward. Therefore, I can guess he's okay with you having it. Is it dangerous?"

"Not on its own, no," I answered. "It could, however, drastically change things between our continents. And yes," I added, "Justin knows and approves of our objective."

"Well, he is certainly more knowledgeable than I about that kind of thing, so I don't suppose I can really press against . . . Ah, the problem is that your group doesn't trust me?"

I nodded in confirmation. "That is the gist of it."

"So, they'll what? Try to recruit me, and if that fails silence me?"

"If you don't want to join up, I hope you'll take this as an opportunity to leave. I can tell them you overpowered me and fled. Could even give you a bit of time."

I was ready to do that for him, to let him flee before he got in too deep.

"They would call you a traitor if they heard that. You might get in a lot of trouble," he cautioned.

"They won't hear it, though. So, what do you say?" I leaned over, perking up an eyebrow at him. "Care to join us and see what we're really up to?"

"Well, this has definitely been an adventure, but I'd like to know what I'd be signing up for."

"You'd be working, indirectly, under Emperor Durin, the man currently trying to rule most of the human continent. Lots of black clothes, references to shadows, stuff like that."

He looked confused. "Sounds kind of . . . evil?"

"It's certainly a little weird, but he's not a bad guy. Much of what he's done has brought a balance of power between those who have magic and those who don't. Before he came along, mages—especially the highborn ones—trampled on the common folk. He's done a lot to stop that, and while I won't say he's perfect, from what I've seen he is doing a lot of good."

"Do you have some examples?" he asked.

"Well, you know the various orders of priests?"

"Not many of our priests subscribe to those, but some do, so yes."

That was not the answer I'd expected, but he was from a different continent.

"Durin made sure that their rules were followed when it came to war. When he took over the kingdom, the bloodshed was kept restrained on his end. And unlike other conquerors, Durin and his men didn't engage in mass pillaging or rape. I was there at the very end, and saw when he even tried to stop the fighting between the weaker forces of the capital. He wanted to save lives."

That was all true enough. Though I'd been in a few places that had almost gotten me killed, Durin's strikes were often precise, taking their targets and little else in the way of casualties. I'd, of course, learned later that the worst offenders had been terrorists who he'd lost control over, and had deserted Durin's forces during their conquest.

"You sound like you like the guy," Ulanion observed.

"He's not a bad guy," I repeated. "At least he wasn't to me."

"You've met your Emperor?"

"Yes," I answered. "And I think he's genuine. He wants to help. But if he is to succeed, he will need help."

Understandably, Ulanion had some questions about our laws. Since almost all of them had some degree of magic, the elves lived differently. When I educated him on the laws—before and after the usurpation—and how I'd lived under both regimes, he didn't seem too unhappy. He did, however, have concerns.

"If I decide to join you," he asked, "there's no going back for me is there?"

"Afraid not," I said, quickly adding, "at least not for a while. From what I've seen, we'll have to keep our work secret for a few years yet." After some moments spent in thought he said, "I've been thinking lately that I need to explore the other side of my lineage. What His Majesty told me shook some of my perceptions about my people and our history. Might be good to see how others live for a while. If I don't like it . . . well, your Emperor is how old?"

I wasn't really sure. "Sixties I think?"

"A couple decades for me, then, even if he is long-lived for a human. Knowing what you know about him now, would you join him if you were given the option? Because you do have the option to leave with me if you want to. We could run off and see this continent instead."

The flirting was unexpected, and I felt myself blush a little at that rather forward suggestion.

"If I knew what I know, I think I would join him. And while your offer is tempting, I do want to return home."

"Good to know that I'm tempting," he laughed. "Well then, I think I'll join you and see what this Emperor of yours is like with my own eyes."

As we returned to the gate, I couldn't help but think about how things might change when we returned.

CHAPTER 36

◆

CONNECTION ESTABLISHED

Selene, bless her heart, was slow as she could be. Much to the conster-nation of our companions, she'd finally managed to add the update to her core and was working on the gate now. I'd finished integrating the stone's mate several days ago and gone to work on the same project, but nobody else knew, or needed to know that just now.

It was slow going, but our work was greatly aided by the fact that who-ever built this particular gate hadn't seen the need to hide the runes they were using. This meant that I just needed to work my way through and check them in order to see what was going on. That prospect was further accelerated by the workup provided in the update, which at this point, of course, nobody else had.

It was weird dealing with the new Guide and the like, since it wasn't properly connected. The whole situation was weird, but I got the feeling that distance was to preserve the integrity of the original core. While Jus-tin hadn't shown back up for me to ask, I got the feeling that he wouldn't make any base changes to that. I could have popped down and asked, but got the feeling that if he were still working in the basement, he wanted to be undisturbed.

I wondered what Justin was doing down in his lair. He was clearly researching the magic that had brought he and I—and those like us— here to this plane, but to what end? Was he trying to return to Earth? Perhaps he was trying to bring someone else from there to here. Some-one specific? In the end it didn't really matter since he seemed more interested in his project than the rest of the world. Which was sad, but what could we do?

On the other hand, I had some practical concerns, the first being our trip home. This gate seemed our best option for that, but after we achieved this, I would begin pushing, quietly, for a public transport network. My first world had been thrust into an age of progress thanks to the quick exchange of ideas and items, and I would much like to see that prosperity and innovation here as well. The basics were already in place, we just needed more trade and better organization then we'd be on our way to a full on industrial revolution.

How would Emperor Durin respond to that idea? I had no clue, but I had good hopes. At any rate, that growth wouldn't be coming all at once, but instead in small increments. The Elven nations had already given me some ideas on how to make those initial improvements. If we pushed for some science, we might even be able to supplement magic with some more traditional technology.

It was safe to say that having seen how the elves lived in their cities—with their running water and lighting for the people—I wanted that for my own people now. I didn't have any delusions of being able to change everything, but such amenities would, perhaps, be feasible.

I ruminated on this while slowly making my way through the gate runes. Even though I was intentionally handicapping what I reported to the others, we could nonetheless see how our project was coming together. The gate created a connection between itself and another using something like the formulas for my radios. Then, the gates linked together and formed a path by manipulating space between the two. Having worked out most of this back home, we understood the concepts, but I learned a few things as I used the new Guide.

We always stayed just below the speed of light. Causality seemed to have some big issues if you tried to make space warp in such a way that it was truly instant, but for planet-side travel that hardly mattered. Any attempts to bypass this universal speed limit, the Guide explained, would fail. Not catastrophically or anything, they just didn't work.

Another new fact I learned was that each gate was also a one-to-one path. A gate pair linked, and could be turned on or off from either side. However, attempting to use a linked gate to travel elsewhere would be quite difficult to accomplish without damaging one or both gates of the pair.

After another long day of work, I declared, "Okay, I think we can turn it on now."

"I'm still unsure on exactly what this is doing," Selene said, pointing to the sequence responsible for the space molding.

"That looks to be the same as back home. I can't work out all the math to it, or why it's doing that, but from what I'm reading here that is the connection."

"Yeah, but we don't know how it works," she complained.

"And we probably won't," I answered bluntly. "That math is beyond me."

And it was, too. There was a description on the update to the Guide that basically said, *This works, Use it like this if you're unsure.* And that was good enough for me.

"How sure are you this isn't going to blow up and kill us or something," Dras asked.

I was very sure, but I couldn't explain why without giving away the game. In any other situation, Selene and Dras would have absolutely been right to question me on this. For now, though, I had to suppress my annoyance and frustration.

"Eighty," I answered, "maybe ninety percent?"

"In my book that's better odds than trying to get back the traditional way," Glen said, shrugging. He then asked, "Can I be the one to turn it on? We should have the rest of you outside in case it goes wrong. With my armor, I can survive anything so long as it's not too extreme."

"Turning it on is easy enough," Selene said. "We'd need to charge it up with some mana, but I have another concern. If this gate links to one of the dead gates in Emperor Durin's home, how do we communicate who and where we are?"

That much remained a mystery. We didn't know where this gate went, and we wouldn't until we turned it on to try. While I suspected that it did, in fact, link up to one of the unused portals beneath Durin's complex, there was no way to be sure until we tried it.

"If I'm remembering correctly," Selene continued, "many of Emperor Durin's gates had portcullises, so we might not be able to just walk through. We'll need some way to send a message that will not be intercepted by anyone else."

"I think I've got an idea on that one," I replied. "I can prepare it by tonight."

"All right Alana, it's on you."

It took some time to gather the necessary materials, but by dinner I'd made a little plate of aluminum. On it was a simple message. *The lost girl from Orsken wishes to speak to her teacher. Use the earpiece.*

The oblique words and the metal itself should provide enough of a hint to those who needed it. Along with the plate, I crafted another radio for when they got around to contacting us. I knew Mystien still had my first attempts at this technology, and those should be able to communicate through the gateway with no problem.

When it was time, Glen had the rest of us move several corridors away while he opened the gate and tossed my message through. With that hard part over, it became a waiting game. I had no delusions that we'd be getting an immediate response if we got one at all. In the event no answer came, though, we would have to consider other methods of investigating the other side without just stepping through.

We decided to wait a week before making any other decisions. We spent our time in the gate research room, puzzling over runes while hoping for a response.

By my guess, that would be more than enough time. The plate would be seen almost instantly, the gate activation probably sending up a whole mess of alarms. From there, the receiver would read it, and look at the metal. Aluminum was rare enough to prick up eyebrows as only a few were known to work with it. Assuming this gate linked to Durin's complex, my message would then travel either to Durin or to Mystien soon enough, both of whom knew I came from Orsken.

Five days into our wait, a buzzing heralded the awakening of our gate. At the sound, all of us startled and fixed our attention on the gate just in time to see the connection take and the portal form.

Spells and blades at the ready, each of us knew there was a chance, however small, that our message might have been received by an enemy.

"Alana," a tired voice asked from my new radio. "Alana, is that you?"

"It is," I confirmed. "Who am I speaking to?"

"Mystien, who else? We need to confirm identities and the situation."

"Agreed." I thought for a moment, finally settling on a simple question with an answer few would know. "Who was the bard you first called to teach me healing magic?"

"That pervert Jackson," he growled immediately. "What is your uncle's name?"

"Barro. I'm satisfied, and you?"

"Confirmed. Where are the team leaders," Mystien asked. "We had an established protocol for secret communications."

"Dead," I announced. "And that protocol might have been worth sharing with the rest of us."

"Dead!? All of them?"

Unsure how to tell them about everything—including Ulanion—I decided that ripping off the metaphorical bandage seemed the best idea. "Yes. All. Our team is now down to six people from the original expedition and one elf who opted to join us and has expressed interest in joining Lord Durin."

"SIX? We sent over twenty people on three vessels! What the hell happened!? Nevermind, we'll brief later. You found a gate on your end, I see. Can we at least confirm that the mission was a success?"

"We succeeded," I answered. Glancing about my fellows, I added. "And we are ready to come home."

"All right," Mystien said. "The way is clear. Come through one at a time and bring your communicator with you. Last thing we need is any more disaster coming from this."

CHAPTER 37

✦

DEBRIEF

After taking a few moments to gather all of our things, we lined up and began the journey home. One by one, we passed. Dras led the way, stepping through the open portal and into the distant beyond. The twins were next, followed by Glen. With a sort of sad expression, Selene took one last look around her before she stepped through the portal. Only Ulanion and I remained.

I looked over at the wolf golem. Though thoroughly annoyed by its verbiage and tendency to call me 'highness,' it was still a really impressive piece of artifice, and a good guardian to boot. It was a shame that we couldn't bring it with us, and I doubted that I'd be able to recreate such a thing on my own.

"This is it then, isn't it," Ulanion asked. Apparently, he'd realized that once he passed through the gate, he might not set foot in his homeland for a long, long time.

"You can still leave," I offered. "I'd understand that, and I think everyone else would, too."

"No, I think I do want to see your people. Just a bit nervous is all."

"I understand," I said. "On our way here, I think we all had a few butterflies at one time or another. I know I did."

He looked confused. "Butterflies?"

"Er, it's an expression," I said. "The sensation of fluttering in your stomach that comes with nervousness. Butterflies."

"Never heard it put like that, but I guess that makes sense. Well, time then."

As he stepped to the opening, a voice from behind us caused us to pause. I heard another voice.

"Good luck, my boy," Justin said softly from behind us.

Both of us took a last look at the Elven mage, the first king himself. I suppose he'd been watching us.

"So, you decided to show? You could join too you know," I offered.

"I plan to seal it after you've left. As for joining you, I'll still pass."

I didn't blame him, knowing that he'd seen some things that I couldn't understand.

Ulanion didn't say anything, just nodded and passed through.

"Perhaps we'll meet again one day," I said, knowing that it was unlikely. I tossed my upgrade stone to him. "Finished with that by the way. Thanks."

"I expected you to ask a lot of questions, but you didn't," he observed. "Do you not wish to be powerful? I could have helped you."

I thought for a moment. He was right, I could have asked a lot, and learned a ton. He probably knew more about magic—even bardic magic—than most people alive, save a few other ancient elves like himself. It just didn't seem right though.

"You said that power didn't make you happy. I like to learn, but I'll learn and grow on my own, and at the pace I think is right for me."

With a shrug for my strange, royal friend, I, too, passed through the gate, a happy chuckle bubbling from behind me.

The world shifted and I was pulled through space. Unlike the almost-instantaneous transport back home, the journey yawned as light blurred around me, swirling and pulling. I stumbled out into a familiar room. One I had first entered on my way to Emperor Durin's wedding.

Disoriented, I tripped, nearly falling over my own feet. Catching myself, I blinked and saw dozens of soldiers and battle mages gathered around. All their weapons aimed in my direction.

Eyeing the guards, I asked, "Everything okay?"

"Sorry," Mystien said from the back ranks. "We might've had a bit of a fit when one of our gates to an unknown location activated. Wanted to make sure it really was you lot." Mystien stood flanked by several of his personal assistants, each of them conjuring layers of shields.

"Don't suppose you've calmed down a bit," I asked.

"Sadly, we're going to have to run a few tests to confirm things. You took longer than the others to make your way through. Something happen?"

"Yeah. The mage who helped us against the Umbral Wolves showed up as we were leaving. Said he plans to—" With a *pop*, the gate closed behind me, much to the surprise of the jittery soldiers. "Seal the gate when we were through," I completed.

My former teacher looked miffed, terribly, horribly miffed. "You could have tried to stop him."

"He makes you look like a weak child barely able to cast your first spell, old man." The number of eyebrows going up at that statement made me sigh internally. I really needed to watch my words better. "Currently, though, he didn't seem ill-disposed toward us, and there was no reason to push that."

"Come on then, you cheeky brat, we need to get you checked, then talk."

I learned then, that our group had been separated, each of us taken within seconds of coming through the portal. I was led out by a number of guards. While that was happening I could see several people cast various spells, ostensibly to check the area for any intrusions. Some of them even had instruments out, scanning the area. I didn't like the paranoia, but it was justified. After all, we'd put a doorway into one of the most secure facilities on the continent, beneath the bedchamber of the emperor himself, and told them there'd been a massive disaster involving most of our people being lost. They'd want answers, and to check us over.

The guards took me to a small room where one member of staff questioned me while another poked and prodded at me with tools to check age, sex, and a few other physical characteristics that might indicate that I wasn't me. After a few hours, when they'd decided I was definitely me and that I could probably be trusted, Mystien returned.

"So, care to give me a full report?"

"I know you've been listening, but sure. After we left the port, we made it some way toward the Elven homelands before we were attacked by a massive, ocean-dwelling monster. The leaders decided that our only real chance was to fight it, and so we did. That's when our other two teams were lost, though we did finally take the beast."

"Afterwards you made your way to our embassy," he asked.

"Yes," I confirmed, "but that was after our encounter with an island with a violent native species. Then we were able to get to the Elven continent, and we met our contact at the embassy." "Where did you pick up the elf?" Mystien seemed particularly concerned about him.

"He somehow knew the ambassador. We needed someone to boost our numbers after taking heavy losses, so Joan suggested him as an addition."

He asked a number of questions about Ulanion. What we knew of him, his behavior. I ran him through the whole incident with the Umbral

Wolves, something that made him furrow his brow. We didn't have any information on those particular beasts, and he took notes on their abilities and tactics. The elf had done a really good job, all things told, I had explained. And I told Mystien that I'd personally asked Ulanion to join us, which he'd agreed to of his own volition.

"I can't make a determination on it myself," Mystien said, "but if he really does want to join with us, I don't think that'll be a problem. What about that mage? I assume you know more about him than you're letting on."

I shrugged. "Anything he said could have been a lie, so there's no telling the truth of his past. What I can tell you is this: if I'm reading the signs right, he's ancient and significantly more pure-blooded than any elf I've ever seen. And having seen him flex his power, it's evident he is far more than we want to deal with. That said, however, I don't think he's likely to be a problem."

"So what? We just drop it?"

"Yes, Mystien. We now have access to the actual gate technology, which was our goal. We take what we got, and stop trying to poke around with elves. From what I've seen, if they decided right now to go to war with us, we'd probably lose. They'd take losses, too, sure, but no matter how much our ambassador would like to brag the elves' use of magic is far beyond us."

"You're a real headache sometimes, girl. We'll have to come up with a whole new protocol around the gates, particularly if there are foreign agents who might be in the know. We now have to assume the elves know about this place."

Mystien rubbed his temples as he pondered it all.

"Enough about me. What's been going on back home while I've been out on the high seas and in distant lands," I asked.

"Hmm? Oh . . . I suppose you'd want to know, huh? Well, your family is doing well. We've had some issues with the remnants of the royals, mostly that they're holed up somewhere and hiding well. Oh! The Queen is expecting the Emperor's first child."

As he went on, it was clear that he wasn't really keeping up too much with personal business. I made a mental note to ask mother when I got to see her.

"When we're done here," I said to that end, "I'd like a few weeks to catch up with my family before we get back to work on those gates."

"Going to be at least a week before you lot go anywhere. Now, let's go over some of the technical information on those new rune sequences. We'll need Selene to get to work on making more, but I understand you made some inroads on the basics."

It was going to be a long, long week.

At least they didn't know that I could make gates yet.

CHAPTER 38

+

THE WORST TIMING

As Mystien predicted, the full debriefing and all its associated paper-work took nearly a week to complete. During that time, I was given access to the stone Selene found so that I could begin the update process on my own core. The powers that be didn't know that I'd already been through that process, so I just spent that time going through the Guide updates again, and making sure I understood things correctly.

I knew that they wanted more of those gates and that I'd be on the shortlist for making them, but the speed was a surprise. It mostly came down to the fact that I'd already demonstrated my understanding and was already experienced with getting a previously-down gate up and run-ning. Few people could question my loyalty because of the positions of my father and mentor, so I was prime to work on them.

During the debrief, I didn't see much of the rest of our group, though I did inquire after them.

Glen was waiting to be cleared, then he would be getting a hefty pro-motion. He'd managed to keep most of us alive in a bad situation that he was in no way properly prepped for, and that made a really good impression on his superiors. Likewise, the twins had reams to do. We'd encountered enough new fauna for Leah to bury herself in descriptions and guides for weeks, or possibly months, while her brother updated our knowledge of the fauna.

With a few of the other researchers from Mystien's lab, Dras, Selene, and I would be taking up the task of getting the gate network going. For now, we needed to get the runes down interpreted. Then we could begin the process of teaching others. Dras busied himself with bringing the newer team members up to speed while Selene tinkered with her first pair of connected gates.

Four days after we returned, I sat in my temporary quarters writing down my observations when a knock sounded at the door. Since our arrival, there had been a steady stream of people coming by, so a visitor wasn't a surprise.

"Come in," I said from my desk.

The door opened to reveal my brother, a crooked smile on his face. "Hey there, how's it going?"

"Good grief," I said, rising to hug my brother. "Took you long enough. I was betting dad would be here the moment he heard I was back." I rose to hug John, it really was weird to have family again.

"Dad's been sent up north for a bit to handle some issues," he said, finding a seat. "Not sure when he'll be back. Otherwise, he would have been here days ago."

"And mom? I know she's not read in on everything, but she knows about the emperor's fortress. Certainly, she could come and say hi."

He shook his head. "Mom's not cleared on a lot of the state secrets, Alana, which is absolutely whatever you're working on. Crap, I don't even know the details, and I am in the loop for lots of that stuff. I think Mystien's trying to find some way to tell people you got back but, being that you somehow traveled across the ocean without a boat and without anyone knowing you did, we'll need to arrange some cover just in case anyone starts looking."

I didn't talk about my work with my family. That was something Mystien had instilled in me as verboten. Sure, my dad could know if he needed to, but portals weren't really his wheelhouse. They knew I was working on magical research under Mystien, and that I hadn't been fond of my previous boss, but little else.

"I suppose that makes sense," I said. "I think you'll be let in soon. Dad, too, probably," I added quickly.

I tried to find a comfy spot to lean back, the wooden chair I used for work being poorly suited to lounging. As an afterthought I hummed a small illusion over my desk.

"Not giving me anything more than that," my brother teased halfheartedly.

"I've been gone most of the past year, John. Tell me what's been going on with you."

"Not much I guess. My unit was doing some work out in the east for a while, but we're off for a few weeks. I got a few commendations from some skirmishes out there . . . and I started officially courting Miss Etia."

"Sorry what!?"

Etia was one of my former teachers, and an elf. My view of her was complicated to say the least.

"You know I knew you'd react like this," he observed.

"React like what? Like you've started hooking up with my completely baby-crazy teacher? Yes, that should be expected. You know she's mostly just looking at you for breeding purposes, right?"

"I noticed, but I'm not particularly bothered by that part."

Looking for something to throw at him, I said, "She's mental, John. Brilliant perhaps, but completely mental. She's also way older than you." This was exhausting.

"I'm aware that she's an elf, Alana, though to be honest she looks about the same age as you do nowadays."

I briefly considered hitting him with a number of different offensive spells. He'd have some hearing damage, sure, but he would survive. I settled, instead, for smacking him with a pillow from my bed. Punching him would be cathartic, but with his level of physical magic I might as well be slamming my fist into a steel cast of his face.

After I landed several halfhearted strikes, he put a hand up, catching the offending cushion and ending my assault.

"One," I said, "screw you. Two, does mom know about this?"

"I was hoping you'd help me tell her," he said.

There was no way I'd even be in the same building when my mother found out. If Mother knew Etia, she'd lose her mind. If she didn't know the professor, she'd soon find out just how off that woman was.

"So, you have gone insane?"

He made a face at me like he was genuinely pleading. "Alana, seriously."

I couldn't judge my brother too harshly. Etia was good looking, and she did have some other merits. "Do you actually pan to marry her or anything, or is this just a fling?"

"I really do like her," he said, seeming earnest. "If I can get mom and dad to not freak out, I think something might come of it."

He has to realize, I thought, *that he is not only a person looking for love, but also the child of a major political figure.*

"Dad will want to know if she's a liability, being that she's not one of our citizens. Unless she plans to stay?" I looked at him questioningly.

"She's said she'll join the empire permanently if we end up marrying." There were so, so many things wrong with all of this. I slumped as I thought about it, trying to come up with what all would need to happen, but just kept drawing blanks.

As I pondered how best to tackle my idiot brother's mix of relationship and romantic issues, another knock came at the door.

I sighed. "Come in." Ulanion entered with a soldier acting as his escort. I hadn't seen him since our return, and had been meaning to speak with him. But I also knew that he was being more thoroughly interrogated than I or my fellows. "Oh! Hello, Alana," he said, nervously eyeing my brother and me. "Hope I'm not disturbing anything."

"Sort of, but it's fine, something you need?"

"Well," he began, "they just finished with me, and I don't really know many of the other people here. I was hoping that . . ." His voice trailed off, seemingly silenced by the glance my brother was flicking back and forth over us

"You have got to be kidding me," John said accusingly.

Ulanion was clearly confused. "What?"

My brother turned to me, brow furrowed. "You're seriously giving me that much of a hard time?"

"This is not what you think," I protested.

"I think it's exactly what I think, little sister. The pot is calling the kettle black."

"It is not like that!" I yelled, frustrated with the whole situation.

John snorted before rising and going to the door. Once there, he gave Ulanion a good hard look before nodding. "All right, you two get on with it. I'll talk to you later, Alana, have fun. Don't forget to think about how to explain things to mom, though."

After he left, a bewildered Ulanion stared at me. "What was that all about?"

I sighed, trying to dispel a headache that I felt forming behind my eyes. "You have just the worst timing."

He cringed. "Sorry. Should I come back later?"

I imagined him doing so, only to have my brother find us together again later. If that happened, I might never live it down. With another sigh, I said, "Won't really help at this point. Though what might help is if you just kill me now."

CHAPTER 39

✦

GARDEN TALK

I wanted a moment out of my room, and there was no point in sending him away at this point; the damage was already done. My brother had run off to who knows where, undoubtedly plotting my imminent demise by Mother. I—with Ulanion and his guard in tow—made my way outside to the large inner courtyard. Since I was last there, the space had seen many changes, a number of lovely gardens chief among them.

"So . . . mind telling me what that was all about," Ulanion asked.

"My brother, idiot that he is, wanted my help explaining his choice of girlfriend to our mom."

"You seem flustered though? Isn't that something to be happy about? Not only has he found someone, but he wants your aid. Is something wrong with her?" He was still a bit confused.

"His choice is one of my former teachers. She's both a bit odd, and an elf, which may be an issue. I don't think mom will care, but if the woman weren't seriously weird it would help."

Ulanion chuckled a bit. "Ah, what's the term? Baby-crazy?"

"Right on target with that one," I confirmed. "How'd you guess?"

"Oh, yes," he said, leaning in a bit conspiratorially. "You see, Alana, I've met one or two Elven women in my years. I've personal experience with the most common of their eccentricities, at least by human standards. With our fertility rates there's a heavy push for girls to make heirs."

I punched him lightly on the arm. Of course he knew what I'd probably see as the weirdest thing for Etia. Pointing out that he'd seen, and was probably related to, similar girls was just a bit crass.

"You don't seem to have those problems," I observed aloud.

He pointed to the side of his head. There were grey hairs there, a light sprinkling not unlike what my father now sported. "Experience."

I snorted. "So, what, back in the day you made lots of little Ulanions to go and do your part or whatever?"

"No comment," he replied with equal amusement.

I was a bit shocked by that. "Seriously?"

"Alana, people with full-blown magic are far more common among elves, but we're still a rarity. Many also want us in their family trees. I've had plenty of chances to pick up women in all my many years, most with no real expectations of me. That is . . . hollow, though. Fun is fun, but it's not really meaningful, if you follow." He shrugged at the end. Clearly, even with my two lives, there was still much I had yet to experience.

I'd had a few flings. Nothing major. Until that torch was taken up by others, my friend Pinea had run a party circuit. With my tattoo and ability to heal anything I might have possibly picked up there was no danger to be found in a night's fun. Though this place had not experienced any sort of sexual revolution like my previous culture's 1960s, I found the morality rather relaxed here. I suspected that was due entirely to magic.

"Anyway," I said, getting back to the point, "John wants me to help him with our mom. And now he thinks we're together. If I say no, he might well tell Mother I'm courting an elf and spent all my time in the Elven lands doing heavens knows what. She's fairly uptight about that kind of thing and will likely have a complete fit."

"I mean, I have seen you sans clothing," he teased.

If the guard hadn't been following, I might have found this funny. The last thing I needed was some random soldier with a loose tongue informing my brother or—for an even bigger mess—my freaking father. He would lose his mind!

When our shadow made a slight choking noise, I quickly blurted out, "By accident! Where nothing happened!"

Ulanion must have seen my eye twitch. He put his hands up, warding off any anger. "Yes, yes. Stumbling on you two in the bath wasn't my intent."

As if that statement wasn't worse.

The guard looked at us with slowly widening eyes.

Ulanion stammered to cover, but only continued to dig. "Er, nothing untoward implied by that, of course. Both parties being women." My family knew that I'd dated a girl before, and this explanation would only confirm their beliefs about my choices.

Our poor chaperone and his strained eyebrows.

"S T O P T A L K I N G!!!" I hissed, driving every syllable hard like a nail.

"Sorry," he quietly replied.

I glared at his guard intensely while considering the value of making some threat or other. In the end, I decided to let my eyes speak all the horrors I would unleash upon him should his lips let any of this slip.

I closed my eyes, rubbing them. "Anyway, the issue is that my brother thinks we're together. He'll probably say something, and I'll have to explain to my parents, or whatever, and in all likelihood they won't believe me, and all that mess, then Mom will almost assuredly insist on meeting my new admirer and then she'll ask lots and lots of questions." I closed my eyes, now fully rubbing them.

"Good grief, I do hope that being associated with me isn't that unpleasant to you." Ulanion shook his head a bit as he spoke. I looked up to see him there.

"I don't have any particular objections to you, just that we're not dating," I answered.

"Good to know. Let's talk again another time."

With that he quickly turned and left, leaving me a bit flustered. His guard, who was both vastly unprofessional and still a bit shocked, took several moments to follow. The elf could have lost him if he really tried, but he didn't.

I stood there just as thrown off as the soldier, if not more.

Did Ulanion seriously like me *like that*? Had he been planning to make some kind of move? Was he seriously going to leave me here on that note?

"Wait what!?"

I spent the next couple of days fuming as I worked. Ulanion didn't come and see me again in that time. Though I considered going to resolve that particular issue myself, I was stubborn. If that stupid, pointy-eared jerk wanted to flirt before leaving, I certainly wasn't going to go and seek him out. If I went to him, who knew what kind of weird ideas he might get.

So instead, I busied myself with mundane tasks. Eventually, I turned over the upgrade stone to Mystien with a letter that I'd finished with it. Soon after, I was sent to aid Selene with gate building.

She'd been doing a rough job of it. Sure, the teleportation sequences and everything were correct since she'd just copied them over from Ristolian's work, copying his methods. But I loathed her design of the surrounding functions. Unlike Ristolian, who'd redone the *on/off* and *mana distribution* methods himself, I was a bit traditional in how I liked my setup. There wasn't any particular reason that his—and now Selene's—way wouldn't work, I just didn't like the inelegant aesthetic.

She and I argued back and forth on those points for a while. She believed that, if it worked, there was no need to change anything, whereas I preferred to move forward by tidying up Ristolian's messy implementation. In the end, I deferred to her for this run. It was a test, after all. However, I was determined to make the necessary changes when we went into full production. Assuming, of course, that I was still on this project at that point.

I wondered how far the update to the core would be spread. It wouldn't be everywhere, of course, and if I had to put forth a theory it would probably be shared among our team, possibly a handful of others, before the stone was locked up tight in a vault somewhere. It was dangerous tech, and if one of us were to betray the empire it could spell disaster. I didn't have to theorize either, I'd seen firsthand what a small, dedicated group could do with even a limited version.

Selene and I had been provided with a modest workshop. We warded our lab in such a way that sound could not escape, allowing us to speak freely. However, our spells allowed us to hear any alarms or noises that might sound in the corridor beyond. We took to our tasks with gusto, working on our first pair of gates together.

I was scribbling down the last bits of our notes when there was a bit of a stir outside the lab. The hallway filled with an excited flurry and the sounds of several boots approaching. The door opened and a man entered, black cloak swaying behind him. His smile was bright as he gazed upon Selene and me with something akin to fatherly pride.

"Good afternoon, ladies," Emperor Durin said. "I do hope I'm not interrupting anything too important?"

CHAPTER 40

EMPEROR'S INTERROGATION

Selene was stunned, as was I. Sure, this was technically the emperor's home, but that didn't mean he was here all that much. As well as having a residence in my former home of Lithere, Emperor Durin and his queen had made their home in the palace in the old imperial capital. We had not expected that the ruler of the country would come to us himself.

"Not at all, Your Majesty," I managed to squeak out after a moment.

"Good, good," he continued. As he moved around our lab, guards shadowing him closely, he fixed his attention on our gates. "I'm quite keen to see what your team has been working on."

"Well, these are our prototypes," I said as I joined him near the pair of gates. "We're working off the existing designs, for now. We're not sure what—if any—quirks we'll need to work out."

"That's to be expected with anything new," he offered with a kind smile. "When should they be ready for their first tests?"

I looked to Selene. If she wanted to pad our timetable, I wouldn't object.

"I think we'll be ready to begin within a week," Selene hedged, adding a couple of days to what we needed. "That is assuming, of course, that we don't run into any issues while putting them together, Your Majesty."

"Excellent. I'll provide personnel for the first test," he said. Firmly, he added, "You two are to stay well away during that test. Observation only. Just in case something goes wrong."

I understood. He didn't want to risk his golden geese, not with eggs this tempting.

"As you command," I agreed. "Testing will take many iterations over time to ensure safety. If that goes well, we can go into full production."

If only to myself, I admitted that though I was as sure as I could be that our sequences would work perfectly, nobody had made one of these devices in hundreds of years.

Durin's smile never faltered. "I have faith that you'll put your all into it, ladies. Is there any risk of the portals being compromised? It's a question my advisors and I have been bouncing back and forth for a long time."

Selene stepped forward and spoke. "We don't believe so. It looks like each pair must be made as a matched set. While it might be possible to alter this, such complex work is, frankly, beyond our current abilities. By a rather large margin," she added. Emperor Durin asked a few more general questions before one of his assistants stepped forward and began spewing incredibly detailed inquiries. These were his personal tech guys, if I had to judge. While I got the feeling the finer points of our work were beyond their exact understanding, these men could follow the general idea of what was going on.

After some general puttering around our workshop, the emperor seemed satisfied. As his tech people gave him their assurances, he nodded politely along.

Facing the room, he beamed and announced, "All seems to be in order. And just in time for lunch. I'd like for you to join me, Miss Alana. Your father is one of my most trusted generals, but I hate to say that you and I have barely spoken."

The other shoe dropped. *He wasn't just here to check on our progress,* I realized, *but for me as well.*

"Certainly," I said. "It would be an honor." There was no denying him this. It would be rude beyond belief and best-case scenario I'd be thrown in a dungeon somewhere until I learned to keep my mouth shut.

I joined his little party and marched with them through the halls. We headed up into the residential areas of the fortress. I had never been to this area myself, and it struck me how much smaller this was than I would have expected of an emperor's quarters. I couldn't help but be a bit nervous. The guards all looked at me as if I were a threat.

Soon enough we made it to a small dining room. The food was excellent, as one might expect. Though not extravagant, the simple ingredients of sweet fish and roasted tubers with herbs had been expertly prepared to the point of delicacy.

As servants took our plates, Emperor Durin gave a brief nod to his people. All but two of them filed out, leaving a mage and a knight to serve as guards. While the knight positioned himself over his master's shoulder, the mage put up a barrier, giving us privacy.

A shudder coursed my spine.

Sitting up straighter in my chair, I asked, "Is something wrong, Your Majesty?"

"Does it need to be?"

"No . . . I just wasn't expecting you to need something private."

"I was hoping I wouldn't, but I have some questions that I feel should be answered personally. I could have one of my people talk to you, but this way looks better if others hear about it. Right now, I'm simply having a conversation with a dear friend's child rather than having her interrogated."

This is bad, I said to myself. *Very bad.*

Aloud, I said, "I see."

"Now, I read the reports that you and your team filed, and I must inform you that there are some odd points. The fact that the gate room was so ignored, and with such an important artifact in it." He quirked his brow up, clearly having a hard time believing it.

"I was not with the team when they found it," I said, relieved that I didn't have to lie. "We were separated and only rejoined later."

"Ah yes, that does match up, doesn't it? You were alone with the elf you recruited, this Ulanion fellow. What do you know about him?" *Is he testing me? Is this what he really wants?* I was unsure.

"Little," I answered, "if I'm honest. But for the limited time I've known him, Ulanion's proven himself to be a decent sort. He fulfilled his job without issue, and even decided to join us." Durin nodded. "He has expressed interest in joining our cause. Do you think him loyal?"

"I don't believe he'd betray you," I said. After taking a second to process my explanation, I continued, "Had that been his aim, he had multiple chances to betray us. He didn't, nor did he take any of the ample opportunities to simply leave. As for his loyalty to you, specifically, he expressed that if he was displeased here, he wouldn't be bothered by waiting the few decades that would constitute any service rendered."

That got a snort of laughter. "Elves! If they don't like you, they don't mind, do they? They just plan to outlive you." After shaking his head, he regarded me with hard eyes. "I need to know now—and I do hate to ask— have you, Alana, had any compromising relations with him?"

My face grew hot as the emperor added, "One of his guards indicated that something might have passed between you. Regardless of this claim's veracity, if something has happened, I urge you to tell me now and I'll not hold it against you. It isn't unknown for people to use such tactics to blackmail otherwise loyal servants."

If I ever find that guard, I will castrate him.

"Nothing," I said. I took a moment to moderate my tone. "Leah and I, after many days on the road, decided to bathe in a rather secluded part of the river. Without knowing, Ulanion stumbled onto us. Nothing more. Also, if I might implore further upon your kindness, please don't discuss this anecdote with my father. My brother, John, already has the wrong idea."

I knew I was beet red. I could not seriously believe that this particular report had made it all the way to the emperor himself. How many people had the story gone through? How many mouths would now be spreading rumors? Surviving a Hurricane Whale, a pack of Umbral Wolves and treacherous journeys, I would instead be brought to my demise by shame.

Durin's words pulled me from my thoughts. "And the extended period you two spent alone together?"

"We were a bit preoccupied with the murderous semi-corporeal beasts keeping a den beneath the massive, heavily-enchanted complex of ancient ruins. Nothing happened."

"I actually believe you on that. If for no other reason than your crimson color," he added cheekily. After a happy sigh, he continued, "There is one other matter. The mage. Your reports indicated this person ended one of the beasts, and it seems that they have disabled a viable path we could have had to another continent. With your knowledge," he added firmly. Internally, I winced.

"He wasn't just passing, or called to the scene by helpless villagers, was he?" My instinct was to lie. Keep Justin's secret, keep us all safe. If I was found out, though, I'd be screwed. And though my punishment would be fierce, I would still have the protections provided by my father, his service and his status. As a practically unknown elf, however, Ulanion had no such aid. Assuming he hadn't already told Durin everything, the emperor could surely extract that information under whatever horrible interrogation methods were at his disposal. "Might I ask you to keep what I say here private," I asked, hoping to mitigate this before my continued silence caused Ulanion to be tortured.

"That will depend on the truth, but that is a truth I want, Alana."

"That Elven mage is ancient and powerful. That facility is under his domain. I let him close the gate without objection because I fear if we were to disturb him, he might retaliate. From what I saw, were we to come to blows against him, our best forces would suffer large losses."

And not a word of it a lie, I congratulated myself. Beyond his magical prowess and ability to create dangerous golems, if he chose, Justin could reveal his presence to the elves. This might reignite the inter-species conflict of ages past.

Durin repeated my words back to me. "Under his domain?"

"I left it out of the report because I feared that word might find its way to someone foolish enough to bother him. Ulanion and I found him living on a lower level, one that the monsters hadn't yet accessed. He was so consumed by his own work that he hadn't noticed them."

"I see." That put him to thinking, apparently. "And, therefore, he would have known about the gate before we arrived."

"We did not discover anything he didn't know about."

Durin tapped his fingers as he thought. "Do you think he knew about that stone, then? The one with the advancements in it?"

"Without a doubt. I suspect he let us find it, possibly even planting it where we'd find it as a way to get us to leave."

"I see." He turned to his mage. "Have the stone locked in one of the secure vaults until further notice."

Then back to me. "I'm at least satisfied that you remain loyal to our empire," he said. "However, that stone worries me. You, your partner Selene, and any other who has worked on adding its advances to their core will be restricted to this facility—and only given access to certain areas, mind—until the necessary testing is done and we can be assured that this technology is not malicious."

He rose and moved to the door. With one last glance, his eyes fell on me and I felt ice creeping beneath my skin. There was at least some amount of anger in his gaze as he said, "Oh, and Alana, my dear, should you find something that alarms you that you do not wish to put it into an official report, that information can be sent either to your father, or directly to me. Do not omit anything again. Am I understood?"

His aura flared, radiating with cold anger.

"Yes, your Majesty," I answered.

I was escorted back to my room, where—finally alone—I collapsed from stress.

CHAPTER 41

✦

IMPERIAL COUPLE

Durin

Nearly a dozen feet stomped down the hall, accompanied by the rustling of robes and light creaking of well-oiled armor. Try as I might, I couldn't help but be bothered as I returned to my current residence. Other than my personal guards and a handful of very trusted servants, few were allowed in this most protected of spaces.

Apparently sensing my sour mood, those following me didn't speak a word as we moved, instead falling into step, scanning the hallways leading to the quarters I shared with the only one I could truly trust.

I could trust her because, at least to an extent, I understood her. My wonderful wife had spent her life as little more than a caged bird, locked away and unable to choose her own fate. I, too, had been trapped. Though my restrictions were not as thorough as hers, perhaps, nor my cage as gilded, my fate had been declared to me from a young age. Had either of us accepted our prescribed lot? No, of course not; we'd turned on our captors and broken the cages. Cutting away all the chains they'd used to bind us, we'd forge a new future together.

Briefly, I mused on my childhood. My older brothers had stood between me and any hope of ever inheriting my father's position. Therefore, from the moment of my birth it had been declared that I would be a servant. In the army, the orders, or at someone's table, the exact manner of my destiny would be decided by my temperament. They'd thought that I would live and die, nothing but another of their inferiors to be ordered around.

It had certainly come as a surprise to them when I'd taken my first unit in the now fallen kingdom's army. That first gathering of men was comprised of soldiers believed to be unworthy, and so they'd been discarded much as I had been. I took them—with all their weaknesses and flaws—and I forged them into a blade, nonetheless. A few still served me, though with their advanced age they were now in cushy positions I'd arranged for their retirement.

Foolish ideas of nobility and privilege had blinded so many to the gems buried in the mud around them. From those humble beginnings, I gathered my real team. No, I'd scoured every village, every town, every unit I came across, looking for the truly skilled, the steel blades that needed only a good sharpening to cut deeply into my enemies.

Wizards, warriors, bards; it mattered not. I never managed to secure the loyalty of any priests, but with their devotion already pledged to their orders, that was no issue to me. My chosen men had joined, one after another, as members of that original team retired or found positions off the front line. I'd molded them into heroes and great men. Oh, how proud they'd all made me. Even now, years later, a few of these first recruits still served me. Though now, with their advanced age, these men held cushy positions I'd arranged for their retirement.

As I reached my rooms, I turned to my entourage. "That is all for today. We've much to do on the morrow, so rest well, my friends."

I entered, knowing that a few guards would stand sentinel while the others slept. Here, in my personal sanctum, I could finally strip off some of the heavy gear that I wore daily, leaving on only a few enchanted trinkets in case of emergencies. I looked at one of the little pendants and frowned, a slight headache forming.

Someone might have informed her of my return, or she might have simply come of her own accord, but before long, I was joined in our suite by my very pregnant wife. Sophia had about her something of the glow so many talked of, but mostly, my queen looked pleased beyond belief. Upon seeing me thinking in one of my favorite chairs, she came to join.

She moved behind where I sat in my chair, and as she rubbed my shoulders, she began to hum. A light wave of healing magic flowed out from her hands, relaxing and reinforcing my tired muscles. "You look troubled, Husband. Care to share your worries with me?"

"A vexing problem," I answered.

She was patient, though, and after making sure I was fully relaxed, Sophia found her own seat and waited. "One of my more useful servants is a headache," I finally said.

"How so?" Sophia inquired.

"She is . . . hiding things."

"That is troubling. Do you suspect betrayal? My brother is still out there, and there are other powers who we know oppose our current expansion."

Her concerns were valid, but I could only frown.

"I do not believe so. All the things she's kept quiet seem to have been for safety, hers or ours. Furthermore, if someone wanted to harm us they could have simply taken her. The frustrating problem is how to deal with her tight-lipped tendencies without causing further issues," I explained.

"There are a number of options, depending on severity required." Sophia's contemplative gaze told me she was pondering a host of rather unkind ways to correct this unwanted behavior. I trusted her, of course, but that made my darling wife no less cunning and lethal. She asked, "What issues could she cause?"

"It's Verren's daughter." She grimaced, and I knew she understood my predicament.

"Troublesome indeed. She's the one who provided the material for your crown, yes," she asked, her hand gesturing toward where the instrument in question sat nearby, the sky-metal shining brightly.

"The material for our crowns," I confirmed, adding, "as well as most of the rune sequences. She's also the one who helped Mystien advance his water magic, and she looks to be a key member of the team working on the new gates." The pressure in my temples built as I listed each of her achievements. To punctuate matters, I dangled the pendant I'd considered moments earlier. "Oh, and not let us forget that she arranged the sequences on these, or, at the very least, provided them."

I had to admit that the pendants had been a useful little trick. They were simple enough to make and protected well against kinetic attacks and falls. I'd seen similar, and superior versions, but those often came with complications that made them difficult to use. For example, the wrong casual touch might set off a series of expensive and dangerous barriers. No, the young lady's design had been more efficient and elegant.

I could see the wheels turning in her mind as she continued, saying, "You're right to worry, though. If she'd betrayed us, keeping a few secrets would be the least of our problems. Similarly, if you keep her locked away, her father will be a sticky thorn. How severe are her transgressions?" There were few who I could share my thoughts with fully, who had all my access to state secrets. A partner was something I'd needed for so long even without realizing the absence.

"Her brother, too," I offered. "He, much like his sire, continues to gain influence and acclaim. As for the daughter, my chief concern is that the elves might have gotten to her. Though I can't fathom why they would bother. They don't seem to care about what we do, so long as we don't try to attack them."

"Are you planning to attack one of the Elven nations," she asked.

The largest of the Elven lands was Atal, but over the years other sects had broken away from their ranks, forming their own countries. Should I desire them, such humble targets did exist.

"No," I reassured her. "Decidedly not. While they don't have the numbers to overtake us, without the mages necessary to fight them, without our forces, we would suffer crippling losses. They know this as well as we do."

My wife appeared concerned at what option I would take. "So, what do you plan to do?"

"For now, I've restricted the irksome daughter's movement. Under the guise of security, of course. There's another matter, a potential agent of the Atali. Until I'm done wringing out the truth from him, I'll need to keep her on a short leash."

An Elven agent was something I seldom got the chance to gain, and a loyal one would be a boon. Therefore, I'd commenced the process of his interrogation with a great deal of care.

"Caution, Husband," she warned. "As we are both well aware, the caged beast often lashes out at those holding the keys."

"I think she understood that her seclusion serves as both a security measure and as a punishment. Regardless, the arrangement shall be temporary. Either she'll prove loyal and be released when her discipline is complete, or . . . Well, if I am to maintain the allegiance of her kin, the solution will need to appear to have been an accident, of course. Truly, though, if it comes to such, I'll hate the loss."

My wife nodded in understanding. She knew as well as I that sometimes one had to dispose of others quietly. No need to incur the enmity of their loved ones, or endure the public concern over executions, or the scrutiny of investigations.

"You seem to have it well in hand, then," she announced.

"Enough about such things, though. Tell me, how fared this morning's appointment with the Lovers? I am eager to know."

"All is well," she said, caressing her belly. "The priestess said everything is progressing as it should, and that within another month, our child will be in our arms."

Sophia could, in theory, do the magic needed to check the health of our child. She was not practiced in such spells, though, and a delicate situation like ours was not a time to learn. We'd been of one mind that she would consult with the best experts available.

For these many months, all such visits to the Lovers ended with similar reports. Though she'd surely been informed, Sophia had yet to tell me if our offspring would be a son or daughter. Perhaps she thought I'd ask, but I saw no point. Though edict required a son to carry the line of my empire, of course, a daughter would be no less of a perfect gift. And so, if it pleased her, I allowed Sophia to keep this secret.

For an hour or two more, she told me of her day spent looking into the work of the many officials who reported to her from several districts in our shared homeland. I checked in every now and then, providing help if asked for, but she kept these lesser nobles in line. The direct subordinates she'd chosen to aid her in these matters were quite skilled. Some she'd even wooed away from my own administrative teams. I'd laughed for nearly half a day when I learned that my own wife had poached several of my most promising lower-level scribes and accountants for her own uses. Their superiors had been displeased, of course. One after the other, they reported to me on the 'theft' of their aides. Finding good replacements was time consuming, but well worth it to know that both I and my queen had the best help to aid in our work.

When she finished recounting her day, we made our way to our bed where we curled up beside one another and drifted off to sleep.

CHAPTER 42

LOCKED

I was . . . really quite stressed. While he hadn't said it, it was clear that Emperor Durin was pissed. If he knew half of the secrets I was still keeping . . . that would be bad. For now I needed to keep my nose clean. Moreover I needed to show results, and quickly.

The next day was when things changed. When I woke up, I was greeted by a guard at my door who handed me a list. There were several new rules pertaining to where I was allowed to go within the facility. The guard would be nearby at all times until the new portal tech was deemed safe. I still had privacy in my room and bathrooms and such, but I was expected not to try and slip away, that much was clear. I was to be contained to my personal quarters, the workshop where we were building the portal, and a few common areas.

I wanted to know how my Elven friend was, but with all the suspicions about me—and us—this seemed a terrible time to inquire after him, let alone to try and go and see him. I'd apologize for my absence later. *He'd understand*, I assured myself. Along with the list of my new restrictions, breakfast was brought to my quarters that morning. Since I'd rather enjoyed taking meals in the communal dining hall, I asked the guard if this delivery would be the new normal. He nodded quietly. If they were going to treat me like a prisoner, at least the food was still good.

After getting ready, I led my guard to the workshop where I found Dras and Selene. Neither looked particularly pleased.

"Okay," Dras began as I entered the room, "why exactly are we now under constant guard and not able to go like . . . anywhere?" It was clear from their matching glares that they'd talked and had come to the proper conclusion that I was, at least in part, responsible for the current state of things. I was, but I still didn't really appreciate being blamed without any evidence.

I sighed. "Well, the emperor has decided that the stone allowing us to make new gates might be a trap or something. My guess is that our new arrangement is his way of trying to keep anything bad from happening until we get a functional gate."

Dras nodded. "Yesterday afternoon several armed guards showed up and took the stone, saying it was on his orders. Any clue as to why he thinks that?"

"I've got some ideas. That's beside the point, though. Until we show a successful test of our gate, that stone is just as impounded as we are."

Selene, looking irritated—which was odd for her—lashed out. "I blame you for this, Alana. I don't know why, but I just feel that you going to talk with him unsupervised was the cause of all this crap. I was enjoying my evenings, you know? There are some excellent baths here, and the library—which I can no longer access, by the way—might just be the best on the continent. So, let's get to work, shall we? Let's finish this shit, and then I can get back to evenings spent in the library after a relaxing soak."

Perhaps because he knew me better, Dras seemed to point his ire away from me, at least, but the current situation still frustrated him. "And what exactly am I supposed to be doing here," he asked angrily. "I never finished with the upgrade, so I can't exactly help with the building process now, can I? And since they're keeping my trainees away for 'safety' reasons, I'm losing time on my own work."

The contrition I felt made my voice go tight and higher pitched. "Well, we've got most of the setup done at this point, but we've never actually done this before, so think of it as a test run maybe?"

"Fine, fine, let's just get to it," Dras said.

It all settled, we got back to work on the gate pair we were making.

The days dragged on. Even if we had all the materials which we could hope for and all the knowledge of what we were doing we still had to make the thing. Layer by layer, Selene, Dras, and I added the necessary enchantments. Once we'd completed that task, we set to work laying out the best possible arrangement around the gates for shielding items, some of which were standard issue while others we wanted to craft ourselves. Magic, particularly the tools used for forming items, seriously helped our progress on the gate itself, but only time would tell if we succeeded.

Two days before our deadline, we sent letters to Mystien and Emperor Durin's assistants requesting an area nearby where we could prepare our first test.

In the city of Ice's End

Far, far to the north, in a city nobody cared about, in a castle overlooking the frigid sea, a host of men sat around a table.

One of the assembled parties, this one with an appearance like that of a serpent, spoke up. "My prince, we know that he is moving, but our reconnaissance shows that his actions are odd."

"I agree," a robed figure added. "This isn't Durin's normal behavior. He's trying to acquire lands for an embassy, and he seeks permission for some major project."

Leaning over the various reports before him, the young man considered matters, eyes darting here and there as he did. "Do we have words on what that is," he asked. "Or why in Linden? What is he doing in the City of Orders? Why . . . ?" his voice trailed off as his thoughts reclaimed him.

"We know he plans to expand," the spymaster continued, "or at least we assume so. The odd thing though is that it would be out of character to attack there. He's let the orders do as they please; even caving to most of their demands as far as we've seen. I believe he wishes to establish contact with The Orders' leadership, and perhaps more, though I don't know what."

The spymaster was rarely so stymied.

The years had not been kind to Emil. His eyes had grown weary as his age finally began to catch up with him, aided by the poor weather this far north. He still resembled a snake, specifically a snake in dire need of a shed. All that aside he was still a master of his craft. Getting this much from his network had been no small task.

The men pored over maps and reports with critical eyes. Long ago abandoned was the discussion of how Durin's special forces seemed to be able to be anywhere they wanted. The most skilled of his operatives seemed to be in one city one day, then halfway across his territory the next. Durin's mobility had lost the war for the prince and his supporters. If they wanted any hope of winning their next battle, Prince Lief and his forces must solve the riddle of this tactic, this particular tool in his enemy's arsenal.

"Track it," the prince ordered, "and find out whatever you can. If there's some advantage to be had, we're likely to only have once chance at claiming it. We must be ready."

Linden

Nestled between a number of constantly warring city-states beyond the eastern border and far to the south of The Empire of Shadows, sat Linden, The City of Orders. So called because it was ruled by the various Orders of priests; the city served as a central hub for their organizations. Training happened in many places, and temples existed in every city of note, but this place was where the major business was decided. The government offices were housed within the temples, each of them austere as befitted those who served the people.

Though few knew the furthest reaches of the Human lands, Linden squatted at its center.

Within the city, however, there was one temple that bore no affiliation. Priests from all of the orders worked here, all of them equal. Deep within the confines of this neutral space, a woman wearing the robes of her order entered a small, simple office. Not a priest herself, but one of the many acolytes who aided priests in their work, she placed a sealed envelope on the desk and turned to leave.

The Elder was a busy man. Though there was an ebb and flow to his tasks, always something begged for his attention. In his own time, the Elder unsealed the envelope then read its contents carefully. With each passing word his brow furrowed, his anger seeping from him.

"This reeks of that bastard," he said.

He put it down, considering his next move.

✦

CHAPTER 43

ICE FIELD

Snow blew across the frozen plain leaving nothing but hard tundra for dozens of miles. The icy wind raged, screaming, howling, against the world, freezing the flesh of any weak creature that might intrude upon the cold waste. For intruders there were, indeed, bustling about like ants.

Even with my shields up and spells going, the chill wind still brushed me now and then. I could walk through a snowbank back home but here, here I experienced a new level of cold. Water would flash-freeze. Still, this was the best place for our work. In such a remote, inhospitable place, nobody would have a chance of stumbling upon us by accident.

I was overseeing the construction of one of our pre-made gates. Erecting the structure itself, then adding the safeties around it was considered a job only a few people were qualified to do, and sadly I was one of them. Selene and one of the others were in a significantly more sheltered valley about a hundred miles to the south.

Once we'd reported our success, orders had come down from on high dictating the placement and teams to put the things up. Either the emperor was still cross with me, or I'd simply drawn the short straw in whatever method had been chosen to place us, because this location sucked. The other team was nestled in a volcanic valley with a lovely little thermal vent to one side that constantly spewed boiling water. Water which, when it rolled downhill a bit, formed the most beautiful pool, providing a warm bath in which anyone might fight the chill.

Instead, I was on a blasted plain, cold, miserable, and desperate for this trip to be over. We were two weeks north of Durin's fortress, having traveled primarily by sled. Though more acclimated to the cold, our beasts of burden—behemoth oxen covered in long, thick pelts— struggled with the weather.

Every member of my team, including the pack animals, had been given an armband designed by our mages to repel the cold. Though the enchantments had held back at the fortress, they proved insufficient in this environment. Worse, the mana use on these things was astronomical, making them terribly inefficient for long hauls like this.

Even with the armbands and heavy winter clothing, I'd still needed to heal almost a dozen cases of minor frostbite.

One by one, I got the wards snapped into place. It was a happy accident that our shielding protocols had the added benefit of fighting the bitter wind. I checked and rechecked our work, nodding on my third pass. To my eyes, everything looked right as rain. At my signal, our team retreated to the safety provided by our heavily insulated wagons.

"All right, Captain Omar," I said to the commander of our team's soldiers. "We're ready as we can be."

"Good to hear," he said. "I understand you can contact the other team?" I nodded as I made my way to the very large magical item at the back of the cart.

Much like my previous models, this radio came with a few alterations here and there. I had not made it, nor had I had any personal knowledge of its creation. I supposed that had been inevitable that Mystien would put some of his people to work on experimenting with and improving the design.

After jabbing in the activation sequence, I spoke into a small receiver, "Calling Team One. Team One this is Team Two. We're set up. What is your status?"

Radio formalities hadn't really been developed yet, as the tech was still in the stage of being brand spanking new. I had no doubt that in a few years there'd be some form of code developed, particularly once the military started using them regularly. The people in charge of that sort of thing liked their protocols.

Around a minute later, Dras' voice answered. "Team Two, this is Team One. We're ready, activate at your leisure."

"Still need to vacate the immediate area, will contact when ready."

"Right, Team Two. Talk to you later."

I nodded to the captain, and he began the process of moving our little convoy to a safe distance. Along with one of the wagons, one or two soldiers remained behind for the testing. If everything went well, one of those poor beasts would be our first living test subject.

Within a few minutes the wheels started turning and I settled back to rest before the big show.

"Should be safe for everyone no matter what happens," the captain reassured me. "Have to say, though, I didn't even know what existed this far north."

I wasn't sure either. No one really came this far with enough regularity to map it. "I don't know. There had to be something up here. With how cold it gets if you go even a few more kilometers to the north, a frozen wasteland seems about right. That or a solid sea, perhaps. Something like that?"

"How far you reckon it goes on? I mean, there's got to be something at the end of it, unless it just goes on forever." His voice carried a spooked tone as he gazed out onto the tundra.

"It doesn't go on forever," I assured him. "The world is round, we even have the math for roughly how big it is."

"Really? I've never heard that. So do we know what's over on the far side," he inquired, curious.

"Unless you went to a formal school or had much to do with sailing, you probably wouldn't have heard. As for what's over there, nobody knows. I imagine there's an ocean at some point, but it's hard to say for sure. Could be another continent. While the elves have mapped their continent pretty well, our cartographers have yet to finish. If you go far enough east, the available maps just sort of say 'there's more people here.' Explorers have gone, but . . ."

He raised an eyebrow. "But?"

"Lots don't return, and those that do talk of impassable mountains. Some have claimed to find hidden passes, or that they sailed around, but they can't agree about what's there. Lot of them seem pretty unreliable, too, so I don't know." I shrugged.

When we rolled to a stop, the military folks performed several checks before I was given the go-ahead to get back on the radio. We were about half a mile out from our test site, still within easy visual range.

"Team One," I said on the radio, "we're in position, and you?"

"All ready, Team Two. Start it on up."

I rummaged around in my things for a few moments. We'd added a remote activator for this model. With multiple safeties to ensure no one accidentally turned it on, the thing was more complex than it needed to be. As I watched, the lights on our end slowly flickered to life. Each light indicated that the safety checks had been successful. When all were lit, we were cleared for activation.

I looked up at Captain Omar. "You ready?"

"Girlie, I was ready to be done with this freezing wasteland a week ago."

I snorted in laughter before pressing the final rune. I pressed my face to the window as the gate begin to glow as it powered on.

CHAPTER 44

✦

TESTS APLENTY

There was a flash of light as the portal came online. As the magic settled into place, I was glad there was no explosion or apocalyptic ripping of space and time. Those weren't really expected options, but it's hard to not imagine the worst-case scenario when you're working with new and dangerous technology.

"It's up," I declared, stare locked on the ring-shaped gate.

"I can see," Captain Omar replied. "Are we ready to begin testing?"

I got on the radio, and we began. First, we needed their verbal confirmation that things were working as desired on the other end, which they were. We contacted the unit sheltering near our gate and asked that they send a man out.

Hesitantly, the soldier approached the gate. It looked the same as those back at the base. For our first test, the soldier produced a small cube marked with a number of colors and sigils on its sides. From as far back as he could, the soldier tossed the cube through the gate.

On the radio, I asked Dras, "Is the cube through?"

"One sec, we'll check it," came the response.

That cube wasn't anything magical or even special. It simply served to test if an item would be noticeably affected by this method of travel. If the material came out on their end with all the colors and scribbles in the right places, we would know that we had succeeded this stage.

"Cube is right," Dras confirmed a moment later. "Proceed with test number two."

Next came one of the aurochs. The poor, shaggy beast was led up to the glowing portal. In the days leading up to our departure, the creature had been taught, using one of Durin's, that passing through one of these gates would lead to a heaping bucket of treats. This lumbering ox, already unhappy with the wasteland, all but dove toward the glowing promise of food.

Captain Omar laughed. "Nearly drug our man through."

"Yeah, we're not at that test . . . yet," I said, a bit nervously. "Kind of feel bad sending him through. He does know this is experimental right?"

"Oh, he knows," the captain confirmed. "This volunteer position is much like being at the head of the non-magical troops in a battle. He's getting a promotion, should he survive."

After a brief back and forth that the test animal was through, I regarded the captain again.

"Is that how it really works?"

"Yeah, anyone brave enough to go at the enemy in the first row is given a rank up at the end. They're almost always all volunteer forces. Some of these men, like our friend out there, are low born, and really want to climb to a higher status. So, while they can't do magic, if they can brave the enemy a few times, and make it through, they rise," he explained.

"That sounds like suicide," I remarked.

"Well, in truth the first rank seldom has many survivors. Once you've been through a few times, though, you're an officer. That means never having to do that dirty work again since you've got men under you. Pay goes up, too, by quite a lot. When you're an officer, you may well be able to get that cute girl from your village to marry you, and all it took was a few brushes with death. It's a risk some of these men are willing to take."

The captain had a look in his eye, like he wanted me to ask if he'd gone through it as well.

I couldn't help but frown, my worry now even worse. "So, no pressure to see that he makes it home, then. Thanks."

"We've got faith in you lot, girlie. Word is that while your team is a bunch of weirdos, you're really good at what you do. Hey," he asked, curiosity brimming again. "Is it true that, like, five of you lot came back from a mission of over twenty?"

"Yeah. Well, seven; six originals and an elf we gained along the way."

I still hadn't seen Ulanion at all. Asking to go see him was still risky. Once we got back, though, I'd take that chance. Since the emperor himself had seemed bothered about Ulanion, I couldn't say for sure he wouldn't be mistreated, and that thought worried me. Getting this job done, however, should be enough to prove my loyalty enough that I could at least check on him.

"The aurochs is alive," squawked the radio, "and our checks indicate it's in good health."

I turned to Omar. "Final test then, Captain?"

I watched nervously as a red ball flew into the air. The sign to proceed was given.

With the attitude of a young man strolling on market day, the soldier stepped to the gate and passed through. Despite all indications to the contrary, I was convinced our work was about to give this man some sort of magic turbo-cancer or something. Sure, cancer was curable with priests around, and I'd do what I could for him if he did get messed up, but I wasn't sure I'd forgive myself. Minutes dragged. I avoided chewing on my nails by nervously twirling a lock of my hair.

"He's through," came the response. "We'll send him off to a priest for a proper checkup, but this test looks like a success to me."

"That's great! We'll be there soon as possible, then," I responded.

Captain Omar sighed. "You know, it's a real shame we can't use that thing yet. I am not looking forward to making that trek again."

"Nor am I, my good Captain, nor am I. Why don't you tell me about your time in the army on the way back, though. A story to pass the time."

I deactivated the gate and soon the group began the process of tearing down and stowing our gear for the return. This process was much less sensitive than the setup, and was, therefore, a whole lot quicker.

Two days later, as we rode across the wasteland and the older man regaled me with tales, there was a creaking. The noise rose in pitch, moment by moment, until the screaming sound of wrenching metal filled the world.

I conjured shields. The beasts panicked and men scrambled into formation. Nearby, there was an explosion. Ice flew in every direction, cracks spreading across the frozen plain as if it were glass. Cracks that grew into fissures.

Something was rising from below . . .

Ulanion

I'd been sequestered in Durin's fortress for weeks. Something about my outing with Alana must have spooked the higher-ups, because since then, I'd been restricted to my quarters. No visitors, no real conversation except a few chats with my assigned guards and the few people who'd arrived to interview me. The interviews seemed constant, always asking personal, probing questions about me, about my home, about my relationship with the team. Everything. As I'd never been a part of it, I couldn't answer their questions about the Atali military. I informed them that I was a ranger and a free agent at that.

These interrogations had continued for quite some time, but more recently I seemed to be in some kind of holding pattern. I'd done nothing wrong, so I hoped this confinement would end soon.

At least the room was nice. The accommodations reminded me of those you'd find at any inn on the roads. My hosts had granted my request for books, and though they were mainly filled with fictional tales rather than anything practical, I was glad to have something to do. As I lounged on my bed waiting for whatever would come, I heard a knock.

"Yes," I answered as I rose, moving to the doorway.

The door opened and I was met with a man who looked suspiciously like me. Though larger than I, his shoulders broad and massive, we had similar features and grey-speckled black hair.

"Good afternoon," he said, stepping in with a small package in hand. "The investigators have cleared you, well as they can, but I have a few questions of my own. You may call me General Verren."

He had the air of a man who'd spent years at war, not one to play around with. "Certainly, General," I said. Stepping out of his way, I indicated that he could sit in the chair. "What would you like to know?"

"First I'd like you to give me your story in person."

I spent the better part of an hour going over, once more, my interactions with the team. He asked a few questions here and there, but nothing nearly as prying as those who'd come before. I got the feeling he was mostly taking my measure, seeing what I was like.

"And then we came through the gate and ended up here," I finished.

"Excellent. I'm glad you and our people made it out all right. And from all accounts, you were a great help. There is one more concern, however, that I'd like to discuss. Something that my son brought to me."

Who is his son, I wondered. *He is too tall to have sired Glen, and looks nothing like the twins. Dras perhaps?* "And what would that be, General?"

His eyes ignited, and an aura like black flames filled the room. "What exactly are your intentions with my daughter, Alana." His son's identity clicked into place. The one who'd yelled at her the day we took our stroll.

General Verren's display was impressive and left no doubts as to his strength. Could I beat him? Not at this range. Perhaps, if I had my bow and a good spot to shoot from, it would be a good fight. Nevertheless, I'd stood before King Justin, and a pack of Umbral Wolves. Sights that would have sent many men screaming in terror, I'd weathered. My years of hunting the beasts of the Elven lands also made me confident in my own skills, my own power.

I loosed my own aura, green vines springing to life to combat the black fire. With our auras, we warred. Keeping my expression rigid and neutral, I pushed as hard as I dared. Backing down would only destroy his perception of me.

"Nothing ignoble," I said, gaze locked with his, "but I intend to pursue her in courtship."

"Many others have tried and failed," he remarked, eyes steely and unforgiving.

"If she rejects me, so be it. I will accept that without objection. But I still plan to try."

General Verren cracked a smile. Both of us allowed our power to fade. He reached over and opened his package that had been a bottle.

"I like you," he declared. "Drink with me." We spent the next hour or so drinking the most foul, most awful liquor that I'd ever tasted. We both smiled, our growing joy only heightened by the knowledge that this disgusting communion was just another of his hazing tactics.

CHAPTER 45

✦

ACROSS THE ICE

From the deep beneath the ice, dozens of purple tentacles poured forth. Each one reached and stretched, trying to grab at whatever it could find. However, its reach seemed to only extend a few meters, and most of our company were already running well away. Regardless, Cthulhu's sudden appearance caused mass alarm.

In our carriage, Captain Omar ordered that we speed up and seconds later we lurched before settling into a noticeably faster pace.

While others scrambled to escape the rising beast, I called out, "Captain, are we good?"

"It's fine," he replied, "but we need to move. Graspers like our friend out there aren't quick. So long as we keep well ahead of it, we shouldn't have a problem."

"You're sure?"

"Absolutely. Seen loads of Graspers. All different kinds," he added, watching the ice below as we moved. "Seen them closer to the Emperor's fortress a few times, too, on some of the ice shelves. This is a biggun, though. We should have noticed before it attacked."

As the cart picked up speed, the ride became more turbulent, jostling me around. I grabbed part of the frame to stabilize myself, struggling to speak. "And . . . how do you . . . see them coming?"

"Look at the ice. You can see the tentacles when they get near. Also, they attack when you get loud. Think they hunt the big furry beasts like our aurochs. They hear the noise of movement topside, pop out when the steps get close. That one seems rather stupid, though. Didn't get anywhere near us." We pushed the caravan as fast as it could go on the roadless tundra. Despite my grip on the carriage frame, I was thrown and jerked by the rough ride. I instantly regretted my inability to use the portal for a hasty retreat. When we finally started to slow down, I felt like a bowl of scrambled eggs. The more relaxed pace made the ride somewhat smoother, the rhythm eventually lulling me to sleep.

A few hours later, I was awoken by rude knocking from Captain Omar. "Come here," he said. "We got something you'll want to see."

I stretched, pulling my spells tight around me to ward off the cold. Sarcastically, I said, "Let me guess. I slept for days and we've miraculously arrived at the hot spring?"

"Not quite."

He led me to a quiet, barren patch of ice away from the carts.

Nervously, I asked, "What are we here for?"

"Look." I followed the line of his finger and attention to a patch of ice. Beneath the milky surface, purplish vein-like structures writhed and stretched, seeming to originate from a central point.

"Is that what I think it is," I asked, panic rising. "Should we even be this close!?"

"It's fine. So long as we don't bring along something heavy that'll shake all this ice over it, the thing should pay us no mind. You and me standing here, we're too light to bother it. But, you asked. That's what they look like."

I stood back a bit as I peered at the undulating pattern in the ice. It was something I would easily have missed if it hadn't been pointed out. I hoped that I'd never need to use this knowledge, but if I got sent to this forsaken place again, it might prove useful.

"Thanks," I said. "Honestly I was a bit worried when you called me out here." The man who'd been cheerful and talkative this entire time hardened his gaze. His voice was cool now, lacking the warm, happy tones I was used to. "Why would you be worried?"

I moved my hands behind my back and let off a series of quick, quiet snaps to a tight rhythm. Should I need to start casting, it should be enough. "I think I pissed a few people off," I explained. "Why else would they send me out here to the middle of nowhere while everyone else got to lounge at a nice hot spring."

He frowned. "I'm not here to hurt you, but to protect you. Let's return to the caravan."

Like a flipped switch, Omar reverted to the jovial, gregarious companion he'd been before.

For the next several days, I got little sleep, and kept my personal shielding spells up. Perhaps I was being paranoid, but I even began checking myself for poison after every meal. I kept my eyes on Captain Omar, unsure about what he'd been told but confident that he had been sent out here to watch me. During that time, I spent a lot of time thinking. Emperor Durin had never done wrong by me. Heck, all the times we'd met, he'd been nice. Despite his outward kindness toward me, Emperor Durin remained a ruler. And every ruler had the capacity for cruelty. Was he angry enough with me to harm me? Honestly, I didn't know. The whole situation had gotten my hackles up.

I figured I'd either have to behave in such a way that I wasn't questioned again, or I would need to begin taking more missions far from home and the emperor's influence.

Maybe I could just fade into the background, I thought. Then I remembered all the inventions I'd created over the years and how much they knew about that work. Disappearing wasn't likely to happen, I realized. I decided that the second I got time alone, I needed to start working on my teleportation along with a few new combat measures.

We approached the volcanic valley to join Team One. It was wild to come up and over the little ridge and feel the temperature spike. The winds blew over the valley, but the depth of the crater protected most of the valley from the biting chill. The insulated area held the vent's heat.

In strong opposition to the vast white fields, greenery climbed the walls of the crater.

Since I'd last visited the site, the crew had built a base of operations the size of a small village. Six or seven buildings in total, from what I could tell. One in particular seemed to be taking in the spring's hot water and releasing a stream gently out of its far side.

As we got closer, I could see that each of the spartan buildings looked to be carved out of stone and moved into place. Like someone had taken the most basic ideas in architecture and begun to build here.

I was not the only one surprised. Most of the soldiers in the retinue were blinking and gawking. Even Captain Omar gave me a bit of a questioning look. I could only shrug. Such feats as we were witnessing were beyond my skill. Though I was still nervous, nothing happened. After the one concerning interaction, Captain Omar had not displayed any odd behavior, nor had any of the soldiers.

We found Dras before too long. He, and another of the mages from his team were working on some kind of aqueduct near the largest, most central building.

"Dras," I called as our cart drew near. "What the heck is all of this?"

"Hey! You're finally back. Good to see you. Well, see," he hesitated. "We got bored. We had plenty of magic users, and the carts weren't really comfortable. Frankly, it started with Selene, see. She wanted a proper place to use the hot spring, and well, we didn't have anything better to do while we waited on you."

I considered the magic needed to do something like this. The mana required, the spells, all of it would be staggering. "So, you built a town? You got bored and built a town. How . . . how did you get all the stones into place? They're huge."

He launched into a long-winded explanation about how all they really had to do was cut the stones out of the ground. Easy enough to do with magic. All that was required then was a bit of shaping. They crafted rollers and brought their materials downhill into the valley. Really, Dras explained, they hadn't done anything more than what would be considered standard practice for many military camps. The only major difference here was that these improvements had been made to increase comfort rather than to fortify a position.

I wanted to punch him. I wanted to punch him so bad.

I'd spent the last few weeks working in the cold, frozen wilderness while they'd been . . . what? Making a miniature resort town for the hell of it? While I'd been spending my days and nights in a tiny wooden icebox on wheels, this guy had been making comfy houses for himself and his crew.

Dras must have seen my scowl. He began to slow his explanations. "And . . . well, we didn't know when you'd show up. So we were diverting water into the dormitories so that we'd have heated floors."

I was sour, and it leaked into my tone. "There are no gates here, Dras, and we are days from anything. All of this is kind of a waste of time."

"Who cares? We've got a gate here right now, and there's no reason we can't put another here in the future, if anyone wants to. The buildings are stone, and it's not like anything could hurt them, so if it takes a few years it's no problem, and it was a fun side project while you were gone."

Before I could explode on him, Selene bounded over to us.

"Hey there!" She missed my expression and asked, "Do you like the town? It's so great! Wow, Alana, you look terrible. Let's get you to the bathhouse to relax. There's time. It's not like we're leaving today." She put her hands on my shoulders and guided me to one of the nearby structures.

I went willingly, but not before yelling over my shoulder, "You've got some nerve playing around like this, Adraias! Some nerve indeed!"

Using his proper name—which I knew he hated—warmed me almost as much as the bathhouse.

✦

CHAPTER 46

SAUNA RUMINATIONS

As I sat soaking in the blissfully warm water, I began to think. This was an optimal place for such things, after all, particularly having spent weeks in the frigid tundra. Regardless of how rushed they may have been, I had to hand it to Dras and Selene. Their construction had been simple, sure, but for something made as a side project to stave off boredom it was functional and well-built. They'd divided the baths, giving one half to the men, and the other to the women. While curious as to what the guys got, we ladies enjoyed a spacious tub with a pair of waterfalls. Sitting under either was comfortable, depending on exactly how hot you wanted the stream to be.

The tub was a blessing. As I ran fingers atop the water's surface, I contemplated my options. I could try to leave the Durin's lands. It would be easy enough to accomplish with my current skill set. As soon as anyone took their eyes off me, I could turn invisible and either walk away or wait until we got back to the fortress. I could use one of the gates. There'd be little way to track me once I was out, and, from there, I could go anywhere.

How would that reflect on my family, though, I wondered to myself. *Or my friends?* I also had to consider that if I did, our esteemed emperor would absolutely send people after me. One didn't let someone wander off freely when that someone could make gates. If I ran, I'd be looking over my shoulder for the rest of my days.

If I left, there were a few places I could go. Eastbound roads would take me to lands Durin hadn't conquered yet, but with his desire for expansion, would that last? If I went back to the Elven lands, I could probably hang out with Justin for a while. I'd certainly be safe there. My last boat trip across that ocean had been harrowing, though, so I wasn't sure if I'd be taking that route.

It wasn't urgent to run, not yet at least. But what was pressing was my need to prepare. I needed new weapons in a bad way. To that end, I considered my options. Poisons were out. I just didn't have enough experience with them. The speed of bard magic meant that most forms of direct attack were either very slow or required a charging period. I gritted my teeth, lamenting this limit for the millionth time. Large energy weapons were out, and the kind of explosive death a priest did was also no good. It wouldn't work with my magic.

Letting out a deep, long groan, I dipped my head underwater, trying to come up with anything. Finally, I started to run out of air, the slow buildup began to get to me until I had to surface again.

Hold on, I thought to myself. *Hold on. Now, that is an idea.* The idea, the process would be slow, insidious. I had more than enough experience holding my own breath that I could try and force the lack of oxygen on others. *Is that possible though?* I'd need to try it on some unfortunate mice or something, but it could work. If it did, I could slowly take people out. By the time a target realized what was happening, it would probably be too late for most of them.

I would just need to make it past the mages' resistances.

I also needed to find methods of casting that were quicker, or less noticeable than singing or snapping my magic into being.

There are only so many ways to perform, I said to myself. *Singing, dancing, acting . . .* I thought about that for a moment. *Could I act?* Surely, someone had tried at some point to work spells through theatrical performance. However, no one had written down the results, or even the attempt. That wasn't odd, though, as a lot of techniques were kept secret, or ignored for perceived uselessness.

"You okay," Selene asked from the other side of the bath.

"Yeah, I'm fine," I responded.

"Right," she scoffed, "and I'm thinking of dying my hair purple."

"Purple would look good on you."

Selene was not to be dissuaded. "Ha! So spill. What's got you in a mood?"

I needed to come up with something workable, and on the spot. I frowned and sank a little lower in the water to blow bubbles. To her, it might look like I was pouting, but in all honesty, I needed time to think.

A lie would be sub-optimal, as lies tended to strike back when least expected. No, I needed a truth, something that bugged me a bit, but not what I was thinking about. I didn't know if she might spill something to the higher ups either on purpose or by accident.

"I'm worried about the other members of our team," I said finally. Truthfully, though I admit most of my worry was saved for a specific elf. "We were quarantined," I continued, "but we don't know about them, how they're doing. I hope they're all right, is all. Nobody even sent a letter."

Selene snorted. "Well, perhaps you should try sending one. I've been keeping a few going back and forth between Leah and myself. They're fine. She's busy writing about the . . . goblins I think you called them? Anyway, she wants to mount another expedition to that island."

That came only as somewhat of a surprise. I knew she'd been interested, but going back there would be incredibly dangerous. *Did she even realize how bad things had been the first time around*, I wondered.

"Well, she did get excited," I said. "But if she goes, she's an idiot."

"At least we can agree on that. Robert is doing what he can to dissuade her, of course, but the idea of another spellcasting sentient species stuck with her. She's intent on keeping records for others, writing as much about them as she can, island location included." Selene finished with a sigh, looking as frustrated as I felt.

"Don't suppose you've heard about Glen or Ulanion," I inquired.

"Sadly, no on both accounts. Glen's military, though, so he's probably off somewhere killing monsters or beating up the emperor's enemies. Well, more than likely working as a living wall while something tries to kill him. He is rather tough. As for the elf," she said, "no idea. He's somewhere, though, for sure. You could ask when we get back."

"I might," I agreed. I'd been planning to do that anyway.

"Good." She switched subjects. "Did you lot find anything neat while out on your little trip? The valley here is nice, but wow is it boring."

"Oh yeah," I said, letting the sarcasm flow from me. "We found ice, and ice, and more ice, and some ice. There was also a worm monster thing, but it just popped up and wiggled around menacingly for a bit."

"Gross," she decided. "Glad I missed that."

"So," I began, "what do you think we'll be doing when we get back? More testing? Or more portals?"

"Depends. The soldier you sent through was sent back already. My guess is that if whatever priest they send to look him over gives him the all clear, they'll have us making gates. But, if not, well, we've got a lot of problems, since I've got no clue where any issues in the rune sequences would be."

"I think the chances of failure are low."

The rest of our bath was spent discussing activation methods. Selene offered suggestions, but they all had complications. Personally, I thought it would be best to keep matters simple and use a simple switch or a pressable rune, much like those used in the gate room. In the end, though, we could speculate all we wanted but the real answer would be whatever the people in charge requested.

That night we slept in proper beds. Well, sort of. We spread our bedrolls over raised stone blocks. It was certainly warmer than the carriages, and that was enough for me. Though I hated to admit it, I slept better in that stone bed than I had in weeks.

Load out went quickly. We casters wanted to go home and so did the soldier. As our higher-ups also wanted us home, everybody agreed. The wizards rigged up a basic door scheme which consisted of big, square stones blocking off the entrances to the now-abandoned buildings. If anyone decided to set up here again, at least they'd have a good head start on the job.

Though better than the blasted wastelands far to the north, the path back to the fortress wasn't what one might call scenic. There were a few boulders strewn about in random piles near frozen lakes.

Near one such lake, Durin's fortress loomed like some sort of spartan castle. For all his many feats, Ristolian sucked at making his home a beautiful place to look at. That said, it was in a strategic position at least, and the ice sheet reflected the light in pretty ways over the surrounding land.

Before we even properly arrived, I could see guards moving about on the parapets. Our homecoming was expected. Hopefully someone had made a meal that didn't include rations or magically summoned food. And I could certainly do with something warm.

CHAPTER 47

✦

HOMECOMING

Though our arrival wasn't scheduled—timing such things in this era could not be too specific if any traveling was involved—however we were expected. The gates quickly opened for us, and as we stepped onto soil the stewards urged us to a small room near the kitchens where hot food awaited us.

There was a thick, hearty stew and some bread that—if I had to guess—had been baked only hours earlier. The baker had taken the time to make it with a sticky honey glaze and it was perfect. Having subsisted on little else as a child, I didn't usually go for bread, but special loaves like this were always a welcome change.

As I was devouring the stew, something contacted me from behind, lifting me out of my chair and whirling me into the air.

I let out a wordless yell and began to charge up a nasty scream.

The spell died in my throat as I saw the man who had lifted me into his arms. I saw the bright smile on his face.

"Gone so long and you couldn't come and see you dear old father?"

"Put me down," I angrily declared. "I didn't even know you were here." I struggled against his embrace. Father or no, he was getting between me and the most pleasant meal I'd had in nearly a month.

"Fine, fine," he said as he lowered me back to my seat. He took a chair opposite me. "Your mother has been asking about you, you know, and I've been a bit concerned myself."

"I've been in quarantine for the last bit. Which I'm guessing, by your presence, is over now?" He nodded and I continued speaking around bites of my meal. "At any rate, Brother certainly could have told you I was fine ages ago."

His face showed a good bit of disappointment in my behavior. "Quarantined or not, you still could have at least sent a letter."

"Er . . . I forgot, and figured you'd be told I was back anyway . . ."

I had never really been much for the whole letter writing thing. Back when I was poor, it wasn't practical as paper and ink could both be costly. In school, we'd had to write things like invitations and basic correspondence as those were integral to high society. At least they had been before the kingdom fell. I, though, had never been overly taken with the practice. To me, it seemed like a chore, and one that was far too formal for me. Perhaps it was because I'd been raised, in my first life, in the age of texts and messaging apps. The concept of a long-winded note just seemed wrong.

"Your brother and I were made aware," Father confirmed, "as we have clearances to know such things. Your mother, however, didn't find out you were back on the continent until you'd already left again. She has, at last, been made aware of how long you've been back."

Those words were less than comforting.

"I'll write her one tonight then."

"You're out of quarantine, dear. The test was successful, and the emperor is satisfied that you and your team weren't compromised by elves or whatever artifact you interacted with. You're free to go see your mother tonight if you want to," he explained. "Which I'd do, were I in your position. Better to get on with it."

I had the distinct feeling that it might be a long night.

"I will. Um . . . another question, could you check in on the members of my team, the ones who made it back with us. I haven't gotten a good chance to, so I'd like to know how the ones we left behind are doing," I said, hoping to appear nonchalant despite my concerns.

"Anyone in particular," he asked, brow elevated. "I imagine that most were sent back to whatever demands their projects now entail."

"Well . . . the elf that we picked up over there. Ulanion? I was a bit worried that since he wasn't part of our original team something might have happened."

Dad smirked, and I couldn't help but feel that he might have been speaking to my brother too much of late. "I'm sure he'll be flattered you were asking about him. He's fine, by the way, and I rather approve."

"You've been speaking to John, haven't you? He's an idiot, you're aware of this, right?"

"He and I talked, yes, but I also spoke to your new friend myself. We had drinks together. Nice guy. Told me about his intentions. I'm having him assigned to one of my training units. We could use more archers like him, and Ulanion is more than willing to teach."

I felt the smallest twitch just over my right eye. It was fortunate that the informal flatware in this world tended to be wooden. As my knuckles tightened, going white, I could have mangled one of the fancy metal spoons used for state dinners.

I wasn't sure who to be mad at. I'd been avoiding Ulanion, but did he have to talk to my father? Then again, he might not have had a choice in that regard. Dad should have known better than to force the issue without talking to me, but I hadn't been around to consult. The old general likely just went on his own instinct. John, though . . . Yes, I'd be mad at John! He'd surely blabbed about things which led to this whole stupid situation. Part of my brain told me that I wasn't entirely logical, but the rest of my rather frustrated mind told that part that it needed to shut up.

"Interesting," I said through my teeth.

"Don't be too mad at him, dear," Dad said, still talking about Ulanion. "For now, you should finish your lunch. I've got a few things to do before returning to Lithere but should be ready to go by this evening. Think you can have your things packed by then?"

"Sure. I'll need to talk to Dras and Selene, too, though. Are we moving back to the previous lab in the city?"

While our place here was certainly secure, my understanding was that our higher-ups intended for us to return to Mystien's place. At least that had been the plan when we'd returned from Atal, but things had gone weird. So incredibly weird.

"That's the plan." he confirmed. "Word has come down that you lot might be getting some more interesting work. The emperor has plans for expansion, and since things are going well . . . Well, I'm not in on all the details, but big things are afoot."

"Excellent," I said, happy to hear we were doing well.

"Right then," he said, rising from his chair. "I'll come by to collect you once I'm finished up. Until then," he added, giving me a light hug before heading off to whatever business required his attention.

While we'd spoken, my stew had gotten cold. Irritated, I hummed a tune, needing only a small bit of spellcraft to bring my meal back to a piping hot temperature.

Our previous project complete, clearing our temporary workshop of anything important took less than an hour. As we hadn't unpacked from our journey, most of our work entailed stacking up the boxes and cleaning up after ourselves. All of us were motivated to get it done.

Upon returning to my quarters, I found the situation to be much the same as that in the workshop. However, I found something that piqued my interest. I had mail, and a fair bit of it. There was a letter from my family, dated one day after our team had left for the frozen wastes. In the stack of envelopes, I found three from a certain elf.

Ulanion's first letter was, at my best guess, from the period we spent in quarantine, after Durin had changed the nature of our confinement. Long and poetic, the letter mostly explained that he wished to speak to me again when it was convenient. The second note was from only a day or two later, explaining that he'd been put into quarantine, and apologizing for his inability to reach me. The third, dated just a couple of days ago, was to tell me that after being released from his quarantine only to find I'd been sent away on a mission, he had taken up a job in Lithere. The elf provided an address at one of the military facilities. He also mentioned the conversation with my dad.

It was clear at some point that I would need to speak to Ulanion, perhaps I should write him when I got home.

I packed my mail with my things, and soon Dad returned. Getting back to Lithere was as simple as strolling through the portal. What was complicated, however, were the many tasks necessary to keep secret our access to the portal network. We arrived just outside of the city and loaded into a carriage which took us the rest of the way home, arriving just as the sun dipped below the horizon.

Mother came down to greet us as Dad and I climbed out of the carriage, both eager to have dinner and sleep. Her face lit up as we saw each other for the first time in far too long. In some ways, I admit, I was distant from my family. We'd spent so much time apart on so many occasions that I didn't feel as close to them as I had my first family. That said, I still loved them. They were still blood and nothing would change that.

"Hi, Mom," I said as we embraced. At some point I'd gotten taller than her, which seemed weird, but the tight hug made me feel small.

"I'm so glad you're home safe, Alana. I was so worried."

"Me too, me too," I answered.

For a moment I was lost in the joy of being some place I could relax for just a bit longer. For now, it was all over.

"You, too, dear," she said to my father. He just smiled.

"It's such a shame," Mom began, her voice sickly sweet. "Had I known you were coming home, I'd have had something special prepared."

I felt my stomach drop. She was clearly peeved. I pulled away ever so slightly only to find that she'd taken both of my hands in hers. Normally that would have been a kind, caring gesture. But it seemed she could sense I'd been thinking of running. She knew my predilection for flight and had, it seemed, taken the initiative to kill that option.

"Something wrong," she asked, grip tightening.

"Um . . . No, just thought I might get some sleep, it's been kind of a long day."

Every cell in my body screamed that I should run.

"I do hope you'll at least have dinner before retiring."

She kept smiling. This was not a request.

"Of course," I said, letting her guide me to the dining room. "Sorry."

CHAPTER 48

✦

A NIGHT IN

I stumbled up to my room, closing the door behind me. The battle had been long and hard. The aggression, passive. Oh, the lessons I'd learned that night as my mother gave a masterclass on telling someone you were pissed without telling them you were pissed. The lessons repeated, and in such rich and varied ways.

My excuses about things like operational security were ignored due to how very long I'd waited while still in Durin's home without telling her I'd returned from the Elven continent. She felt—rightfully so, I had to admit—that had I truly wanted to, I could have informed her that I was back in the country albeit indisposed for the time being.

I lamented the fact that Dad had brought me home so soon.

Mother's war games even applied to the meal itself. My plate had been piled high with all the things she knew I liked the least. The featured dish seemed to be a broccoli variant that, when cooked, smelled like death. For some reason, my parents loved it. Normally, I'd eat almost anything, convinced by a few years of near starvation that most food is good food. But my mother knew the exact buttons to push. When I'd been a bit slow to eat, she'd launched into a whole grief routine.

"What? Are you not hungry? Perhaps I shouldn't have seen to dinner myself if you ate before . . . Did you lose your taste for home-cooked meals while wandering the world, dear?"

Eventually, I surrendered and ate my food

She'd even sent me to my room. I'd made a mistake, it seemed, by claiming tiredness and using that as an attempt to hide. As we finished our meal, when Mom declared that I looked absolutely ghastly, and that I simply must go to my room to rest. That meant, however, that I was stuck in a room that was still in storage mode.

Wait, I wondered, *am I?* I was a powerful bard, skilled and experienced. I'd killed monsters, traveled to other lands far abroad. I'd come face-to-face with some of the most powerful archmages in the world and had appointed myself well. I'd brought military strategy to new heights and had discovered new avenues to explore. Perhaps, one day, I might be one of the most respected bards in history.

I should go down there, tell her that I am an adult, I said to myself, *and that I decide when I rest. I could stay up with them if I choose.*

I rose from my bed, laid my hands on my hips in a power pose, and stalked to my door.

I'd go down there and tell her that I had a number of things that needed doing tonight other than sleep. Important things! Letters to write, spells to practice, a few things to set up for more magical research. Big things needed doing and I would do them.

From my room.

Nevermind. I chickened out halfway to the door. There really was no reason to get in another fight against a force who had a clear advantage against me tonight. I had lots of things that needed doing, and I could take care of them without wading into a battle with Mother.

Then—only after finishing my highly sensitive work—I *might* go to bed. But only because I chose to for myself. And if I did, it would be because of the late hour and my exhaustion, not for any other reason.

I spun up a pair of portals on either side of my room. Even when I didn't have anything going through them, they were a mana drain. The only way to solve that issue, unfortunately, was practice. So, I'd be practicing, ready should I ever need to flee or use them in a real fight.

I then moved to my desk which, luckily, still had a few sheets of paper, some pens and an inkwell. I started scribbling a supply order for some mice and the necessary materials for keeping them. As any bard or priest who needed to practice healing spells would often use mice or some other small animal for that purpose, this wasn't odd at all. Mice were cheap, easy to keep, and nobody really cared if they were hurt or killed. My explanation, should anyone care to ask, would be that after my experiences abroad I wanted to work on more advanced healing spells, particularly those for limb regrowth. That wasn't a bad idea.

If things with Durin and the empire went poorly, I might need those spells.

In actuality, though, I would be trying to develop a spell to suffocate the mice. I found it kinda dark that I was thinking of killing the little furry guys, but I needed more offensive options. I couldn't practice such magic on people, but perhaps I could arrange my experiments in such a way that I wouldn't cause undue pain or suffering. Perhaps I could find a way to make them sleep first? Since the people in this world didn't care for animals too much, I couldn't buy a tincture to knock them out. Spells would be used for such things, and typically required a priest.

As I finished writing my lists, I dropped the portals. The drain on those was still too high to keep them going for long, and I had scant practice at longer ranges. I wasn't immediately passing out from the effort as I had with my first attempt. But it was obvious I needed more practice. And a larger area to work than my storage closet of a bedroom.

Briefly, I considered developing a teleportation spell like Justin had used, but I had a working model now I could use for a while at least. Starting over from scratch to mimic the Elven king's work seemed too much effort. Finding a way to put portals in places I couldn't see, however, was added to the list. *How had he managed that? Was he using some kind of detection spell? Could I use something like that to see places out of view?* Every issue seemed to add more to my plate.

I sighed. The methods I'd used to pass Battle Magic courses had been effective, but certainly weren't the end-all be-all. Mostly, those methods leaned heavily on magic for misdirection and control. Though these spells certainly had their uses, I couldn't get complacent. I needed to keep working, keep developing new tools. To stand still might well be to die.

I had another task to take to first though, one that I dreaded. Going back over the mail I'd received while away, I picked up Ulanion's letters. I didn't know how I felt or what I wanted where the elf was concerned, but it would be rude to not respond at all.

Taking my time, I composed a letter telling him that I was well, and glad to hear that he was too. Then I scrapped it. Too formal. I composed another. This one felt a little too flirty, something I definitely wasn't going for right now. The third, oh the third! That one was a disaster that I hurled into my fireplace with extra vigor. This process repeated itself several times until I finally had something that felt right. Though dishearteningly similar to my first attempt, this one I'd composed in Atali. I'd spent years learning the language so I was damn well going to keep using it. Besides, he might like that I'd gone through the trouble to do so.

As the failed letters curled in the fire, it occurred to me that I was a walking trope, a realization that rankled a bit. Some things just had to be done right, and the right way was often a pain in the neck.

A knock came from the door, causing me to startle. I slowly rose to see who it was and, upon opening the door, I found my mother, a bowl of ice cream in hand and a thoughtful look on her face. How and from where she'd gotten ice cream I didn't know, but with a few magical items it wouldn't be too problematic to make.

"Your father and I had a bit of dessert after you retired. I came to see if you were still up," she declared.

"Yeah, I had some correspondence to see to." As she offered out the bowl, I added, "Thanks."

She hugged me, far tighter and for longer than when I'd first arrived. "I am glad you're home, Alana," she said, sounding a bit sad. "But I worry. The boys are off to . . . well war! Constantly! Most of the time you're here, I'm not even told where you are and then you disappeared for nearly a year. Again."

"Mom, you know I can't talk about a lot of it."

"I don't suppose you'd consider settling down and taking a quiet job," she asked, though her tone told me she hadn't even managed to convince herself such a miracle was possible. I had always entertained a few ideas in that regard, but this seemed the wrong time to want such things.

"I'm afraid that option isn't really there for me right now." That got me a frown, and I continued. "Even if it were, though, I'd go nuts if I weren't getting up to something. That would just be . . . kind of boring, I think. Maybe one day, but not now."

She gave me a big sigh. "Very well. Eat your ice cream and go to bed, dear. You do really look tired."

She wasn't wrong, I was exhausted from the day, and all the mana I'd burned practicing my portals only exacerbated that condition.

"I will go to bed when I'm good and ready," I declared with a huff. "Which, I mean, is actually in just a bit, but because I want to, not because you told me to."

She looked at me, dead silent and neutral, for a solid ten seconds before she started laughing. "All right then Alana, do as you please. Tomorrow is going to be busy, though, what with unpacking and all." She turned and started walking down the hall, calling over her shoulder, "Oh, and you've yet to tell me about this nice Elven boy your brother mentioned."

I would kill John, and it would be justified. Through dinner, Father had kept his mouth shut while I similarly—expertly!— avoided that subject all through dinner only to find out that John had run his big mouth.

Maybe running away now would be best, after all.

No, I chided myself. *I can't run when there's ice cream.* It was flavored with one of my favorite fruits, one that my brothers had taken me to pick all those years ago. Each spoonful reminded me of easier times, happy days in the village when there were no wars, no palace intrigue or geopolitical strife. Just my family, content and whole. Before the war, and the famine, back when Rod was still alive.

When I fell asleep, I dreamed of those times. My brothers, dumb as they could be, were there with me, roaming the forest once again. We looked for fruit and gathered mushrooms.

And I was happy.

ABOUT THE AUTHOR

Wandering Agent is the North Carolina–based author of the Melody of Mana series as well as other fantasy and isekai stories.

Podium
DISCOVER
STORIES UNBOUND
PodiumAudio.com

www.ingramcontent.com/pod-product-compliance
Lightning Source LLC
Chambersburg PA
CBHW020655120726
47906CB00001B/275